Edgar Wallace was born illegitimately [...] adopted by George Freeman, a porter a[...] eleven, Wallace sold newspapers at Ludgate Circus and on leaving school took a job with a printer. He enlisted in the Royal West Kent Regiment, later transferring to the Medical Staff Corps and was sent to South Africa. In 1898 he published a collection of poems called *The Mission that Failed*, left the army and became a correspondent for Reuters.

Wallace became the South African war correspondent for *The Daily Mail*. His articles were later published as *Unofficial Dispatches* and his outspokenness infuriated Kitchener, who banned him as a war correspondent until the First World War. He edited the *Rand Daily Mail*, but gambled disastrously on the South African Stock Market, returning to England to report on crimes and hanging trials. He became editor of *The Evening News*, then in 1905 founded the Tallis Press, publishing *Smith*, a collection of soldier stories, and *Four Just Men*. At various times he worked on *The Standard*, *The Star*, *The Week-End Racing Supplement* and *The Story Journal*.

In 1917 he became a Special Constable at Lincoln's Inn and also a special interrogator for the War Office. His first marriage to Ivy Caldecott, daughter of a missionary, had ended in divorce and he married his much younger secretary, Violet King.

The Daily Mail sent Wallace to investigate atrocities in the Belgian Congo, a trip that provided material for his *Sanders of the River* books. In 1923 he became Chairman of the Press Club and in 1931 stood as a Liberal candidate at Blackpool. On being offered a scriptwriting contract at RKO, Wallace went to Hollywood. He died in 1932, on his way to work on the screenplay for *King Kong*.

BY THE SAME AUTHOR
ALL PUBLISHED BY HOUSE OF STRATUS

The Devil
Man

HOUSE OF
STRATUS

This edition published in 2001 by House of Stratus, an imprint of Stratus Holdings plc, 24c Old Burlington Street, London, W1X 1RL, UK.

www.houseofstratus.com

Typeset, printed and bound by House of Stratus.

A catalogue record for this book is available from the British Library.

ISBN 1-84232-676-7

1

On the western outskirts of Sheffield – the Sheffield of 1875 – there was a dingy red factory that had seen the bankruptcies of at least three concerns which had been housed within its high walls. In this year it was occupied by the staff of a Mr Wertheimer, who produced nothing that was of commercial value, and was rather secretive about what he hoped to produce at all. He called himself and his partner, known and unknown, "The Silver Steel Company", which, as Baldy said subsequently, was a contradiction of terms.

On a certain wintry night a young man dropped a rope ladder from one of the walls and came gingerly to the ground. His name was Kuhl, he was a Swiss from the Canton de Vaud, by profession an engineer, and by disposition an admirer of attractive ladies.

He picked his way across the uneven ground towards the road and was met halfway by two men. A woman, driving into Sheffield, saw the three talking by the side of the road where a closed wagonette, drawn by two horses, was standing. The men were talking loudly and gesticulating at one another. Looking back over her shoulder, she saw what was apparently a free fight in progress, and whipped up her horse.

She did not inform the police because, as she said, it was none of her business, and, besides, fights were pretty frequent in those days and in that part of the world. Later she informed Sergeant Eltham, but could give no satisfactory account of how the fight finished.

This Sergeant Eltham was a police officer who never ceased to apologise for being seen in public without his uniform. But for this it might almost have been forgotten that he had ever worn a uniform at all, since he was the most astute of the "plain-clothes men" that ever went on the roll of the Sheffield Police Force. He was tall, broad-shouldered, bushy-bearded, bald. Wrongdoers, who did not like him and never spoke of him except in the lurid terms, called him "Baldy" or "Whiskers" as the fancy seized them.

He was a man who was seldom at a loss even in the most baffling situation, but he confessed to being beaten when the Silver Steel Company called upon him, for the second time in three months, to ask him to solve the mystery of a lost employé.

He came into Alan Mainford's surgery one cold night in December to drink hot rum and water and gossip about people and things, as was his practice. The sergeant was a bachelor living with a widowed sister, and his recreations were few. Dr Mainford often wondered what he did to pass the time before the beginning of their friendship – it had its genesis in a violent toothache which Alan ended summarily and in the early hours of the morning with a No. 3 forcep and a muscular forearm.

"I don't know about these Silver Steel people, doctor," he said.

He had a deliberate method of speaking and a weakness for long words, was known as an orator at social functions, held important office in the Order of Oddfellows, and was a Buffalo of the highest grade.

Alan smiled as he filled his pipe.

He was a good-looking young man, who sacrificed a certain amount of confidence amongst elderly patients because he shaved clean, a habit that made him look even younger; so that people often referred to him as a "bit of a boy", and expressed their firm determination of never allowing him so much as to bandage a cut finger. He had hardly lost the tan of India, spent more time out of doors than his brother professionals, kept a couple of hunters in the Melton country and might, had he desired, have found an easier and a more lucrative practice in more pleasant surroundings, for he enjoyed a good income and had expectations which must inevitably be realised.

"What don't you know about the Silver Steel Company?" he asked.

Baldy shook his shiny head.

"In the first place, silver is silver and steel's steel," he said. "It's ridiculous and absurd to mix 'em up. In the second place, they're foreigners. I don't like foreigners. Give me the true-born Briton!"

Alan chuckled.

"You are what Mr Gladstone calls 'insular'," he began, and Baldy snorted.

"Gladstone! Don't talk about that man! He'll ruin the country one of these days, mark my words! Now, Dizzy – "

"Don't let's talk politics. Go on with your foreigners."

Baldy sipped his rum and made a little face.

"Sheffield's full of 'em lately. There's this Silver Steel lot and there's Madame What's-her-name over in – "

He snapped his fingers in an effort to recall the location. Baldy could never remember names, that was the most colossal of all his weaknesses.

"Anyway, there's her, and that German lot that are experimenting at what-do-you-call-the-place? Taking the bread out of our mouths."

"We're probably taking the bread out of their mouths, too," said Alan good-humouredly. "Don't forget, Baldy – "

"Say Eltham, or say sergeant," pleaded the other. "Baldy is low."

"Well, don't forget that Sheffield is the centre of the steel world and people come here from all over Europe to pick up wrinkles. What are the Silver Steel people doing?"

"The Lord knows," said Baldy piously. "Turnin' silver into steel or *vice versa* – a Latin expression. Only a little factory, and all the workmen sleep in cottages inside the walls – the cottages were built by a feller in Eccleshall who got sixty pounds apiece for 'em. Foreigners all of 'em. Can't speak a word of English. Works guarded by men with guns. I've seen it with my own eyes! I've warned 'em about that."

Alan picked up a small log and put it carefully on the top of the glowing coals in the grate.

"It's a secret process, I expect," he said. "Sheffield is packed tight with mysterious factories trying some new-fangled scheme."

Baldy nodded.

"With electricity, according to what I hear. It doesn't seem possible. Electricity is lights and cures rheumatism. I had a penn'orth at the winter fair. You hold two brass handles and a feller pulls out a piston and you have pins and needles all up your arm. I don't know how it's done, there's a trick in it somewhere. But what's electricity got to do with steel? It's absurd, ridiculous and confusing. It's against the laws of nature, too."

There had been, he explained, some rum things happening at the Silver Steel works. One of the workmen went for a walk on a Sunday night and had not been seen since. Then a month later another workman, who had learnt enough English to correspond with a Sheffield young lady, had climbed over the wall and gone to see her "clandestinely". He had not been seen since, except by a woman who saw him in the company of two men.

"Fightin', accordin' to this witness, a woman named...bless my life, I'll forget my own name next! Anyway, he's gone. And why not? According to Mr What's-his-name, who owns the works, this man lives in Switzerland among the Alps. Who would live in Sheffield if he had an Alp to go to?"

"I know Wertheimer," nodded Alan. "One of his men had a hand crushed and I attended him. What do you suspect about the missing men – foul play?"

"Foul grandmothers!" snorted Baldy. "Gone home – that's all. Run away with gels. This feller was writing to a girl – a Miss – dear me! I've got it on the tip of my tongue! She went away the same night. Nobody knows where. It's the old story – marry in haste and repent at leisure."

"Who is Mr Dyson?" asked Alan.

Baldy frowned.

"Dyson? Don't know him. Who is he?"

"He's an engineer, I think. I met him at the works. An enormously tall man. He's been in America and seemed to know Wertheimer."

"Dyson – I know him. A long un! He's all right – a gentleman. He's with the railway. Got a pretty sharp tongue, too."

Baldy mixed another glass of grog, using his own bottle – he insisted upon this act of partnership.

"Too many foreigners – not enough good Yorkshiremen in Sheffield. What's the use of foreigners to us? Nothing."

Alan was interested in the missing men and asked questions.

"I don't know any more than that. I've got too much work to do to bother about 'em. There's a regular outbreak of burglary in this neighbourhood and I pretty well know the man that's doing it. When I say 'man', I ask pardon of my Maker, for this chap is no man. He's a monstrosity. He oughtn't to be on the face of the earth."

"In fact, he's no gentleman," laughed Alan. "I am going to turn you out, Baldy. Don't scowl – it's a term of affection. I'm off to bed. And perhaps tonight a few expected babies will postpone their arrival until I've had a spell of sleep."

No maternity case brought Alan out of his warm bed. The hammerings on his door that woke him were the hammer blows of fate. He went out into the raw night to face new and tremendous factors which were to change and reshape his life.

2

Dr Alan Mainford was at the age when even a night call from an unknown patient had in it the stuff of adventure. Dixon brought round the pony trap and offered a few bitter comments on the weather, the hour, the difficulty of harnessing the cob by the light of a lantern which the wind blew out every few minutes, and, above all, and most insistently, the futility of obeying every summons that comes out of the night.

"The old doctor used to say: 'If they can't last till mornin' I can't save 'em tonight' – that's what the old doctor used to say," he said darkly.

Dixon was stocky and bow-legged, as became a groom. On the finest summer morning he would have been disgruntled, for it was his habit to complain.

"The old doctor – " he began again.

"Blow the old doctor!" said Alan.

"He's dead," said Dixon, hurt and reproachful.

"Of course he's dead – your grousing killed him."

Dixon never liked the word "grousing"; it was an army word and outlandish. He resented Alan's three years of service as an army doctor, did his best to hide from the world that his employer had ever had that experience. It was a tradition of the medical profession in the year 1875 that army doctors were without quality, and Dixon had been brought up in the traditions of the profession.

Alan took the reins in his hand and looked up and down the dreary street. Snow and sleet were driving down from the north-west; the gas-lamps were dim nebulae of foggy light.

"Thank Gawd I rough-shod him yesterday!" said Dixon, his mind, as ever, on the impatient and rather annoyed animal between the shafts. "Mind that hill near the Cross – he's fresh tonight, poor little feller."

He held the horse's head as Alan stepped up into the trap, wrapped a leather-covered rug waist-high about him and sat on the driver's seat.

"All right – let go his head."

The cob slipped, recovered, found his feet and his gait and went swiftly down the white-covered road. Wet snow beat into Alan's face, blinding him. Clear of Banner Cross the street lights vanished, and he drove into a black void which the faint light of his trap lamps did little to illuminate.

Happily, the cob knew the road, knew, in his peculiar way, every hedge, every isolated house. Where the road turned sharply he checked of his own will; he fell into a walk at every sharp rise and picked his way cautiously down every declivity.

Alan dreamed his waking dreams, which were in the main as fantastical and unreal as the shadows about him. He dreamed of a day when the railroad would run to the least village; perhaps there would some day be road locomotives on the lines of traction engines and steam rollers, but less cumbersome and cheaper. Perhaps a time would come when every man would have his own little engine which ran at incredible speeds – twenty miles an hour possibly – along every highway.

He hoped Mrs Stahm's servants would be able to give him tea or coffee – the latter for choice. The Germans made good coffee, or was she Swedish? He had seen her often, riding in the foreign-looking victoria with her coachman and her footman on the box, a dark-eyed, inscrutable woman of uncertain age. Nobody knew her; his small circle of friends used to speculate upon her identity and wonder what brought her to the outskirts of Sheffield and the loneliness of Brinley Hall, until they learnt that she was the widow of a Swiss engineer who had invented a new steel which was yet in its experimental stage. Apparently she lived near to the scene of the experiments, not because her interest in her husband's invention was academic or sentimental, but because she herself had had something of a scientific training.

Young Dibden, whose father was senior partner of the firm that were trying out the invention, spoke of her with respect.

"By gad, she's clever! A woman, too…! You wouldn't expect a woman to know anything about the chemistry of steel, but she does. Got the process from A to Z…told Furley that he was old fashioned…what was the word? Archaic! But she's odd – deuced odd. None of the women likes her – they loathe her. She doesn't ask 'em to tea and they don't ask her. She makes 'em shiver, and by heavens she makes me shiver too!"

Alan grinned into the dark night. Would Madame Stahm make him shiver? He saw humanity from his own peculiar angle. Men and women could be majestic and terrifying and all the things that impress, but usually they were never really interesting until he was called in to see them: rather pitiful creatures who had shed their majesty and were neither impressive nor awe-inspiring.

The cob went at a steady gait, clop-clopping through the snow covering of the road. Once he shied at something Alan could not immediately see. Snatching up the pony, he brought him to the centre of the road and, as he did so, he saw the figure which had startled the animal: the shape of a man trudging through the street. He shouted abusively in a harsh voice. Alan heard the word "lift", but he was giving no lifts that night. There were some queer people in this neighbourhood – burglaries had been numerous; it was not a night to invite any unknown pedestrian to share the trap.

His gloved hands were stiff and numbed with cold when he turned the cob's head towards the two stone pillars that flanked the drive. It wound up through an avenue of anaemic-looking trees to the big house. No lights showed in any of the windows. Stiffly he descended, gathered up the reins.

"I'll take the horse."

Alan almost jumped.

The voice came from the darkness of the porch. Now he was dimly aware, not only of the figure in the dark porch, but that the door of the house was open. The hall was in darkness.

The man spoke again in a language which Alan did not understand. It sounded like one of the Scandinavian tongues. A second man came shambling into the open and went to the cob's head.

"He will stable the horse and look after him, doctor. Will you come this way?"

Suddenly the lantern he was carrying threw out a strong yellow beam. Electricity was in the days of its infancy, and this was the first hand-lamp that Alan had ever seen – the famous Stahm lamp that was an object of curiosity for many years afterwards.

They passed into the hall, and the heavy door closed behind them.

"One moment – I will strike a lucifer and light the gas," said the guide.

Mainford waited. A match spluttered, and in a second the hall was illuminated.

The guide was a man of forty. He was well, even foppishly dressed. The long, yellow face was framed in side whiskers; there hung about him the nidor of stale cigar smoke.

"Before you go up, doctor" – he stood squarely between Alan and the broad staircase which led to the upper part of the house – "let me tell you that Madame is not ill – not ill as you would say that a person is ill, eh?"

English was not his native tongue, Alan realised. Though his accent was pure, the construction of his sentences, no less than his choice of words, betrayed him.

"She has storms in her brain; fears of death groundless. She is too clever. In woman that is terrible. For a long while she will go on, but sometimes there comes to her a sense of…bafflement. There is no such word, eh? But you understood. Good! A wall confronts her. She screams, she tries to climb up, she tries to burrow beneath, she tears at the stones with her pretty fingers. Absurd! Wait, I say, and the wall she will vanish. Mind" – he tapped his narrow forehead – "always mind will triumph! In such times the nasty little man can soothe her. You know him? I am sure you know him. Ach! Such a man! But the good Lord makes them in all shapes and sizes."

He went on, hardly stopping to find his breath, and all the time his long, white hands gesticulated every emphasis.

"What is the matter with her now?" asked Alan, a little bewildered to discover that "Madame" was not ill.

It was a cool greeting after a six-mile drive on a stormy night. He did not trouble to wonder who this man was, or in what relationship he stood to his patient. Such matters did not greatly interest him. The name of his companion and his profession he was to learn immediately.

"Hysteria – no more. It is alarming, but I would not have sent for you. Madame thinks she will die. A doctor and a priest and the nasty little man. The priest, no! She shall not die, but she shall be ill if I do not bring her relief. I am Baumgarten – engineer. Dr Stahm was my master – I his disciple. Eckhardt was also his disciple. He is dead. All thieves die sometime. He died in America of consumption. There is a God!"

Abruptly he turned and walked up the stairs, Alan, carrying the bag he had taken from underneath the seat of the trap, following. Who was Eckhardt? Why the malignant satisfaction that he had died so painfully? Eckhardt was a thief; what had he stolen?

At the head of the stairs was a wide landing. The walls were hung with tapestries; there was a suggestion of luxury, of immense wealth, and with it went an air of neglect and decay. There was a certain mustiness about the house which betokened a total disregard for fresh air or ventilation. Two of the tapestries hung crookedly; Alan saw that they were supported on loops of string from tenpenny nails driven into the panels.

"This way, my dear sir."

Baumgarten opened a recessed door and they passed, not into a bedroom, as Alan had expected, but into a great drawing-room. Though from the centre of the black ceiling hung a gas chandelier, where three yellow flames were burning within glass globes, it was almost as if he had walked into the outer dark. The walls, the carpets, the curtains were papered or draped in black. The furniture, when he could pick it out, was upholstered and lacquered in the same gloomy hue. The only relief to this manufactured gloom were the woman in pale green velvet who sat on the raised dais at one end of the long room, and the white-clad nurse who stood by her side, watching Alan with a relief in her eyes which she did not attempt to disguise.

It was not on the patient, but on the nurse, that Dr Mainford's attention was riveted. In her simple uniform she looked like some exquisite creature of the Renaissance with her dull gold hair which the nurse's bonnet could not hide, and her slim, perfectly poised figure. The exquisite moulding of her face, the red rose lips, the firm little chin, the ivory whiteness of her skin, left him breathless.

He knew most of the nurses in Sheffield, but this was a stranger to him.

"Well, well, well." It was Baumgarten's impatient voice. "There is Madame to be seen, is it not?"

And then, almost with a wrench, Alan turned his attention to the woman in green. It was difficult to believe that she was human. Her face was an enamelled white, the dark eyes stared ahead of her; she seemed oblivious of her surroundings, of his presence, of anything that was earthly.

From her face, plastered thick with powder, he could not judge her age. It was only when he saw the hands, tightly clenched on the arms of her velvet chair, that he judged her to be over fifty. She sat, stiff, motionless, bolt upright, her chin raised, her face expressionless. About her neck was a great circle of green stones. From their size he was satisfied they could not be emeralds; but here he was mistaken. A big emerald ring glittered on one finger. About each arm was bracelet upon bracelet, until she glittered from wrist to elbow.

Alan experienced a queer sense of embarrassment as he went to her and tried to take her hand. The clutching fingers could not be pried loose from their grip. He pushed up the jewelled circles, found her pulse and took out his watch. The pulse was faint but regular.

"Are you feeling ill?" he asked.

Madame Stahm made no answer, and he looked at the nurse inquiringly.

"She has been like this for nearly an hour," said the girl in a low voice. "I have tried everything. It looks like a cataleptic seizure, but Mr Baumgarten says it is not unusual and that she will recover in time. She was taken ill last night at about seven," she went on. "It was dreadful!"

"Screaming?"

She nodded. He heard her quick sigh.

"Yes…dreadful. Mr Baumgarten was alarmed. But the attack passed off, and he thought it was over. At eleven o'clock it came on again, worse."

She did not take her eyes from his when she spoke, and he saw in them the shadow of fear, which is very rarely met with in the eyes of a woman of her profession.

"What is your name?" he asked.

"Jane Garden. I am from St Mary's Hospital in London. I've been here a month."

She glanced past him towards Baumgarten, who stood motionless, his head bent, a frank and unabashed listener.

Alan stooped and looked at the woman's eyes. They were set; the pupils were pin-pointed, and he made a little grimace.

"It is either hysteria or drugs – " he began.

"Neither – fool!"

It was the green woman who almost snarled the words, and he was so startled that he dropped the stethoscope he was fitting.

She did not move, did not even turn her eyes in his direction. Only the thin lips moved.

"You have no sense, no brains! You see only material things! You do not examine the soul! I project myself into the infinite, and you say 'hysteria'! I walk with Stahm and his shadow, Eckhardt, and you say 'drugs'! I live in the shades, I go out of the world, and you feel my pulse and listen to my heart and say: 'Ah, well, she is mad.' "

And then the dead figure came to life. He saw the bosom rise as she inhaled a deep breath; the eyes moved slowly in his direction. The figure became suddenly alive.

"Who sent for this man? Who sent for him?" She almost screamed the words.

"I sent for him," said Baumgarten calmly. "You said you were dying, you asked for a doctor, a priest and the ugly man. Here is your doctor. The ugly man is coming – the priest, no."

She began speaking rapidly to him in a language which was neither Scandinavian nor German. One word gave him the clue. They were talking in Russian. Both Baumgarten and Madame Stahm were Russian by birth, he discovered later.

The first part of her speech was obviously a flood of abuse; but gradually her voice and manner grew calmer, and the thin lips curled in a smile. When she turned to the doctor and spoke her manner was entirely changed.

"Most stupid of me, doctor," she said, so graciously that he was staggered. "I have these – what is the word? – fits! Hysteria? It is possible. But drugs – I do not think I have taken drugs – no, Baumgarten?"

He shook his head slowly, his eyes upon her.

"That is the truth," she said. "Now you shall feel my pulse."

She held out her hand almost gaily, and Alan's fingers closed upon a wrist that pulsated so strongly that it might not have been the same woman he had examined a few seconds before.

"It is hysteria possibly. I am a great trial to all my friends. But then, what woman is not? You are psychic, doctor?"

It was a word not very commonly used, and he frowned.

"Psychic? Do you mean seeing spooks and things?"

"Spooks and things," she repeated with an ironic little smile. "Eh? That is your idea of the psychic? Well, perhaps you are right, doctor. My nerves are bad."

She turned abruptly to Baumgarten.

"The ugly man, is he coming?"

Baumgarten looked at his watch.

"He should be here," he said, and went out of the room.

Madame Stahm regarded her professional caller with a quizzical smile.

"You do not know my nasty little man, I suppose? Or does everybody know him? He is a seer. People do not believe so, but he has divinity!"

Alan for the moment was not interested in psychic things, or even ugly men who had divine qualities. He was intensely practical.

"Don't you think you should undress and go to bed?" he said. "I can give you a bromide draught which can be made up at the chemists – there is one at the village two miles away."

She laughed a low, amused laugh.

"You say I take drugs, so you give me more, eh. That is funny!"

"Rest will be very good for you," he said.

The nurse started from her contemplation of Alan.

"It will be very good for you," she urged. "You remember, I suggested a sleeping draught – "

"A sleeping draught, ach!" Madame Stahm snapped her jewelled fingers. "No, I will have my ugly man and he will rest me. Jane doesn't like my ugly man."

There was no need for the girl to confirm this – her face told the story.

The squeak of the door handle made Alan Mainford turn, and then he saw Madame's seer.

3

He was a queer, incongruous figure of a man. His height could not have been more than five feet; the big, dark, deep-set eyes were the one pleasant feature in a face which was utterly repulsive. They were the eyes of an intelligent animal. The forehead was grotesquely high, running in furrows almost to where, at the crown of the head, a mop of gray hair rolled back. The unshaven cheeks were cadaverous, deeply lined and hollow. There was a ferocity in the overthrust jaw as the little man moved it from side to side. His thick, rough coat was soddened with sleet, his boots left little pools of water on the black carpet. He wore home-knitted mittens, and in one hand clutched an ancient violin case.

"Delighted!" murmured Madame. "You are a good man to come. I am in need of your inspiration. Play, play, play!"

The little man was glaring malignantly at Alan.

"You couldn't stop and gimme a lift, mister?" he demanded resentfully. "I must trudge through the muck and the mire. I called to tha', but no, he goes on – him ridin' – me walkin'!"

Alan's eyes had wandered to the nurse. She stood rigid, and in her face was a look of horror that helped to tell a story he intended knowing before he left the house that night.

"Play!"

The order was imperious. The little man squatted down on a chair and opened the case on his knees. He took out an old violin and a bow and cuddled the fiddle under his chin.

15

Then he began to play, and all the time those animal eyes of his were fixed on Jane Garden's face. He played a queer obbligato and he was extemporising every note. There were moments when he defied every law of harmony, when he became so musically illiterate that Alan, who was no music-lover, winced. There were times when he achieved a breath-taking peak of beauty, when the very soul of humanity trembled on the taut strings of the instrument.

And always he looked at Jane, and it came to Alan Mainford that this man was playing her as though she were a piece of music, translating thought, discordant fear, jarring uncertainty, wild despair, into the terms of melody.

"Play me, ugly man! Leaf her! You hear, play me!"

Madame's voice was an angry wail. It was true then – that was what this ugly little devil was doing – playing souls.

He saw the violinist turn his eyes to the older woman and the pace of the music quickened, became distorted, wild, dreamy and strident. Then, suddenly, in a discord that set Alan's teeth on edge, the music ceased.

"Out of me head!"

The ugly man pronounced his boast loudly. He was pleased with himself, triumphant was the better word. His deep chest swelled, he wiped his streaming forehead with a brightly coloured handkerchief, and the thick lips were unlatched in a grin.

"Out of me head! You're an educated man. I'm self-learnt – but I got more cleverness in me than you! Next time I say give me a lift, you give it!"

He had become suddenly a bully, overbearing. Alan, who had reason for being annoyed, was amused: for all this bluster was for the benefit of Jane Garden. The little ugly man was showing off.

"I can sing, recite, do a dance," he went on. "I bin before public in real theatres. I can whistle like a bird – "

He pursed his lips and of a sudden there was a blackbird in the room, singing with the joy of life and the unborn spring in its little heart. Alan listened, fascinated.

"No more, you have done well, my dear little friend." Madame arrested a further demonstration. "Here is the money."

She thrust her hand into a bag that hung from her wrist. They heard the jingle of gold and then she held out two sovereigns to the whistler. He accepted the gift with an odd air of condescension: it was as though he was the donor and she the recipient.

"You are a truly great man" – her tone was almost caressing. "Some day you shall be the greatest man in the world. I love you, because you are so ugly and dirty. Tomorrow – or on Sunday – I will send for you. Goodbye."

He hesitated, his dark eyes again sought Jane Garden.

"I don't walk back, missus. You ain't going to let a poor old man walk back?"

"I'll give you a lift as far as the city," said Alan, still amused. "I didn't know you were coming to this house or I would have picked you up."

The little man's lips curled in a sneer.

"I daresay you would," he said.

And then Alan caught the girl's eyes, saw the urgency of the summons in them, and went across to her. To his amazement she was breathless, hardly able to speak.

"I want you to get me away from here," she said in a low tone. "Can you – will you?"

"But how –?"

"I don't care how you do it. I know you can't take me away tonight, but can't you send for me tomorrow and give me some instructions about Mrs Stahm's treatment? They won't let me go near Sheffield – please!"

Mainford thought quickly. Both Madame Stahm and Baumgarten were watching him closely. It almost seemed as though they had expected her to approach him.

"I'll send the trap over for you tomorrow, Nurse Garden," he said in a loud voice. "The test won't take very long, and I think that it should – "

"Send the trap over?" repeated Madame sharply. "Why?"

He looked at her steadily.

"Because Nurse Garden is not particularly well, and I would like to make a blood test," he said.

"It can be made here," said Baumgarten quickly.

"It will be made just where I want it to be made!"

Here was the imperious army doctor speaking, authority in his tone.

There was a brief and embarrassing silence.

"I'm afraid I can't spare the nurse," said Madame Stahm acidly, and quailed under Alan Mainford's cold gaze.

He had that effect upon some people; this woman might not be a coward, but she was incapable of resisting authority.

"Is there any reason why she should not go into Sheffield?" he asked.

"None at all," snapped Madame. "But I think a sick patient is entitled to be consulted before a nurse is taken away from her."

Alan smiled.

"You are consulted, Madame Stahm. I will send the trap for this young lady at three o'clock tomorrow afternoon. Either my groom will drive over or my friend Sergeant Eltham, who is an expert driver, will call for her."

It was a threat; nobody in that room mistook the significance of Alan's alternative suggestion. He heard a low grumble behind him, like the growl of an animal, and out of the corner of his eye he saw the little man's face pucker in anger.

"Very good," said Madame Stahm hastily. "There is no reason why the nurse should not go, though it will be very inconvenient. Mr Baumgarten will pay you your fee, doctor. I shall not require you again."

Alan bowed.

"That is for you to decide, Madame Stahm. But I would advise you, if you have another such attack as you had today, not to let your prejudice against me stand in the way of calling me in. You have a very bad heart, but I suppose you know that?"

She glared down at him malignantly from her raised seat.

"It's a lie!" She spoke with difficulty. "I have goot health – goot health! You shall not say that I am sick because I have visions…you said this to anger me? Tell me, doctor, you said this to anger me, and I will forgive you."

"You have a bad heart," repeated Alan quietly. "Your pulse is not at all as it should be, and you have certain facial symptoms which are rather alarming. I repeat, don't let the fact that I have annoyed you stop you from calling me in if you cannot get another doctor."

He nodded to the girl, made another little bow to Madame Stahm and walked out of the room, followed by Baumgarten. At the door he turned to look back at Jane. She had already disappeared, but the ugly little man had made his way to Madame Stahm's side and was talking to her eagerly in a low voice. She nodded, nodded again, shook her head and smiled.

"Have no fear, little friend," she said. "You shall have all you desire."

As the man came towards them, Baumgarten, with some ostentation, opened a purse which he took from his trousers' pocket and put a golden sovereign and a shilling in Alan's palm.

"That, I think, is a generous fee," he said, a little pompously. And then his voice changed. "Do you think she's ill – yes? Really, with her heart?" He tapped his own anxiously.

"I think so," replied Alan.

He was not anxious to discuss the symptoms of his patient with the mysterious Mr Baumgarten and made his way down the stairs into the dimly lit hall.

"One question, doctor – Do you know a dull, stupid man – a Swiss – who has a factory: the Silver Steel Company, eh?"

"No," said Alan shortly.

The cob and the trap were standing at the door and Alan mounted to his seat. He had just taken up the reins when there came a sound that made his blood run cold. It was a long, muffled shriek, that ended in an agonised wail, and it came from somewhere in the house.

"What was that?" he asked quickly.

"It is the railway whistle, my friend," said Baumgarten's voice. He could hardly see him in the darkness. "You are nervous!"

"That was no railway whistle," said Alan, and waited, listening, but the scream was not repeated.

He had forgotten all about the little man until he began clambering up on the opposite side and fell into the more comfortable seat.

"Give me some of that apron, will you?" he growled. "Haven't you got any heart for an old man?... Ought to be ashamed of yourself."

Alan unwrapped the driving apron which he had drawn around himself; slipping one of the leather loops round the iron batten at his side, he passed the rest of the cover to his unwelcome passenger. A touch of the reins and the cob was heading down the drive.

He was half annoyed, half amused with himself. Why on earth had he taken this line with Madame Stahm? He had deliberately tried to frighten her, and he had most certainly antagonised her beyond forgiveness, though this was a matter of no account.

He was amused also to find himself acting in the role of champion to distressed nurses, but there was something behind that girl's terror, something peculiarly sinister in the atmosphere of the house. He had not hesitated; the only uneasiness he had in his mind was whether he should leave her there for another night.

All the time he had been in that queer habitation he had a sense that it was over-tenanted. He was conscious of the presence of men whom he did not see, and had a feeling that strange and unfriendly eyes had watched him all the time he had been there...

That shriek — it was a shriek; it could not have been anything else. Was Mrs Stahm passing through another hysterical crisis? The little man at his side fidgeted uneasily, grumbling under his breath.

"You've got too much of the apron." He tugged at it savagely. "Do you want to make me ill so as you can cure me? I wouldn't have you for a doctor! I hate the sight of doctors. They go round telling people they're sick when there's nowt wrong with 'em."

"Why did you come out at this hour of the night?" asked Alan, ignoring the abuse. "Is it a practice of yours?"

"Mind your own business," snarled the other. "I go out any hour of the night I like — do you see?"

"If you're not civil I'll stop the trap and throw you out," said Alan angrily.

"It'd take a better man than you – " began the other, when the young doctor pulled his horse to a standstill.

"Get out and walk," he said curtly.

"See this?"

The little man stretched out his arm. In the rereflected light of the lamp Alan saw, dangling from his wrist, a snub-nosed revolver, evidently fastened by a strap to his wrist.

"That's a shooter, young man. You know what a shooter is – hold hard, don't hit!"

He had seen Alan's hand go back, and the bullying tone became suddenly a supplicating whine.

"You wouldn't hit an old man, would you? Mind you, I could throw you out of this trap as easy as cutting butter! But I don't want to get into any trouble with you or with anybody else. I'm an old man, and all I want is peace and quietness."

"Then sit quiet," said Alan savagely.

He flung the apron back over the man's knees and tchk-ed to the cob.

"And shut your mouth," he added.

The latter injunction was instantly disobeyed.

"I don't wonder you're surprised seeing me here," said the little man. "But I go out when I'm sent for. And they send for me all hours of the day and night – women! They take a liking to me – they go off their heads about me. There was a girl in Sheffield – "

He told a story to which Alan found it difficult to listen with patience.

"Madame is a lady bred and born," he went on. "That woman knows me better than I know myself. I heard what you said, mister – I play her! I can play anybody! I see inside 'em and put it into the fiddle. There ain't another man in England could do that. There ain't another man in England who can recite like I can recite. I've been on the stage."

21

He went on in this strain for ten minutes, and then abruptly broke off and asked: "What do you think of my girl?"

"Your girl?"

"That's what I said," said the other; "the young nurse lady; the one you're going to operate on tomorrow."

"I'm not operating on anybody tomorrow, but if you mean the nurse, will you explain what you mean by 'your girl'?" asked Alan in a cold fury.

The little man chuckled continuously, beating his knees in the ecstasy of his humour.

"She'll be mine," he said at last. "I don't say she is at the minute. Notice her looking at me as if I was a snake? I've seen dozens of 'em do that, and how have they ended up?"

"I don't particularly want to know," said Alan.

But his passenger could not be snubbed.

"There's a lady bred and born coming to live near me. Her husband's a gentleman, but she's coming to live next door to me, and for why? Because she's off her head about me – and a lady! You ought to see her, mister – young–" He smacked his lips and became physically descriptive.

Alan was not easily revolted. He was not revolted even now. He listened with a sort of resentful amazement to the boasting of this little blackguard, and if once or twice he had the temptation to hit him on the head with the butt of his whip he restrained himself.

"Where do you work?" he asked, more to turn the conversation than to elicit the information.

"Work? What – me? I'm a master man. I don't work for nobody. I'm independent. I can earn my living in a dozen ways. My wood-carving is better than any wood-carving you've ever seen. I can frame pictures, I can make a cabinet – there's nothing I couldn't do. Some of these lah-de-da-dy swells in Sheffield think they're clever, but I've forgot more than they knew. You're not going to drop me here, are you?"

Alan pulled up the cob before his house.

"Take me on to Darnell, mister: it's only a couple of miles."

"Walk," said Alan laconically.

"I'm an old man," wailed his dogged passenger. "You wouldn't let an old man walk through the slush and the snow on a night like this? It's not human!"

"You're not human either. Get down!"

Out of the shadow of the porch before Alan's house came a burly figure.

"Hullo, doctor! You're the man I wanted to see."

It was Sergeant Eltham, and at the sound of his voice the little man slipped from the trap on the offside and vanished into the night.

"Thought you had somebody with you? He went quickly enough – not so quick that I didn't see him," said Sergeant Eltham. "What kind of persons are you picking up at night, doctor?"

"Do you know him?" asked Alan, in surprise.

"Know him?" scoffed Baldy. "I should say I did know him! The cleverest burglar in the north of England, the nastiest little brute in the world."

"What is his name?" asked Alan, suspecting another demonstration of Baldy's weakness, but for once Sergeant Eltham had the name on the tip of his tongue and could pronounce it.

"His name is Charles Peace," he said.

4

Charles Peace? The name meant nothing to Dr Mainford.

"He's certainly a nasty fellow. Come in and have some coffee. What are you doing out in the middle of the night?"

"I'll tell you later."

The sergeant stopped to stamp the snow from his feet on the doorstep, and heaved a sigh of relief as he came into the snug warmth of Alan's study.

"Have a look to see that you haven't lost your watch," he said. "Peace is as good a pickpocket as he is a burglar. There's nothing he can't do, from shove-ha'penny to murder. Did he give you any trouble?"

Alan laughed.

"A little bit," he said. "I nearly threw him out of the trap."

"I'm glad you didn't try." Baldy was very serious. "That man has got the strength of ten. I went for him once in Sheffield, and it took seven policemen to get him to the station, and then we had to frog-march him."

Alan was not convinced.

"He didn't give me that impression. He showed me a revolver when I threatened him."

"A revolver, eh?" said the other quickly. "By gum, I wish I'd known that, I'd have pinched him. I've always heard he carried a pistol, but I never found one on him. How did you come to meet him?"

Briefly Alan told the story of his visit to Madame Stahm, though he made no reference to the beautiful nurse or to the shriek he had heard. When he had finished, Baldy nodded.

"Yes, I know all about his fiddle playing. Personally, I know nothing about music and harmony, but I'm told he plays well enough to go on the stage. In fact, he has been on the stage. Did he tell you anything about wild beasts?"

"Wild beasts?" repeated the startled young doctor. "Is he an animal tamer, too?" he asked ironically.

To his surprise Baldy nodded.

"He can tame wild elephants! I've seen him go into a lions' den at Wombwell's menagerie and take a bone from under the nose of a lion. His father was in the animal training business, and so was Peace – that's why he's a good burglar: dogs never bark at him."

"Are you serious?" asked Alan, pausing as he poured out the coffee which the sleepy-eyed Dixon had brought in.

"It's the truth," said Sergeant Eltham. "Dogs never bark at Peace. You can get the most savage retriever and chain him in a kennel outside your door, and Peace will come in in the middle of the night, pat the dog and send him back to sleep. He plays the piano – in fact, there's nothing he can't do in the musical line. And they tell me he can make up poetry."

Out of curiosity Alan repeated some of the man's boasts of conquests, and was amazed when Baldy confirmed the little man's claims.

"You wouldn't think it possible, but it's a fact. I could tell you some pretty bad cases – decent women who've left their homes for him. He's lame – did you notice that? And one of his fingers was shot off when he was a boy, and his face – good Lord! Well, you've seen him!"

"He's a pretty old man, isn't he?"

Baldy shook his head.

"No, sir. Peace can't be much more than forty-three. He looks seventy, but round about forty is his real age. Did he cry to you about being a poor old man? He always does."

He told Alan something of the man's record. He had started as a pickpocket, gone on to be a burglar.

"I pinched him twenty years ago, when he burgled a house in this city. He got a stretch of four years, but that wasn't his first conviction.

He got one dose of six years at Manchester, and then went back and got another. In fact, he knows more prisons than any bad character I've ever met with."

Alan listened, fascinated.

"He's been out three years now," explained Baldy in answer to his question. "I don't often see him, except when I'm making inquiries about a job, and then he's got an alibi tied to his left ear! Funny you met him tonight. What was he doing at Mrs Stahm's? That's the puzzle."

The sergeant ran his fingers through his long beard.

"She's very kind and charitable, by all accounts. I think somebody ought to see her and warn her."

Alan shook his head.

"I don't think that's necessary," he said quietly. "Madame Stahm has a pretty good idea of the kind of man he is. Now, tell me what you want to see me about."

Baldy sat for a little while, ordering his brief narrative.

"Do you remember that fellow I spoke to you about – the foreigner, who disappeared from the Silver Gilt works?"

"Silver Steel," suggested Alan.

Sergeant Eltham brushed aside the correction impatiently.

"Whatever it is. Well, it appears he hasn't turned up in Switzerland. His relations have written to Mr What's-his-name – "

"Wertheimer?"

"That's the feller – asking for the allowance he used to make to his sister. What's more, the first man that ran away hasn't been seen at his home since he disappeared from Sheffield. I've got a few facts about the business that you might like to know, doctor. You've been a good friend of mine, and your brain and education have helped me when I've been stuck before."

He opened his book, turned the leaves slowly to refresh his memory, closed the book and slipped it in his pocket, and began.

"Over in Switzerland there was a man, whose name I can't exactly remember and can't read, who got an idea he could make steel that wouldn't rust. Which, on the face of it, is absurd and ridiculous. This

Professor What's-his-name had a lab – what's the word? It begins with an 'l'."

"Laboratory?" suggested Alan.

The sergeant nodded.

"That's the thing. He was pretty high up in science and he built or borrowed or rented this lab – the word you said – and got a lot of young professors to come in and help him. They didn't quite make what they were looking for, but they got near enough to it for them to see that they were near the secret. Then one of the young men who were helping the old man bolted to America, and took away with him all the papers and calculations and the likes of that, thinking that he could invent the thing himself and get all the money there was for inventing it."

A light dawned on Alan Mainford.

"Is the professor alive?" he asked.

"No," said Baldy. "This feller running away so much upset the old man, Professor What's-his-name, that he took sick and died. Another assistant carried on the work, but the widow of the professor was so suspicious that she kicked him out, and he came to England and started experimenting on his own. That is the man at the Silver Steel works."

"Wertheimer?"

"That's him, Wertheimer. In the meantime the feller that went away to America and opened a sort of lab – whatever it is – on his own, died. The man at the Silver Steel works heard about this, sent to America and brought over two or three of the head men who had been working for the American fellow, and two out of the three have already disappeared. Wertheimer (don't say I can't remember names) is very upset about it, because he was sure that both these men had the secret of the new steel, and would have worked it out for him if they had remained. What is worrying him is that they may have gone over to this very woman you're speaking about."

"Madame Stahm? Why, of course. Eckhardt was the man who ran away – "

"That's his name," said Baldy, as triumphantly as though he had himself remembered it. "Eckhardt!"

And Wertheimer was the dull, stupid man about whom he had been questioned.

"I'm going to drive over to see the lady tomorrow," Baldy went on, "and I was wondering if you could lend me your trap."

"I'll lend you my trap, and you can bring back the nurse who is there, a Miss Jane Garden," said Alan quickly. "Have any inquiries been made at Dibdens, where Mrs Stahm is having her experiments made?"

Baldy nodded.

"Yes, according to Mr – the Silver Steel man – he's been into that. He's had a chat with Mr Dibden himself, and neither of the two men are employed at the works. My own theory is that they've gone off with girls – they're foreigners, and naturally they run after women."

"I know a few Englishmen who do that," said Alan dryly. "Your friend Peace – "

"Don't call him my friend." Baldy raised his voice protestingly. "There's a dirty little skunk if you like! I remember once he fell into the river: he couldn't swim, but, bless your heart, I said to the people on the bank: 'Don't worry about him: he's born to be hung, and a man who's born to be hung can never be drowned.' It's a funny thing – have you ever noticed it as a medical man?"

"I can't say that I have," said Alan, yawning. "But I still don't know why you go out in the middle of the night to pursue these inquiries of yours."

"The Silver Steel man came round and knocked me up. I've been with him for two hours, and I was so wide awake when he'd gone that I popped round to see if there was a light in the surgery."

Alan dozed off that morning with an uneasy consciousness that there was a vital something that he had forgotten to tell the sergeant. In the first hour of waking he realised that that something was – the scream in the night.

5

Baumgarten waited until the sound of the trap wheels had passed beyond his hearing, closed the half-open door through which he had watched the departure, and went swiftly upstairs to Madame Stahm. Madame was alone; she had dismissed the nurse, and was half sitting, half reclining in her big throne chair. She saw something in the man's face that brought her bolt upright.

"What is wrong?" she asked.

"Did you hear it?" His black eyebrows made an inquiring arch. "If you did not, our doctor did."

"Lamonte?"

"The ventilator must have been left open. I will go and see. Tomorrow we shall have the police here, and that will be extremely awkward."

She was galvanised to life by the words and came instantly to her feet.

"The police?" she said shrilly. "You are mad! And if they come it will be your fault. You are careless, Peter."

He said no word, but, passing down into the hall, took the lantern from the table and descended a flight of stone stairs, through an underground kitchen and along a passage, the end of which was barred by an ironclad door. He unlocked this; beyond was a chamber that had once been a wine cellar, a large, low-vaulted room, lined with iron shelves. He stopped here to light a gas bracket and went on through another door to a smaller cellar.

It was part of a much older building. The stone-vaulted roofs were supported on pillars that seemed over-massive in that confined space. Again he lit a gas bracket and looked round. A table, a chair and a bed practically comprised the furnishing of the room. On the bed lay a man, and from beneath the blanket ran a thin, steel chain which was fastened to a staple in the wall.

The man on the bed lay on his back, his white, disfigured face upturned. He glared at Baumgarten as he approached.

"Why did you make that noise, you pig?" demanded Baumgarten without heat.

The man blinked at him.

"I am cold, and there are rats here," he said thickly. "I must have been dreaming."

He stretched out his hand, took a mug of water from the table and drank eagerly, supporting himself on his elbow.

"It is very cold," he said again. "You must give me some more blankets."

"I will give you something else to warm you." Baumgarten showed his white teeth in a smile from which mirth was absent. "You are fortunate to be alive, my breaker of oaths!"

The man on the bed passed his thin hand over his face wearily, and turned on his side.

"I took no oaths; I am not a traitor," he said. "I was little more than a workman – you know that, Herr Baumgarten. It is true that I worked for Eckhardt, but would Eckhardt give me any of his secrets? It is true that I worked for Wertheimer, but does he tell me his formula? A hundred and fifty francs a week, Herr Baumgarten – that is my salary. Is it the pay of a genius to whom you trust formulas?"

"You're a liar," said Baumgarten dispassionately. "Every month you sent a thousand francs to your bank in Lausanne. We shall make you talk, my friend."

The face of Lamonte puckered with rage.

"Your whip – no. Some day I shall talk, Baumgarten, before an English judge – and I shall tell them of the man who was here before, and who left a message written on the wall…ah, you did not know that. Where is he – you devil!"

Suddenly he leaped from the bed. Baumgarten had just time to throw himself out of reach before the chain about the man's ankles caught him and flung him to the stone floor.

Peter Baumgarten was no coward. He could meet violence with violence, but this news the man had given him threw him off his balance.

"My friend, you had him here; what did you do with him?" screamed the prisoner, straining at the chain. "You murdered him – you and that hag! I will have you on the scaffold with a rope round your necks!"

"Your friend is in Switzerland." Baumgarten was practically breathless, panic-stricken by the discovery of his secret. "He was very foolish; he could have had a lot of money. Instead, he preferred to be a traitor."

"He is dead," wailed Lamonte.

"He is alive – I swear it. He went from here a very sick man, but he is alive."

Here he spoke the truth, for the prisoner this cell had held was alive and on the Continent in the mental hospital for which his sufferings had qualified him.

"Go back to bed. Be sensible. We have not hurt you. What is a little whip? You are the better for it. Tell us all that Eckhardt told you, and you will be a rich man and free."

The man crawled back to bed with a groan and pulled the blankets over him.

"I know nothing, I can tell nothing," he said.

Baumgarten went out, extinguished the light and locked the doors behind him. He found Madame sitting as he had left her.

"Well?" she asked.

He shrugged his shoulders.

"I am worried about this man. His mentality is stronger. We cannot present him to the alienist and say: 'His mind is deranged; do not believe anything he says.' "

"He may die," she said indifferently.

"I hope not."

Baumgarten's voice was curt, emphatic.

"What use is it to you or to me, Clarice, if we have millions in our hands, and after be locked up behind an iron door, with an English judge eating his eggs and bacon and saying: 'I think I will send these people to the gallows today,' *hein*? That is no end for a gentleman! All the money in the world is not worth it. We have already gone too far, spent too much, chasing this miracle dream of ours."

"You're a fool, too," she snapped. And then, after a moment's thought: "The little man would kill him."

"Peace?" He laughed. "You do not know that man, Madame! He could not kill Lamonte — he must dramatise his every action. If Lamonte were part of a drama — yes. But if you took him down to a cold cellar and said: 'Kill this man,' he would be horrified. He is highly moral, a little religious."

She stared at him in amazement.

"Peace I am talking about," she said.

He nodded.

"That is Peace. I mean, this dirty little man has a peculiar moral standard. Strange that you have not noticed that. It is the standard of sentiment, a little elastic, but very real. And yet, he is loathsome; and I feel that I could put my foot on him every time I see him."

She smiled to herself.

"He is very admirable. Some day he will be very useful."

"To calm your nerves?" He could not resist the sneer.

"To save us all," she replied.

6

While Alan was shaving next morning, he sent Dixon round to find the police officer, but Baldy was out on one of those mysterious missions which made up his life. He would see him later in the day, when he brought Jane Garden back; and here a new train of thought started.

Jane Garden was a problem which had to be solved, and the solution of this particular difficulty did not immediately present itself.

This ugly burglar Peace had excited his curiosity and interest, and these were big enough to overcome the natural revulsion he felt towards the man. He was something of a humanist, and had all the detachment of the scientific observer. He could regard the little man as foul beyond tolerance, and yet could find the same interest in him as he discovered in the obscure diseases which came under his notice at rare intervals.

Alan, despite his youth, had retained and enlarged the practice of the old doctor from whose executors he had acquired it. In the main it was an upper middle-class clientele, and none of these could be expected to give a first-hand impression of the little nondescript. It was not until he began his charity calls in the poorer suburbs that he learned that Peace was quite a well-known character, had a reputation none too savoury, but on the whole was reluctantly admired by his law-abiding friends and neighbours.

Peace himself lived in a poor-class district, and was by all accounts a great lover of animals: his canaries and parrots were famous in the neighbourhood. He was believed to be a man of superior education, and was credited with gifts to which, to Alan personally, he had made no claim.

If these poor people looked askance at him at all, their distrust was based on other causes than his anti-social activities. There were mothers of daughters who did not call his name blessed; but if he was hated in such quarters as these he was also feared. Alan confirmed the stories of his extraordinary strength. He was a frequent attraction at local sing-songs, and was believed to have not only written his own lyrics but composed the music.

Nobody loved him; nobody even liked him; the most that could be said of him was that he was respected. Hereabouts his boastfulness was not regarded as such, but rather as a statement of fact offered by the only person who could be an authority.

By a coincidence, Alan came upon some of his handiwork: a wooden crucifix, carved from cedar, and, despite certain crudities, a beautiful piece of work. In another house the mention of the man's name produced an ingenious mechanical toy, which he had made for a child. Alan had a chat with a doctor who did most of his work amongst this particular class.

"A terrible little beast," said the other medico, and, speaking as doctor to doctor, he explained why. "He's done time, too, but his neighbours don't know that."

"Would it make any difference?" asked Alan, and to his surprise the other doctor was emphatic.

"Good heavens, yes! The respectable poor are terribly proper, and would have nothing to do with a man who'd been in the jug, as they call it."

Alan was again to hear of Peace, for when he got back from his afternoon calls, which he did on foot, since he had lent the cob and the trap to Baldy, he found that gentleman waiting for him.

"I've brought the young lady. She's gone upstairs to her room – is she staying here?"

"For a little while."

Alan had made this eleventh-hour arrangement with his housekeeper, and had scrawled a hurried note to the girl telling her his plans.

"A very nice young person," said Baldy. "Very nice. That Madame What's-her-name wasn't too pleased to see me, doctor, although she seemed to be expecting me."

Alan started guiltily.

"Good heavens, yes! I'd forgotten that I half threatened her with you – at least, I said I'd probably send you out to bring back Nurse Garden. The spirit of prophecy was on me, Baldy!"

Sergeant Eltham closed his eyes in resignation.

"Don't call me Baldy," he murmured.

"Sorry. She wasn't pleased to see you, eh? What do you think of her?"

Baldy pursed his bearded lips.

"She may be, and she may not be," he said cryptically. "I'm not sure. She must have been a fine woman when she was young, but, of course, she's a foreigner, and that makes all the difference. She's got a rough side to her tongue, doctor; when I started inquiring about the missing men she let me have it in French, German, Russian, Eyetalian, Spanish and Chinese – at least, that's what it sounded like. When she got back to English she started to tell me what she was going to do when she saw my superintendent. Naturally, I shook in my shoes: I always do when I'm threatened."

"Whom did you see?" asked Alan curiously. "Baumgarten?"

"I wouldn't remember the names even if I'd heard 'em," confessed Baldy. "I saw a couple of menservants, and tough-looking customers they were. And, of course, I saw the lady and the nurse, but I didn't see her till I was going. And I saw three or four rough-looking loafers walking about the grounds. They might have been gardeners, but they didn't look like it. Well, the long and the short of it is, doctor, she knows nothing about the missing men, and has never employed them. She said Mr What's-his-name of the Silver Steel Company was a thief and a dull man and other abusive epitaphs – "

"Epithets," suggested Alan.

"Well, whatever it is. Rum-looking woman, not my idea of something to come home to. I saw that other woman this morning – the farmer's wife, Mrs How-d'you-call-him – the woman who saw the fight the day the man disappeared. She said one of the men who was talking to this young feller on the night that he disappeared was a little man with an ugly face. Recognise the description?"

"You mean Peace?"

Baldy nodded.

"I'm taking her round tonight to see if she can identify him. Of course, Peace will swear he wasn't anywhere near the spot – he's the man who invented alibis. He's poisonous."

He took his leave soon after to go in search of the farmer's wife. Mrs Haggerty, the housekeeper, had laid tea and had brought in the pot and the muffin dish when Jane Garden came down the narrow staircase through the hall and into the little study.

Alan looked at her and gasped. She wore a dark, closely-fitting taffeta dress, with a little white lace collar, and her deep gold hair was uncovered. Beauty sometimes owes some of its quality to the frame in which it is set. Alan always said that a nurse who was not pretty in uniform must be very plain without; but the radiant beauty of this girl was enhanced by the severity of her "civilian" attire.

There was a new light in her eyes; her face was transformed. The haggard fear which had sat on her on the previous night had departed, and there was now an assurance in her poise and a radiance in the smile that parted her red lips.

"Well, doctor, you certainly got me away! What are you going to do with me?" she said almost gaily.

"You're not going back to Madame Stahm's?"

She shook her head.

"Never," she said emphatically. "I may return to London; I expect the institution that sent me will be very angry that I left Madame in a hurry, but I must risk that. Is there no place in Yorkshire where I could find work?"

"Must you work?" he asked.

She nodded.

"Yes," she said quietly. "I have to earn my living, and it's the only way I know."

She sat down and, at his invitation, began pouring out the tea.

"What was the trouble at Brinley Hall?" he asked,

She did not reply immediately. She handed him his cup, sliced a muffin upon his plate, and then: "Everything," she said. "The atmosphere was terrible – sinister. That's a dramatic word, but I can't think of anything better. And all those dreadful men…"

"Are there many there?"

She hesitated.

"About ten, I think," she said, to his surprise. "Madame Stahm has a private laboratory in the grounds. Some of them work there, some of them are servants; one is always meeting them in the house, and they're rather – well, embarrassing."

"Baumgarten – what of him?"

She dropped her eyes quickly.

"I don't know. He's not very nice – rather friendly – too friendly – and he's absolutely all-powerful there; he rules the house and rules Madame Stahm, although he pretends all the time that he's a sort of upper servant. Actually he is her secretary. I don't know what correspondence she has, but he seems to be with her all the time, except when that horrid little man Peace is there – "

"Does he come often?" asked Alan quickly.

"Very often. He's an amazing little creature, isn't he? I confess that the sight of him makes me sick here" – she laid her hand on her diaphragm. "He's the only man in the world I couldn't be alone with without screaming. But Madame Stahm is never tired of him, says he's a genius – 'God-gifted' is her word. What makes him more terrible is the delusion he seems to hold that he is irresistible to all women."

She gave a little shiver, and her pretty face puckered into a grimace.

"He must belong to absolutely the lowest grade of mankind. I've seen the type in hospitals, but never quite so bad as he. His face in itself is extraordinary. He can make it change so that you would never recognise it – from hideous to more hideous!"

And then her sense of humour overcame her disgust, and she laughed softly.

"He asked if he might take me out one afternoon."

"Asked whom?" demanded Alan, aghast.

"Madame Stahm – and she gave permission! Not immediately, but in the future. She told me it was one of the rewards she was holding out to the little man, and practically commanded me to grant his request. I told her I would sooner go walking with a large family of snakes, but that only seemed to amuse her."

"He goes there very often, does he?" said Alan thoughtfully. "That will be news to Baldy."

"Who is Baldy? Oh, you mean Sergeant Eltham? Isn't he wonderful? He must have pointed out fifty people or places on the way back, and didn't know the name of any! Am I staying here tonight?"

"Yes. It's quite proper," said Alan hastily. "My housekeeper sleeps on the premises – "

"Don't be silly," she interrupted. "I'm supposed to be a trained nurse, and I've been alone in a house all night with a lunatic!"

Usually Alan Mainford took his time when he made his evening calls, but this night he found himself hurrying one after the other, skipping unimportant cases where ordinarily he would have called if only to gossip, and he was back in the house within an hour, and found, to his disappointment, that she was just going to bed.

"And I'll sleep well tonight. No screams – "

"Screams?" he said quickly. "What do you mean?"

She was annoyed with herself.

"I shouldn't have said that. But there were screams – hideous noises sometimes. I thought it was Madame Stahm shouting in her sleep, but once I heard it when I was talking with her, and she was so agitated that I knew she had heard the sound before."

"What did she do?" asked Alan.

"She sent for Baumgarten and talked to him vigorously in Russian; and when I say 'vigorously' I mean – vigorously! The night you left – you heard it?"

He nodded.

"It was dreadful, wasn't it? It made my blood run cold."

She was looking a little white and peaked again, and Alan summarily ordered her off to bed. He sat for a long time turning in his mind the problem of Madame Stahm, weaving about her the most fantastic theories, none of which was perhaps as fantastic as the truth.

Thought passed quickly to dream. Alan jerked up his head with a start, and was conscious of coldness. The fire was out; the clock on the mantelpiece pointed to half-past two. With a yawn he walked upstairs, opened the door of his room, and stepped in. A soft voice from the darkness said: "Is this your room, doctor? I'm so sorry."

With an incoherent apology he shut the door and went into the back room that his housekeeper had prepared for him.

He carried his embarrassment into his dreams.

7

At Brinley Hall Madame Stahm sat at a black-lacquered table, resting her elbows on its polished surface, her long chin in the palm of her hand. At the far end of the table Baumgarten half sat, half sprawled.

"Twelve o'clock. The doctor's cart was to bring her back."

Madame Stahm spoke in Russian.

Baumgarten sat up and stretched, flicked a speck from his immaculate evening coat and yawned.

"And I, my dear Clarice, told you that she would never come back."

A deep frown gathered on Madame's brow.

"Another spy to combat," she said, her eyes glowering. "And a woman! They are the worst!"

Baumgarten yawned again.

"She is no spy. She is frightened, partly of the beast, partly of the noises, but mainly of the beast, I think. You were very stupid to let her see him."

Madame shrugged.

"She is a spy; she has been listening at doors. I have found her in my bureau when she was not supposed to be there. If she does not come back – " She looked at the jewelled watch that lay on the table before her.

"She will not come back – have no fear."

"She could have sent a message – " began the woman.

"The doctor could have sent the message, but he did not. We are a long way out. If these barbarians had telephones we could speak to

Sheffield. To be sure, I will myself go to the doctor, but I know exactly what he will tell me – that he has taken a blood test of the beautiful nurse and that she is unable to continue her work for a week or two."

Madame Stahm brooded for ten minutes.

"I did not send for her –" she began.

"I sent for her, yes," said Baumgarten calmly. "If you die without medical attention, what will people say? They will say: 'Baumgarten, to whom this dear, good lady has left all her money, must have poisoned her.' The English are ready to believe anything of foreigners."

Again that brooding silence.

"The little man would bring her back," she said.

Mr Baumgarten smiled, and stroked his long face reflectively.

"Indeed? You overrate the beast. He can do many things; he is very strong, cunning and wicked. I myself have never met a worse man. He can play divinely and bring you out of your tantrums, Clarice, and that in itself is wonderful. He can do other things that require violence. How shall he bring the girl here? Shall he hit her on the head, lift her into a wagonette, and will your doctor do nothing? Beware of that young man, Clarice. He is clever and he is a soldier. Mr Dibden, who knows him, tells me he is the cleverest revolver shot in the country. Also he has killed his man. That to me is very important. Kill one – the rest are so easy, even though the one be a marauding Somali. Also he heard the noise."

She shrugged.

"So you said."

"I told you the truth," said Baumgarten coolly, "because I could not afford to have another night of nerves and screamings and teeth-grindings. I did not emphasise the fact, but he heard."

Another ten minutes passed by, the silence broken only by the periodical puffs of his cigar.

"Was there any result?" she asked.

He shook his head.

"The result was negative – for the moment. I am not so sure that Lamonte knows nothing. He was with Eckhardt in America. One thing he told us, and that is important, that Eckhardt had a friend in Cleveland, an engineer, a man who is now in Yorkshire, and has been in communication with Wertheimer. Eckhardt and this man spent many evenings together, especially when Eckhardt was ill. This gentleman is an engineer by profession and a draughtsman. He took notes. He is apparently the kind of man who would take notes methodically. Also – and this I learned from our friend – Dyson (which is his name) has offered to help Wertheimer on certain conditions which that treacherous dog has not granted. He could only bargain if he had something to bargain with. Also certain observers of mine, who have shadowed him, say that Dyson boasts that he has in his narrow head a secret that would revolutionise the world. That can only be the formula."

"Is it possible to get his notes?" asked Madame Stahm. "Who is this man? What does he do for a living? Where does he work?"

Baumgarten sighed wearily.

"I have told you a hundred times, Clarice, that you are so not of this world that you refuse to hear me. He is an engineer; his name is Dyson ; he lived or worked in Cleveland, Ohio – "

"But if he has the documents they can be found."

Her voice had risen to a shrill treble, a certain symptom of her growing excitement, which the man did not fail to notice.

"If you keep calm and quiet I will tell you more, but if you are going to scream and clench your hands and be mystic, I am going to bed."

She was breathing deeply through her nose, and that, too, was symptomatic of the grip she had taken on herself.

"It is a waste of time to find his notes if he carries the vital information here." Baumgarten tapped his forehead. "We are prepared to make him an offer, I suppose?"

"Of course," impatiently. "What are you doing about this, Peter?"

He shrugged his shapely shoulders.

"I don't know. It is all in the realms of conjecture. Dyson has a very charming wife, a pretty woman who drinks a little – which means she has vulgar tastes. She is a woman, I should imagine, on whom the beast would make a great impression."

A look of disgust wrinkled Madame Stahm's face.

"Ach! Who but you would think that, Peter?"

"You might," he said calmly. "I am paying compliments to your little horror – you should be grateful to me! Always he tells me that he is attractive to women, and I believe him. There are stories about him in the city. I speak often with the workmen, and I have discussed him. Your little man is irresistible."

She struck the table with the flat of her palm.

"Bring him now," she said imperiously. "Let him be sent for. Have the horses harnessed in the victoria, and let him be brought at once."

There was an amused look in the tired eyes of the Russian.

"*Manana!*" he said. "Tomorrow is also a day, beloved."

He rose from the table and stretched himself, his arms outflung tautly.

"I don't like your doctor – he is too intelligent, and he doesn't like me, which is unfortunate. He will give you trouble, especially if the nurse arouses him. He is in love with her."

"*Glouposti!*"

"It is not rubbish," said Baumgarten.

He walked behind her, dropped his hands on her thin shoulders and swayed her to and fro.

"Beloved, while there is money left shall we go back to a country of clean snow and blue skies? These English are a peculiarly unimaginative people. They hang men rather too readily, and women too. They have no emotion, no sentiment, no romance. Think of it, Clarice – in a day and a night we could be in the shadow of the Matterhorn!"

"Never!" she stormed. "Never! Until I recover the work of John Stahm's life, and the secret they stole from him, I will never rest. If you are too soft for this work, go, Peter. I am not afraid of prisons and ropes. I will go on to the end."

"Very well." Baumgarten was calmness itself. "If you stay, I must, for I adore you! I will do as you desire – everything, except engage myself to work with the nasty little man. There I cry 'Never!' He offends me, socially and aesthetically. There is nothing in him that is not – what is the English word? They have a fine one – ah, squalid. He is squalor, he is foul, he is something to be decently burnt and turned into clean ashes."

He heard her low, amused laugh.

"He is divine," she said, with a little gurgle of laughter, "beyond price. Also extraordinarily useful, Peter, as you have proved. He may be more useful yet."

In the morning Baumgarten sent a messenger to Peace. He was not at home; he had left on the previous night for Manchester, a city in which he took a very great interest, though it had sent him to penal servitude for twelve years. None the less, the lure of the cotton city never failed. In every moment of financial crisis Manchester was the city.

Charles Peace limped to the railway station, took a third-class ticket to the northern city, and spent a profitable and instructive two hours of the journey arguing theology. For Charles Peace held strong and orthodox views, though it was his boast that he believed in God and the devil but feared neither.

He went away with the amount of his return fare and a golden sovereign in his pocket; he came back with a small bag filled with miscellaneous articles, some of which he put into the fire. Most precious of all the loot was a new and beautifully fitted concertina, and throughout the day of his return his neighbours heard strange melodies issue from the Peace house, for he was improvising a hymn, making up the lyric as he went along. It was all about love and heaven and beautiful white angels, and dear little children waiting to receive their earthly parents. Mr Peace had lost a child; it had been born and died whilst he was in prison. But to him it was a dream child, surprising and dazzlingly lovely. He often wept over the baby he had never seen, and composed poetry about him; for he was a sentiment-alist and easily moved by a vision of angels playing harps. He himself was always on the look-out for a harp, for he was certain he would excel upon it, but never found one.

"There's no instrument I can't play," was his boast.

Since there was no harp, a concertina was an effective substitute.

When he sat back in the chair tilted against the kitchen wall, manipulating the keys under his fingers, his eyes closed dreamily, he could almost imagine harp-like qualities in the wailing harmonies that the little leather bellows blew.

"I value that concertina," the owner of the burgled house was telling a sympathetic policeman. "I paid a lot of money for it."

"Have you lost anything else?" asked the police officer.

The other compiled a list of spoons, clocks and portable silverware. Mr Peace could have compiled a fuller list and have claimed greater accuracy, for all the articles which had been lost lay snug in the coal cellar, and that night would be fenced for a tenth of their value.

He had no friends, this lone wolf. His dowdy wife feared him; his stepson hated him; the child of his marriage was petrified in his presence. He had a quick and heavy hand for wife or child, though he could be generous. Sometimes he would be unaccountably flush with money; golden sovereigns would jingle in his pockets; the bar of his favourite public-house would yield him a sycophantic audience.

"There's no instrument I couldn't play, sitha. Piano? I can an' all. Trumpet, bugle, organ – "

"Harp?" suggested somebody at random.

The ugly face grew uglier.

"We'll say nowt about religion, lad. I'm religious."

He was particularly religious at that moment, for he had escaped arrest by the skin of his teeth, and by luck was without his six-shooter.

Subsequently he told a chaplain that he ascribed his escape from justice to a direct answer to prayer. He prayed for things and got them, he said, and related how he once paid his addresses to a sweetheart, who had received them coldly, and after an evening spent in supplication he had changed her attitude to him in twenty-four hours.

Madame Stahm, who never prayed, sent for her faithful servant, and he, hiring a car, drove out to her in the dark of the night, smoking a cigar which was wholly distasteful to him, but which seemed consistent with his importance.

A plain-clothes man saw him as he left the outskirts of the city, and reported his movements to headquarters on a dial telegraph. Baldy, who was at the station, took the report and sniffed at it.

"Let him go," he said. "If there's any burglary in that direction, pull him in, and ask the patrol to pick him up on his return."

Baldy Eltham was taking an unusual interest in his pet abomination. Curiously enough, Peace at that moment was especially interested in Sergeant Eltham.

8

A remarkable woman was Madame Stahm. She was indefatigable, tireless. Baumgarten, who, curiously enough, never spoke good German, called her the *Wonderfrau*. She could live on the minimum of sleep; she ate no more than would have kept a canary alive; and, except for these hysterical outbreaks of hers, did not know a day's sickness. She had an unusual knowledge of mechanics, was a particularly brilliant chemist, though she had taken no degree in the subject, and during her married life had acquired some of her husband's uncanny instinct which is nine-tenths of inspiration.

She was a wealthy woman, too, could afford, as Baumgarten reminded her at frequent intervals, to drop this quest of hers and, retiring, live an amusing and comfortable life. But the attainment of the goal which her husband had set forth to reach was her life's passion. Without it, life could have no meaning.

Her interest in Peace was no affectation. There was in her a leaning towards the bizarre, and there was this creditable factor in her perversity, that she saw through the ugly coating of things and detected qualities which were hidden from the normal eye.

"Dirt? Show me dirt, and I will show you the most delightful chemical constituents," was her favourite saying.

Baumgarten was a man of vision, but could never see, in the slouching little man with the repulsive face, more than something slightly removed from the baser form of animal life. He conceded to him a genius for music, for Baumgarten was not musical, and he was fair. For all he knew, the little man was a prodigy.

He received Peace in the bare ante-room that led off the square stone hall, and the visitor came in, rubbing his mittened hands.

"It's cold here," he croaked. "Ain't you got a fire here anywhere?

"Attend to me!"

Baumgarten barked the words. He never attempted to disguise his antipathy to the man he employed.

"Madame wishes to ask you questions and to give you some work. You may earn ten or twenty pounds – more than you will ever make from a burglary."

Peace scowled at him.

"I don't know what you mean by burglary. That's a nice word to use to a respectable man, I must say! I wouldn't have come out if I thought you was going to jaw me! Twenty pounds! A friend of mine makes hundreds – thousands!"

He carried under his arm a bundle wrapped in a piece of calico, obviously torn from a bedsheet.

"I've brought her something that'll surprise her – look at this!"

He unwrapped the bundle and showed a small violin of an unusual shape. Most unusual feature of all, it had only one string.

"I invented it. When you hear it you'll be surprised. It will cause a bit of a stir in London when they hear it, though I'll have to learn 'em how to play it. I've learnt some of the biggest fiddlers in England – do you know what they call me? 'The Second Paganini.' I've got playbills to prove it. 'Charles Peace, the Second Paganini.' I've had some of the highest people in the land come up to me and say 'Why don't you go on the stage, Mr Peace?' I can prove that too."

"I daresay you can," interrupted the other impatiently. "But I am not interested in fiddles, nor does Madame desire music. It is on another matter I wish to speak to you before you see her. She will ask you to do something in Sheffield – possibly to take somebody away. Nothing you must do without first consulting me – you understand? You must take no steps until I have gone over every detail of your plans."

Peace shifted his movable jaw restlessly, his deep-set eyes on the Russian.

"Is she here?" he asked suddenly.

"Madame – oh, no, you mean the Nurse Garden?"

The little man nodded.

"No, she has gone – the Sergeant Eltham came yesterday and drove her into Sheffield to see the doctor."

"Sergeant Eltham…a bald man with whiskers?" Peace scratched his chin uneasily.

"Do you know him?"

A moment's hesitation.

"Yes, I know the old hound! He swore my life away – stood up in the witness box and perjured himself so that I wonder the roof didn't fall in. They say these London detectives are liars, but this man could teach 'em something! Ain't she coming back, the nurse?"

"She is staying with Dr Mainford."

The jaw of the little man thrust out.

"That puppy! Said he'd throw me out of the trap, and I could have put him across my knee and broken his back! Nobody knows how strong I am. I once took a six-foot navvy and threw him over a hedge, and I've got people to prove it. There was a lord who bet I couldn't carry a twenty-stone pig for half a mile, and I done it for a mile, and nobody would have thought, to look at me, that I'd – "

"Yes, yes – you are wonderful, but that is not the point. This young woman must not be hurted – hurt – you understand? Whatever Madame says."

Peace looked at him cunningly through half-closed eyes.

"You tell me what I got to do and what I ain't got to do? Suppose I tell her ladyship what you're telling me, you'd get into a bit of a row, wouldn't you?"

If Baumgarten had followed his natural inclination he would have taken the long-barrelled pistol that he could see in the drawer of his desk and wiped out of existence the man who was an offence to him.

"You may tell Madame if you wish. She already knows my views. Now you may see her. You need not bring your fiddle, for she does not require music."

He led the way up the stairs, Peace following, carrying, in spite of his instructions, the one-string fiddle and its bow.

It was into a smaller room, which he had never seen before, that he was ushered. Madame sat at her secretaire, wearing a padded gown. She was smoking a brown cigarette, a remarkable spectacle. Peace had never seen a woman smoking before, though he had seen men indulging in the offensive practice of cigarette smoking.

"Sit down, nice man," she said. "Give him the stool, Peter. He will look so odd! What have you there?"

Peace handed the fiddle to her with a smirk.

"He said you wouldn't want to see it."

She examined the home-made instrument curiously. "I have seen such things in Russia," she said, as she handed it back, and the little man's face fell.

"I invented that out of me head – " he began.

"I have seen it in Russia, my man. It is very interesting and some day you shall play it for me."

She swept the secretaire clear of papers and rested her elbows upon it, staring at her visitor thoughtfully.

"Sergeant Elt'am – do you know him? Is he important?"

"He is a liar," said Peace promptly.

"All policemen are liars," said Madame. "I am not interested in their moral characters. But is he of great importance?"

"He is nobody," said Peace. "He's only a copper, a sergeant. Would he be only a sergeant if he was clever? Suppose he had my brains, where would he be? Chief Constable of England – that's where he'd be, sitting in a grand office in Parliament, ordering people about."

"Nobody has your brains, little man," she cooed.

"Nor his modesty," muttered Baumgarten, and Peace shot a baleful glare in his direction.

"And Dr Mainford – what of him? Is he clever?"

"A whippersnapper," said Peace. "I could break him in two across my knee. I've got the strength of ten men."

"Is he well known?" she persisted patiently. "Suppose he went away, said nothing to anybody, would he be missed very much?"

"There's hundreds of doctors in Sheffield," said Peace. "They'd go to somebody else."

"That is not what I want to know." She drummed her fingers irritably upon the mahogany writing desk.

"Is his – what do you call it? – practice very large?"

Here Mr Peace was at sea. He knew nothing of practices, had only the vaguest idea of the system under which doctors work.

"I told you it was useless to ask him this," interrupted Baumgarten, a touch of asperity in his tone. "The man can only tell you what he knows, and he knows nothing."

The face of the little man went livid. Baumgarten had touched him on the raw. His colossal vanity was hurt. To question his omniscience was to commit a deadly offence.

"Know nothing, don't I?" he spluttered, but she calmed him again.

"I see that you have not studied the doctor, and why should you? Now, my friend, listen."

From a pigeon-hole she took a slip of paper.

"You can read, of course?"

"I went to the best school in England – " began Peace.

"Here are some names and some addresses. They are friends of the man Wertheimer. The first one is the young woman to whom he has paid his addresses."

"Courting her?"

She nodded.

"They are engaged perhaps – I am not sure. He writes to her regularly. Do you know Manchester?"

Peace leered at her.

"Do I know me own right hand?" he asked.

"I see you do," she went on. "She lives there. She is young and romantic. Possibly she keeps all his letters – where I do not know. The bureau, under her pillow, near to her heart – God knows! You are a clever little man; I have always said so. You are adorable. I am your friend and your disciple, isn't it – is that not so? You will make inquiries in your own way. You are too clever to be told. Possibly a servant will tell you where the young lady keeps her letters. I would like those."

He eyed her suspiciously, a little resentfully. Nobody must think ill of him or regard him disparagingly.

"Any one would think I was a burglar, the way you're talking!" he complained, and she smiled at him.

"How absurd! Of course you are not a burglar; you are a very clever man, and you are a wonderful spy. In Russia you would be a great man, earning thousands of roubles."

Peace considered the matter. He was a little ruffled. The polite fiction of his integrity had to be maintained. Burglary was vulgar and low, but spying –

He could dramatise himself into any role. Already he was slinking through the snowy streets of St Petersburg in pursuit of Nihilists.

"Can you do this for me, my dear friend?"

He hesitated.

"I know a man," he said slowly, "a common man who does a bit of burglaring. I ain't seen him for years, but he'd do anything to oblige me. I saved his life – jumped into the river when he'd gone down for the third time and brought him out. They wanted to give me a medal, but I got away – never even so much as left me name."

"Modesty again," murmured the irrepressible Baumgarten.

"There is another thing I want to speak to you about," Madame went on quickly, to check the little man's snarling retort. "You remember the girl – the nurse? You wanted to take her for a walk. You remember you asked me?"

"I'd have treated her like a lady," said Peace vehemently. "I always treat ladies as such. I'd have took her into the best public-house and given her nothing but wine. Nobody's ever said I wasn't a gentleman – "

"Yes, yes, yes, that I know. But she has run away from me, to the doctor. I think he is her lover."

The man's face became distorted with rage.

"If he does any harm to that young girl I'll smash his head in!" he growled. "I can't abear seeing women treated cruel."

She was secretly amused, but did not show it. She knew something of Mr Peace and his private reputation; knew, though he was not aware of this, that he had so beaten his wife that her face was permanently disfigured; knew other unwholesome facts which did not accord with this profession of chivalry.

"You are quite right," she said. "It is admirable of you! You have the heart of a chevalier, my little man. She is in bad hands. I would like to bring her back to me. She may tell stories about us − about you, for example. This doctor is a busybody, very arrogant and unscrupulous. Also he is a friend of your Sergeant Elt'am. That is very bad for us all."

"I'll get her back," interjected Peace excitedly. "It's just come to me how I can do it! That's how my mind works, my ladyship. Other people think hours and days and months − it comes to me of a sudden! I'll follow her round when she goes out for a walk; I'll talk to her. She can't shake me off. Then I'll have a handsome pony chaise and ask her to go for a ride and bring her here."

"Very clever," said Baumgarten. "And suppose the doctor is out walking with her?"

"I'll settle him," said Peace with an ugly grin. "You mark my words, mister."

Baumgarten and the woman exchanged a glance. He shook his head slightly, and he saw agreement in her eyes.

"That will not be good, I think. We must try some other plan. But in the meantime these letters − I must have them. There is twenty pounds for you − ten pounds today and ten pounds when the letters come. The girl in Manchester, I mean. Afterwards you must try this man." She pointed to the second name on the list. "He is a friend also of Wertheimer. Do you know Mr Dyson?"

"I know everybody in Sheffield," said Peace, and ignored the sarcastic click of Mr Baumgarten's lips. "Dyson? He's got a greengrocer's shop in − "

"He is an engineer on the railway," said Madame. "He has a very attractive wife."

"Leave it to me," said the little man.

EDGAR WALLACE

That satyr smile of his sickened Baumgarten, and he was a man with a strong stomach.

"I will tell you about him later," said Madame. "First" – her finger went to the top of the list – "this girl. Here is the address. I do not know what kind of house it is, but that you will find out. If anything happens you will not, of course, speak of me."

"Don't worry."

Peace would have taken the slip of paper, but she held it under her hand.

"Have you a book? I will write it for you."

"I can write," he said gruffly.

He was very touchy on the point of his education,

She watched him whilst laboriously he copied the name and address in a little notebook with a stub of pencil. He wrote as a child writes, letter by letter, muttering each as he set it down.

"That's good writing." He showed her the illiterate scrawl triumphantly. "There's people been to Oxford and Cambridge that couldn't write better than that."

9

Half an hour later Peace left the house, driving back through the silent country lanes and the deserted streets of Sheffield with a sense of importance that he had never experienced before. He was going to prove himself an expert craftsman.

He was in bed by four o'clock, up again at eight in his dingy little workroom, littered with gluepots and frame mouldings. He selected his tools with the greatest care, and left by the last train that night for Manchester with a pleasing sense of his own exalted value.

Nor had the day been spent idly. Dyson he located and observed: a tall, thin, querulous man, who spoke occasionally with an American accent, in the manner of Englishmen who have lived in the United States. Peace wondered what the wife was like, and hoped that she was a lady. He had a weakness for real ladies who wore rings and silk dresses and scented themselves lavishly.

He reached Manchester late at night, and was slipping through the barrier when a commanding voice hailed him.

"Hi, come here!"

He turned with a scowl, and, recognising the military-looking man in the long ulster as a member of the Manchester police force, he went towards him with an ingratiating smile.

"What are you doing here?"

"Why, inspector, who'd have thought of seeing you? This is a joyful surprise!"

"You look happy about it," said the other sarcastically. "You were in Manchester two nights ago."

55

Peace shook his head.

"No, sir, I was here last week; I'm doing a bit of business."

"Somebody cracked a nice little crib in Victoria Park. Was that the business?"

The eyes of the ugly little man opened, his big mouth drooped.

"Me, sir? I'm going straight now! No more of the narrow path that leadeth to destruction, as the Good Book says. No, sir, I've got a trade of my own – I'm picture-framing, making a living. What I say is, thank Gawd I've got a trade in my hands! People come to me and say: 'Charlie, come and help crack a crib,' but I'll have nowt of it. I've seen prison for the last time, inspector. It's a mug's game."

"How long are you going to be in Manchester?" interrupted the sceptical police officer.

Peace hesitated.

"A couple of days. I'm trying to get a contract from one of the big firms."

"Where will you be staying?"

This time without hesitation Peace gave an address: one of the three lodgings he used, but not that at which he had stayed on his previous visit.

"Come into the station inspector's office," said the police officer abruptly.

He pushed the man ahead of him until they came to a tiny, ill-lit room with a desk and a couple of chairs.

"Now let's have a look inside that bag of yours," he suggested.

Meekly the little man opened the big carpet-bag he carried, and the inspector pulled out a few articles of clothing. Beneath these was an assortment of picture-frame mouldings and such tools as were proper to the craft Peace was following.

"That's a nice, handy-looking chisel. And what do you want a centre bit for?"

"I'm a joiner," said Peace. "There's a gimlet there, too."

The inspector looked at the chisel; it was broad, sharp, an instrument of tempered steel that could be used for the carving of wood, but would also make an effective jemmy to force a window. But there, also, were the samples of mouldings. Peace never travelled without them. They were the articles which cancelled out the instruments of his trade, his sure defence in case of arrest on suspicion.

The inspector threw the tools back into the bag and did not attempt to disguise his disappointment.

"Have you got a shooter?" he asked.

"A what, sir?" Peace was amazed and hurt. "You don't mean firearms, do you, sir? Good Gawd, I've never heard of such things! I wouldn't dare carry one, I'd be afraid of it going off."

The tall inspector in the ulster looked at him straightly.

"If anything's cracked while you're here, Peace, we shall pull you in. By the way, what are you calling yourself now, Ward or Peace?"

"By my own name, sir – Charles Peace, the same as I was christened by according to law and the Gospel."

He hurried with his bag from the station, got on to a 'bus and was driven two miles. He lodged in a dingy little house in a street remarkable for its griminess. Not until he was in the privacy of his own room, with the blinds drawn down, did he take off his hard felt hat and remove from the webbing that held it the snubnosed little revolver with the leather wrist-band. He broke the pistol, carefully examined the old-fashioned pin-fire cartridges, and put the revolver under his pillow.

He did not go out that night, but spent the evening carving the head of a cherub; he had begun the work in Sheffield and designed it as a present for the lady of Brinley Hall, or, alternatively, for the pretty nurse. He was an opportunist, though he had never heard the word.

10

Long after he had left, Madame Stahm sat at her writing desk, chin in hand, discussing certain urgent matters with her secretary. She seemed to be impervious to fatigue, and Baumgarten, who was cast in more normal mould, had learned to snatch what sleep he could in the middle of the day, in preparation for these midnight and early morning conferences.

"We are so near to everything, it is madness," he said, for the fourth time.

"Inspiration will come," said the other.

And then: "This doctor – what will you do with him?"

"Dr Mainford?" She shrugged her lean shoulders. "I don't know. If he is troublesome – "

She did not complete the sentence.

"You must find another method." Baumgarten was firm on this. "This doctor is not like the others. He has friends; he knows the police station, who will miss him. He is well born, too. It is not easy, Clarice. Do you think you are wise in trusting this little devil of yours?"

He stopped suddenly. Madame had raised her finger to enjoin silence. He, too, had heard the sound, a curious swish as if somebody had brushed against the wooden panels which lined the room.

"What was that?" she asked in a low voice.

"Rats, I think. The house is full of them," said Baumgarten.

He looked uneasily towards one ancient, panelled wall.

"It came from there, didn't it?"

Again she put her finger to her lips, and they were quiet for a few minutes. The sound was not repeated.

"Did you not say there was a passage behind that panel?"

"There is a passage behind most of the panels," said Baumgarten sourly. "The place is honeycombed with them! It is a very old house – one of the men found a tunnel in the garden; it leads heaven knows where. I will have it blocked up one day."

They listened again, but there was no sound.

Suddenly a thought occurred to Baumgarten. He hurried from the room, ran down the stairs, through the kitchen, unlocked the door of the cellar and passed through the door of the cell. That, too, was locked, and almost he turned back, reassured. Then a thought struck him, and he went into the cell.

A light was burning, though he distinctly remembered turning it out when he had gone down to give the prisoner his evening meal. The bed was humped up. At first sight it seemed as if somebody was in it, but a closer glance showed that there was nothing more substantial than the bolster and the bed – the prisoner was gone!

But where? He looked round. There was no place he could possibly be hiding; the walls were of solid stone. He looked under the bed. There was nobody there –

Then he saw in a corner of the floor a square aperture. A grey flagstone had evidently been lifted. He pulled aside the bed, struck a match and looked down. Six feet below he saw the floor of a small passage. He had no light, and less inclination to explore. He did not doubt that the sound he had heard was the man threading his way between the panelling and Madame Stahm's bedroom.

A new surprise awaited him when he reached the hall. The door was wide open. Somebody had gone out in the brief space of time it had taken for him to reach the cellar and return; somebody who had probably been watching him. A panel swung idly on the wall where it had appeared solid. One of the worm-eaten panels was a secret door.

Flying up the stairs two at a time, he burst into Madame Stahm's presence.

"He's gone!" he said. His voice was unsteady, his hands shaking. "Now, Madame, I think we must decide – prison or the Continent."

She did not answer. Her dark eyes were fixed on his.

"We will go to neither place," she said.

She shivered, brushed her correspondence towards the pigeon-holes and closed the flap of her desk, locking it with two keys.

"Send somebody to remove the bed and the chain – and let Weiss and Bermans go out in search of him – they must take riding horses."

"But suppose Lamonte – " he began.

"He will go straight to Wertheimer – and Wertheimer will do nothing. He would not dare. He would do no more than use his information to buy reconciliation with me. Now, go and do as I say!"

He hurried to convey her orders. When he came back she was staring gloomily into the little fire that burnt on the hearth. She looked round with a start as he came in.

"Yes? You have done this? Good! Now listen. I am worried about the girl Garden. Could you not see her, Peter? You have finesse, you could tell her I am ill – dying, if you like."

He made a grimace at this.

"The doctor would come with her. How would you explain if I said I did not want the doctor? Besides, he has written, saying that she is not in a fit state to work. I'll see her if you wish. What is Mainford's address?"

She had to unlock her bureau to find her book and read it to him. He repeated, writing it down on his white shirt cuff.

"That man is our worst enemy," were her parting words.

Baumgarten could have laughed. He had met so many worst enemies that one more or less did not seem worth while bothering about. Worst enemy of all might be Lamonte...

All that day Alan Mainford had turned over and over in his mind the superlatively important question of Jane Garden's future. He had made several calls at nursing institutions and the local hospitals, without finding the employment which he felt her abilities deserved. He had been surprised to discover the importance of her qualifications. If his practice were larger…

He coquetted with this idea, trying to convince himself that he was justified in the extravagance of employing a private nurse on the off-chance of his own patients requiring her. It was not an unusual practice: he could name three doctors who maintained their own nursing staff; and he became enthusiastic as he reconciled himself to the extravagance.

He put his suggestion to her at dinner that night, and she took the view that he had expected of her.

"Will there be enough work for me to do?"

"Frankly, I don't know," he said. "Of course, I shall have to find some lodgings for you."

She nodded.

"I've been thinking about that. Would you let me the coachman's flat over your second stable?"

He stared at her.

"Why, that's a hovel!"

She laughed.

"No, it isn't; there are three nice rooms there – there's even a bathroom. Dixon was telling me that the old doctor – of whom, by the way, he never speaks except with awe – kept four horses and two grooms. It's the second groom's rooms I want. I'll have my own front door; I needn't bother to come near the house, and I know I shall be awfully comfortable. Some girls at St Mary's had a room over some stables in Devonshire Mews, and they made a very charming home of it."

Here was a way out of one difficulty, though he was dubious as to its possibilities. To tell the truth, he had never explored the rooms of the second groom. The old doctor, whose practice he had bought, was something of an aristocrat, and from what he knew of the conveniences of his own house, Alan was certain that the rooms would be at least habitable. He said he would see them in the morning, and gave a tentative agreement, haggled for an hour over the rent she would pay – a delightful hour – and altogether had a pleasant evening.

He could get her to say very little about the life at Brinley Hall. She came here against a sense of loyalty to her late employer. She was very vague about Baumgarten and about his employer. Apparently she knew nothing about the business side of Madame Stahm's life, except that she went three or four times a week to Sheffield, where, at the works of Dibden and Payne, two small outbuildings had been equipped and set apart for her experiments. Dibden and Payne had a lien upon the patent – if it ever materialised.

At a quarter past ten the maternity case which Alan had been expecting for three days arrived urgently, in the shape of an agitated, perspiring young father, who almost dragged Alan into the street. He had not far to go, and, as he was to discover, arrived some two or three hours before his presence was necessary.

In one respect his coming was providential. The slatternly nurse, who was not a nurse at all but a woman who engaged herself in these delicate functions, was slightly the worse for drink, and her uselessness became more apparent as the night progressed. He scribbled a note and sent it round to Jane Garden, and in half an hour she appeared, cool, immensely capable, able to deal not only with the case but with the inebriated lady she was replacing, and who eventually had to be thrown into the street and handed to the paternal care of the police. At two o'clock a howling morsel of humanity qualified for the English census. He left Jane to look after the woman and walked home.

Very capable, very sweet, very wonderful. He mused upon the phenomenon as he walked slowly homewards. She had dropped beautifully into her appointed place. It was true that the people he was attending could not afford the services of a highly trained nurse, but this was in the nature of an experiment, and from his point of view the experiment had already succeeded.

He was not a bit tired when he unlocked the door and went into his house. He took his casebook from the shelf, entered up and amplified the particulars of one or two interesting cases he had visited that day, and had just finished when he heard a knock at the door.

Whoever it was did not ring, but hammered with a fist on the panel. Somebody in a hurry, for he or she knocked again, frantically.

He jumped to his feet. Something must have gone wrong with the woman he had just left. He strode into the passage and pulled open the door. A man fell forward into his arms. The weight of him and the force of the fall almost threw Alan off his feet. Recovering, he caught him round the armpits, dragged him into the surgery where he received his patients, and laid him on the floor before he struck a match and lit the gas.

The man was grimy, unwashed. Despite the coldness of the night, he wore only shirt and trousers. It was raining outside, but there was no sign of moisture on his shoulders, and this was accounted for later when outside the house was discovered the big, brown blanket that had covered him, and which had dropped off as he fell forward. His unshaven face was drawn and blue. On one side of his head were the marks of an old wound that had not properly healed, and across his bony face were three red weals.

Alan looked at the grimy, emaciated hands and felt the pulse. It was so faint as to be almost imperceptible. His feet were bare, blue with cold and streaked with blood.

Going into his little dispensary, he filled a hypodermic syringe and shot its contents into the man's forearm. He made no sign, lying apparently lifeless.

The doctor was puzzled. Who was this stranger? Whence had he come? Leaving the man on the floor, he ran through the kitchen into the stable yard and called Dixon. When he returned the man had recovered consciousness. He was staring up at the ceiling from wide-open eyes.

"Are you feeling better?"

Slowly the wreck turned his eyes on him and muttered something in a cracked voice which Alan could not distinguish. He bent down and listened. Again the man spoke, in French.

"This cannot go on. I cannot endure…"

Alan heard a heavy footstep in the hall. At first he thought it was Dixon, but when over his shoulder he saw the burly figure of Sergeant Eltham: "You're the very man I could have prayed for."

"What's this?" Eltham had over his arm a big blanket. "I saw your door was open and found this outside. I wondered if Mr Peace had been doing a little burglary. Hullo! Has he been run over?"

Briefly Alan told him what had happened and how the man had come. The wreck on the floor had subsided into unconsiousness.

"Do you know him?"

Baldy shook his head.

"No, he's a stranger to me."

He threw the rug over the man's feet.

"We ought to get him to hospital. What's the matter with him?"

"Exhaustion, and he's got a scorching temperature."

Baldy lifted the thin hand and examined the wrist curiously.

"He's had the darbies on. Look!"

Round the wrist was a raw, red mark. They found its fellow on the other wrist.

"That's funny."

He pulled up the trousers' leg, and here the marking was unmistakable. The flesh had been rubbed raw round the bone of the ankle.

The two men looked at one another.

"What do you make of it?"

For a little while the sergeant did not speak; then, with a cry, he thrust his hand into his inside pocket, and, taking out a photograph, examined it intently, looking from the man's face to the picture in his hand.

"By God, it's him!" he gasped.

"Who?" asked Alan.

"The man who disappeared from the Silver Steel works a couple of weeks ago!"

11

"It's him all right," said the agitated sergeant, bending down and scrutinising the wasted face. "Look, doctor."

He handed the photograph to Alan, who identified the original the more readily because he had seen him when his eyes were open.

"I don't know his name – " began the sergeant.

Alan looked at the back of the photograph, where some particulars had been scribbled.

"Lamonte, isn't it?"

"That's right, Lamonte. Now, where did he come from?"

Baldy examined the wounded feet of the man.

"A long way, a devil of a long way. Look at his trousers – the mud's still wet. He must have had this blanket over him. I'll go out and find a policeman, and we'll get a stretcher and take him to the hospital."

He blundered out of the house, and came back in five minutes to find Alan forcing brandy down the throat of the unconscious man.

"He's pretty bad, isn't he?

"Very bad," said Alan gravely. "I don't think there's a possible hope for him. He has acute pneumonia, amongst other things, and his heart's just about finished."

At that moment Lamonte opened his eyes and stared about him wildly.

"I have told you everything – everything there is to be told," he said shrilly. "I can tell you no more – I know no more – I am a workman; I do not know the technique…"

"What is he saying?" asked Baldy urgently.

Alan was scribbling down the words, and roughly translated them.

"Listen to everything he says," urged Baldy. Don't make any mistake, doctor. This may mean hanging dues for somebody."

The man did not speak again. He lay very quietly, scarcely breathing. Once he murmured something indistinguishable. Then, there was a little grimace of pain and he lay quiet, and it seemed to Sergeant Eltham, as he watched the poor, stricken thing, that all the anguish that was in the thin face suddenly smoothed itself out into a marvellous serenity.

The ambulance came; two policemen clumped into the passage and stood, watching, at the door.

"Ought we to move him?" asked the sergeant anxiously.

Alan nodded.

"He's dead," he said.

Henri Lamonte, sometime technical engineer in the employ of the Silver Steel Company, had gone, carrying his great and painful secret with him.

Jane Garden came into breakfast the next morning, looking as fresh as though she had risen from a perfect night of rest. There was little or nothing for her to report. The baby's grandmother had arrived and had taken charge.

"A very normal case," she said.

Alan speared a piece of bacon from the dish.

"I had a case that was not quite so normal," he said grimly, and told her of the coming and passing of Lamonte. "In fact, I've had a hectic night and feel like a wet rag trying to walk a tight-rope," he said. "I suppose you've never seen this fellow?"

Baldy had inadvertently left behind the photograph of the man, and Alan had propped it on the mantelpiece so that the sergeant could not miss it when he called again. She rose and took it down, looked at it for a long time, then shook her head.

"No, I've never seen him — I have never met him in Madame's house. Didn't you sleep at all?"

He had gone to bed at four, and had been awakened by Dixon at eight.

"You must tell me how you manage to look as you do without sleep," he bantered her.

She explained that she had slept all the previous afternoon. Apparently at Brinley Hall Madame was never active until nearly midnight, unless she were going to the city. The affairs and routine of the household had been adjusted to meet Madame Stahm's activities, and the afternoon sleep was part of the general routine.

"I promised I would go back tonight. There is a little trouble in that household. They're terribly poor, aren't they?"

Alan nodded.

"That kind of trouble is fairly general in Sheffield," he said, "though, as a town, we're progressing at such a tremendous rate that we shall be a city before we know where we are!"

She sipped her tea, looking at him.

"It isn't the poverty. Apparently the wife is a little flighty – do you mind the scandals of the poor? When he had recovered from his hysteria, the father wasn't as happy about the child as you might have expected, remembering it is their first baby. She has a friend to whom he very much objects and is very much afraid of – guess who it is?"

He looked up, startled.

"Not Peace?" he said in amazement.

She nodded.

"Charles Peace." Then, with a twinkle in her eye, she added: "Squire of dames!"

After breakfast came Baldy, acting for the moment as coroner's officer. He served a notice upon the doctor.

"We've fixed the inquest for three o'clock tomorrow, doctor. The old boy wanted to have it in the morning, but I knew you'd be busy."

"Have you found out anything about Lamonte?"

"A lot of things," said the sergeant. "I had Mr What's-his-name of the Silver Steel Company over – "

"It's a wonder to me that you can remember Silver Steel. You mean Wertheimer, of course?"

67

"That's the fellow. He knew him at once. Terribly upset he was. He's wondering what happened to that other fellow of his who disappeared."

"Does this upset your theory that Lamonte ran away with a girl? You remember that there was a girl missing?"

"A mistake on my part," said Baldy, unabashed. "She's gone away to see some friends in the country. I knew that, but I didn't tell anybody. This fellow from the Silver Steel cried – actually cried, doctor. Broke down when he saw this fellow. Foreigners often cry; they kiss one another too – men! I've seen it done at Victoria Station in London. It oughtn't to be allowed."

"What else did you learn?"

"He'd come a very long way. One of our mounted men saw him trudging through the snow – thought it was a woman with a shawl round her. That was just outside the town. The mounted man was at a cross-roads and wasn't sure which way he had come, and didn't trouble to inquire. That's mounted men all over! The moment you put a policeman on horseback he seems to lose his intelligence. I've said it before, and I'll say it again."

"What else did you discover?"

The sergeant consulted his notebook.

"He'd been thrashed. There were marks on his body. There were marks also on his face. The police surgeon says they're whip marks, too. The thing's a mystery to me."

Alan thought for a long time, then he asked slowly: "Do you connect Madame Stahm with this man's death?"

Sergeant Eltham opened his mouth and eyes.

"Good heavens, no!"

"I'll tell you something," said Alan, and related in greater detail the story of his visit to Brinley Hall and the scream he had heard.

Baldy tugged at his beard.

"It might have been a railway whistle – " he began.

"That was the half-witted explanation offered to me by one who knew better," said Alan acidly. "No, if I were you I'd make inquiries. See Madame Stahm and Baumgarten – you'd better write those names down: you'll never remember them – and if you can find any excuse, search the house."

Baldy demurred at this. It was a high matter, to be undertaken only by his superiors. For his own part he would not like to interfere or even to suggest such a thing. It was a terrible thing to accuse a woman, even if she was a foreigner, and the police just then were not popular. All these views he offered.

"The police never are popular – don't be silly," said Alan tersely. "If you're clever, you might even associate your friend Charles Peace with the death. Do you remember, you told me a small man was one of the two people who were seen attacking Lamonte?"

"It was not Peace," said the other. "He wasn't in town. He went to Manchester the night before last. Why they don't pinch him the minute he arrives at the station I can't find out. I've got a friend of mine – an inspector – and I always notify him when Peace goes to Manchester, but nothing ever happens. And while he's there there's generally a burglary or two."

"There's probably a few when he's not there," smiled Alan. And then, more seriously: "What does the police surgeon think about Lamonte?"

"Starvation, exhaustion, ill-treatment," said Baldy. "It's murder within the meaning of the Act. If we caught the fellow that did it he'd be meeting Mr Marwood – nice fellow, Marwood: you'd never think he was a hangman, to talk to him. He's a true blue Tory, and what he says about Mr Gladstone would make your hair curl."

The politics of hangmen did not interest Alan, and he said as much.

He spent the brief time between the departure of Eltham and the beginning of his "round" in drafting a rough report for the coroner. Baldy had promised to convey Alan's suspicions of Madame Stahm and her household to his superior officer. Whether he did so or not, no steps were taken to explore that avenue.

In all probability Sergeant Eltham had not pressed the point with his chief, for he made no secret of the fact that he regarded the suggestion as fantastical.

Throughout his rounds that morning Alan was considering the possibility of pursuing an independent line of investigation, and had half made up his mind to call on Madame Stahm, when he returned to the house for lunch. His housekeeper opened the door to him.

"There is a lady to see you. She is in the waiting-room – Madame Stahm."

"Indeed and indeed!" said Alan, a little staggered. "The mountain has come to the prophet, eh?" And then, in a low voice: "If Miss Garden wakes up, do not let her come down until Madame Stahm has gone."

Madame Stahm had a trick of enthroning herself in the most prosaic surroundings. She sat on a high chair that was in the very centre of the room, her magenta silk frock outspread, her hands primly folded in her lap. She carried with her the atmosphere of a court and greeted Alan with a quizzical smile, which was not without its queenly consideration.

"The invalid has come to you," she said gaily. "The lady with a bad heart, eh? But I have a good heart for you, doctor. My poor Jane, is she better?"

There was a hint of sarcasm in this which was not overlooked by Alan.

"Much better," he said. "So much better that she is in bed!"

Madame Stahm smiled.

"Young ladies who are out all night, attending maternity cases, must sleep sometimes. Her blood was too bad to look after me, but not too bad to look after the mother of little brats – it is too unkind of you, doctor."

He returned no answer to this. Evidently she had made a very judicious use of the time she had been waiting; also his housekeeper was a little loquacious.

"You have had a terrible case here, I am told, last night, eh? How trying to be a doctor!"

"A man who died in this room," said Alan untruthfully.

But, if he had hoped to impress Madame Stahm with a sense of tragedy, he was disappointed.

70

"It is a very nice room to die in," she said.

"Did you know Lamonte?"

She frowned at this.

"Lamonte? The name is familiar. My husband had a workman named Lamonte. It is very common in Vaud. All names there are French. They become German when you cross the mountains into the Oberland, and Italian in the Trentino. In Basel they are German."

"Madame Stahm," Alan was smiling, "you haven't come here to discuss the ethnological divisions of Switzerland, have you? Do you know anything about the death of Lamonte?"

She lifted her shoulder.

"I? How absurd! Why should I know? The poor man was killed by an accident, I understand. I knew nothing about him till your housekeeper spoke to me. You do not like me, Herr Doctor? You think I am a bad woman, eh? You think I killed Lamonte – cut his t'roat or something? Absurd! Presently you will say that I am in love with Peace, that ugly little man. You are unreasonable, my dear frien', because you are prejudiced. You are like that funny policeman who does not remember names. You think I am bad because I am foreign!"

She had a very musical laugh when she was amused, and she seemed amused now.

"I came here, first" – she ticked off the items delicately on her fingers – "first, to ask after my dear Jane. Naturally, I am attached to the girl, and I have her good name to think of. You are a doctor, a man of the world; is it good that a young woman should live in your house, where you have no mother, no sister, aunt, Gott knows what, to look after her? Two, I came because I owe you an apology. I was very, very rude to you. I was angry with you. Peter Baumgarten told me I should be ashamed, so I came to apologise and ask you please to continue seeing me."

Alan shook his head.

"That is not why you came. Lamonte was alive when he reached here; he was able to speak. You want to know what he said."

A look of blank astonishment was his answer.

"Why should I care what he said? How does it interest me, my friend, what any man in the delirium of death may say? When people are dying they are not sensible; they say wild things. Is it not true? You are a doctor and you know."

She waited a while, but Alan was silent, and she went on.

"He might have spoken about me – why should he not? If he was one of my husband's employees, it would be very likely. He might also speak about Mr Wertheimer, for whom he worked, or Mr Eckhardt, whom he joined in America, or about you, doctor – what would it matter? Nothing. If he said anything – "

She paused expectantly.

"What he said you will read in the account of the inquest which will be published in the *Sheffield Telegraph*."

"Why not at the court?" she asked.

"Will you attend?" he asked, and instantly realised the mistake he had made.

There was triumph in her smile.

"Then I am not to be called as a witness? And he said nothing about me at all! Not even in his dying delirium. My dear doctor, you are almost simple. I shall never dare trust your advice again!"

She had learned all she wanted to know. As she rose, pulling on her gloves and adjusting her bonnet before the square of looking-glass, she was still smiling.

"You must not think I am a wicked woman, or blame me for everything. If I had lived here in those days you would have said: 'This woman made the Bradfield flood' – and that wouldn't be true! No, no, there are quite a number of my acts which are innocent."

When he took her to the door, her victoria was there, with its footman standing, rug on arm, to assist her into the carriage.

"You will come and see me, doctor, and bring me all the news, eh? My friend Baumgarten likes you – and bring my little nurse. We are lonely without her. But she must come back without scandal to her name, you understand?"

There was a malicious little smile on her lips as she drove off. Alan went into the house and had a lot to think about during his frugal lunch.

He did not see the mother and the child until late in the evening, and then found another patient. The husband of the woman sat in the tiny, stone-flagged kitchen, nursing a bruised face. It was the anxious wife who asked Alan to see him, for she feared some permanent injury to an eye. The eyesight was unaffected, however, though the flesh surrounding the priceless organ was blue and purple.

"Had a fight," mumbled the man. "He hit me when I wasn't looking…up at the railway station. I waited all day for him to come back."

"Who is 'him'?" asked Alan. "Peace?"

The man looked up with a scowl.

"You heard about it, too, did you? I won't have him near my house."

"You're a fool – leave him alone," said Alan, "especially while your wife is ill. If she runs a temperature I'll have her taken to the infirmary."

The man winced at this. Like all his class, the very proximity of the workhouse was in itself a disgrace.

The woman's mother had arrived, and there was no necessity for Jane Garden to return to her nursing, he decided. He arrived home in time to stop her going out.

They had an uninterrupted evening, when he taught her écarté. She was an apt pupil, but the game for him had less interest than the player. He realised this night that he was desperately in love, and when, on the following day, she suggested she should go round the shops, trying to find a few simple articles of furniture, he insisted on placing at her disposal the very considerable quantity of his own household goods that was stored in the town.

12

Medical men loathe inquests: they are time wasters of the worst kind, and there is always the possibility that the ordeal may be interrupted by the too zealous questionings of a juryman. For it is a peculiar delusion of coroner's juries that something is being kept from them.

The inquest on Lamonte, however, was a brief affair, the verdict being an open one. There was not sufficient evidence to justify a verdict of wilful murder, and the jury, after the way of all juries, played for safety, and returned one of those curiously obscure pronouncements which mean nothing.

He did not see Charles Peace, though he had reason to know he had returned. Baldy told him that Peace had been stopped on his departure from Manchester and his bag searched, for during his stay there had been two flagrant burglaries. In one case a house had been broken into, a desk forced and all its contents taken away. Curiously enough, although there were many valuable articles in the house and within the burglar's reach, he had taken nothing.

The second burglary was a more serious affair; nearly five hundred pounds' worth of property, mainly silver, had been stolen. The search of Peace and his few belongings at the station had revealed nothing. Indubitably he had been engaged in legitimate business, for he showed orders that he had given and paid for, to a wholesale manufacturer of mouldings. No trace of the stolen property could be found.

If the police had gone to the booking clerk they would have discovered that the man had taken two tickets from Manchester to

Sheffield, and that the second was for a boy who passed the barrier well ahead of Peace, carrying a heavy parcel under his arm.

"Don't you pretend you know me, boy," warned Peace. "When we get to Sheffield you just follow me home, and there's a golden sovereign for you."

In this way the stolen property passed under the nose of a strong force of police that were gathered to intercept the burglar at the station, and the three plain-clothes officers who awaited the arrival of the train at Sheffield.

Peace sat in the bosom of his family that night, tuning his fiddle and discoursing upon his favourite subject, which was Charles Peace.

"I'm too clever for 'em. If they had people like me in the police force there'd be no crime. I'd fill the prisons, but they wouldn't be prisons like they are now. All the screws would have to treat men like men, and the prisoners would have beds to sleep on and good food to eat, and they'd be able to smoke and read the newspapers, and their families could come and stay with 'em for a few days every month."

His worn wife said nothing. She was sewing a garment by the shaded light of a paraffin lamp.

"Hear what I said?" he snarled.

"I hear you, Charles," she said meekly.

"Well, say something," he said savagely. "Don't sit there like a stuffed image! I don't know why I've come home to this place at all. I could have the best home in the land if I wanted it. All the lovely women are off their heads about me. Not ugly old devils like you, but lovely ones – put that in your pipe and smoke it!"

"I'm sure, Charles," she said with a sigh.

"There's a lady bred and born out there" – he pointed vaguely – "who says I'm God. What do you think of that?"

"I think it's blasphemy," she said, and in his whimsical mood he agreed.

He had certain deep religious convictions, and though he did not believe in the hereafter, or think that he would develop such a belief, he had a keen desire to be on the safe side. He had moments of enthusiastic frenzy, when he composed hymns and prayers, and on one occasion went to the length of asking a prison chaplain to publish some examples of the latter activity, "for the good of the world".

He packed his family off to bed; he had some private work to do, he said. This was no new experience. His private work took him out late at night. Twice he had not come back for six years, and at odd intervals there had come to them letters written on blue paper, bearing the superscription of various of Her Majesty's prisons. They usually began: "Dear Wife and Children, this comes hoping to find you quite well as it leaves me, thank God." Usually the letters were filled with pious and praiseworthy promises as to his future, and plentifully sprinkled with samples of more intensive piety, for they were written for the prison chaplain to read and for the prison governor to censor. A man who expresses penitence, gives nobody any trouble, calls warders "sir" punctiliously, and is ready and willing to pass on a little private information that he has acquired from his fellow prisoners, has a better chance of getting his ticket than one who is unregenerate.

At half-past one Peace slipped the key of his house into his pocket, fastened the revolver inside his high-crowned hat, and, pulling on a new ulster he had bought, went out to the rendezvous where Madame Stahm's victoria, drawn by two dashing bays, was waiting for him. He covered himself up well, and shrank back inside the hood, though, if he had had his wish, he would have made the journey in daylight under the admiring or astonished eyes of the multitude. Some day he would have a pair of horses, but the carriage would be a bit different. He invented a new victoria as he drove through the night, for he could not resist improving on the best. He would turn a carriage like this into a little room where he could change his clothing when the necessity arose; he would have candle lamps to read by, and india rubber tyres – why not? If bicycles had india-rubber tyres why should carriages run on steel? He had once tried to ride a bicycle and had fallen off. It had a very high, big wheel and a little wheel behind it, and you wore frogged tunics and little round caps – nobody knew why. There were several in Sheffield; it was a nine days' wonder, people said, and would pass away. Peace thought it would last, that everybody would have bicycles, and was laughed at for his pains.

When he had got into the carriage he had tucked away a small packet of letters under one of the cushions. You never knew what the police were going to do. He had been searched twice that day, and maybe they were watching him when he came out of the house and were following him. He lifted the leather flap of the little window at the back of the hood, but saw no lamps in view. They weren't clever enough to follow him. That was the trouble with the police: they hadn't his intelligence.

He reached Brinley Hall behind the sweating horses in an incredibly short space of time, retrieved his letters and went importantly into Madame Stahm's bureau. The first question she asked him was if he had been followed.

"They'd have to come fast to follow me, my lady, behind them horses of yours."

"Did you get what I sent you for?"

He took out the letters and laid them down.

"All the rest was bills," he said.

He had also found six five-pound notes, but he did not mention these. He would sell them on the morrow for two pounds apiece to a fence who would send them to the Continent.

"Give me the letters."

She was impatient and almost snatched them from his hand.

Turning them over, she scanned them one by one, her brow furrowed.

"These are not what I want," she said. "The girl's name isn't Emily."

The man's face fell.

"I did what you told me to do. You gave me the address – I got it here."

He fumbled in his pocket for his book, and she gave it one glance.

"Thirty-nine, you fool. You've written 'fifty-nine'. You went to the wrong house."

"My friend must have made a mistake – " began Peace.

"Don't exasperate me, little man. Your friend! Why should you be afraid of my knowing? Of course it was you!"

The crestfallen man was staring at the notebook. There were almost tears in his eyes.

"It was a hard crib, too," he whined. "Took me all day to find the servant girl, and the best part of a night to do the place. I thought it was funny. There was nothing in the letters about love – I read 'em careful, too!"

She mastered her fury with an effort.

"It is lamentable, but you must try again. These letters have no value whatever. They are stupid letters from a woman to another woman."

"There was no young lady stayin' in the place," began Peace.

"Then why did you go there?" she snapped. "I told you there was a young lady living in the house."

The man bridled. He had been called a fool, touched in his tenderest place, that sensitive vanity of his.

"All I can say is, missus, you'd better do the job yourself," he growled. "I'm not used to havin' females call me names."

Baumgarten, who, as a rule, took no attitude sympathetic with Peace, tried to pour oil on troubled waters.

"It was an error anybody could make, Clarice," he said suavely. "Our friend here made a pardonable mistake. I might have done the same, so might you."

Madame recovered an appearance of calm. She caught and heeded the warning in her "secretary's" tone.

"Yes, yes, it is stupid of me, but my heart was set on this thing. I am sorry, little man. You shall be paid just as if you had given me what I wanted."

If she had read the mind of Charles Peace she could have made no stronger appeal.

"Not me – I don't take a penny till I give you the letters. Thirty-nine, was it? I know the layout of the whole street, but I've got to get into Manchester some other way. I'll go down to London and take a train to Manchester, and get out at the station before where they examine the tickets. And I'll come back the same way. If I say I'll do a thing, I do it! That's me! It's not money that makes me — it's pride!"

She let him talk about himself for a little while and then she gave him news, and incidentally unfolded a part of her plan.

"The woman I spoke to you about, and the tall man, are moving to Darnall. There are two empty houses in a terrace there; she has taken one. Would it be a good idea if you moved into the other, supposing I paid your rent and the expenses of moving?"

The idea appealed to Peace. He was by nature a restive soul, and had never lived long in any place. Darnall was an old haunt of his and a place of pleasant associations. Moving meant nothing more than exchanging one brick box, with all its inconveniences, for another. And there was adventure in it — human adventure, which was very pleasing to him.

He had never seen Mrs Dyson, and could therefore create the image of her in his mind. It made the early morning journey to London pass in a very little time, and carried him into the outskirts of Manchester almost before the journey seemed begun.

There was no time to scrape acquaintance with any of the household staff of the house in Seymour Grove. He must take his chance.

He reached Whalley Range in the dusk of the evening, and reconnoitred the house. Luck was with him: he saw a light appear in one of the upper windows, and a girl of twenty-five or twenty-six pull down the blinds. By the light of the lamp her shadow was thrown against the white window blind, and he saw that she was writing. This was luck with a vengeance. Greater luck was his when, later, he saw a man call at the house. He was in there half an hour, and both came out together. Peace gathered, from what he overheard, that the man was some relation.

As they passed him where he crouched behind the bushes in the garden, he heard the girl say something in a foreign language. The man with her laughed and then she said in English, "I don't like leaving the house empty, even for an evening. Papa will not be home till midnight."

Empty? That meant no servants. And so it proved. The back door was easily forced. He reached the bedroom, broke the bureau and took the letters. They were tied together with blue ribbon. Subsequently he discovered, to his disgust, that they were written in French. At least, he supposed they were French. He had looked forward to reading them: he had that kind of mentality.

Carefully buttoning them into a pocket on the inside of his coat pocket, he came out of the back door, passed up a side passage and into the front garden.

There was on that beat an officious police constable who was not particularly popular with such of the lower orders as lived in the neighbourhood. Peace, who could see in the dark, saw the uniformed man from a long distance, and crossed the road. The policeman crossed to meet him.

"Hullo! Where are you going?"

"Home, sir."

It was a great mistake for him to say "sir". The policeman, a shrewd man, sensed a member of the criminal classes.

"Where have you been?"

"I have come from Manchester; I'm going back."

"Let's have a look at you."

The constable caught him by the lapel of his coat, not too gently, and at that moment Peace struck out with all his strength, and with all the concentrated hatred he had in his heart for authority. The blow caught the policeman under the jaw, and he went down like a log.

13

In an instant Peace ran.

He turned down a side lane, clambered over a fence, crossed a field and came on to the main road. He saw a horse 'bus coming along and swung himself on to the step, clambered up the iron rungs of a perpendicular ladder on to the top.

If the policeman had recognised him, or could describe him, it might mean a stretch for him. He reached a station where he knew the trains would stop, and, learning that a fast train for Sheffield was due in a few minutes, he concealed himself on the dingy platform, got into an empty carriage and hid himself under the seat.

To take a ticket would be fatal. Booking clerks and ticket inspectors would be able to describe him, and whether he was journeying to London or Sheffield, but particularly if he was going to Sheffield.

The train was evidently an express. After a while he came out of his place of concealment and began examining the letters. Then it was he had his disappointment, for the most amorous passages were as Greek to him.

The signals were against the engine driver outside a station five miles north-west of Sheffield, and the train slowed down and stopped.

The opportunity was too good to be lost: opening the carriage door he dropped on to the permanent way, climbed down a steep embankment, and, after half an hour's tramping through snowy fields, reached a deserted highway.

It was a coincidence that the only man who saw him that night was Sergeant Eltham, and Baldy's not too friendly greeting took a load off the little man's mind.

"Didn't I see you outside the Norfolk Hall this afternoon?"

"Yes, sir," said Peace promptly.

"Why did you run away?"

Peace replied glibly. His alibi was established; and he had need of it, for Police Constable Cock had circulated a fair description of him, which did not come to Sheffield, however, until the following morning.

Peace was pulled into the station as a matter of routine. He could triumphantly produce his arch-enemy to testify that he was in Sheffield that afternoon.

"And when I come to think it over," said the disgruntled Baldy, "I'm not so sure that it was him! The little devil answered so quick that I ought to have known he was kidding me. Anyway, he didn't arrive at the railway station, and so far as I know, he didn't leave for Manchester. That Peace is as artful as a waggon load of monkeys!"

When Baldy accosted him that night, near the Town Hall, he was standing on the edge of the kerb, running his hands up and down his long trousers' pockets, listening to the musical jingle of golden coins.

"I'm not so sure I saw you outside the Norfolk Hall – "began Baldy.

"Then you should be sure," snarled the other. "You shouldn't go making statements if you ain't prepared to stick to 'em. You saw me and I saw you."

Sergeant Eltham swallowed something.

"They tell me you're moving – going over to Darnall?"

"I don't like this neighbourhood. It's low."

It had been agreed that if he succeeded in getting the letters he would send a message notifying Madame Stahm, and that Baumgarten should come over and collect them. This was not to Peace's liking. He wanted to parade his success and his efficiency before the woman who had condemned him. But her orders were imperative. There were very excellent reasons why he should keep away since the death of Lamonte.

He met Baumgarten at a little wayside inn a few miles out of Sheffield, and the packet was handed over. Baumgarten took one look at the letters and his eyes sparkled.

"Can you read it, mister?" And, when the other nodded: "Read us a bit – a courting bit!" said Peace eagerly.

"My friend" – Baumgarten tapped him on the shoulder benignly – "you require no lessons in the art of writing love letters."

The little man almost purred at the compliment.

Madame Stahm very graciously consented to receive him a week later. He had to come with three picture-frames and go through the formalities of being a tradesman calling for orders, a proceeding which, for some reason or other, irked him.

He was a very vain little man. Nothing pleased him better than to be described as a gentleman; nothing drove him to such fury as a suggestion of his illiteracy. If he could play her emotions, no less could she play him.

An ingenious woman was Madame Stahm. She would sit for hours, dreaming great schemes, ingenious schemes, unbelievably clever in their intricacy. She had thought a lot about Jane Garden and the doctor, and she had woven into her fanciful stories this crude, ugly man.

Thoroughness was her keynote. She had not been content to discover the antecedents of the girl and her history so far as the hospital could supply it; she went farther afield, made inquiries in the little Midland village where the girl had been born. Jane's mother and father were dead. They had been an unhappy pair, and had separated a few months before Jane's birth. Mr Garden had married beneath him, a pretty girl from a travelling circus. There was some talk of a former lover – the whole matter had to be thrashed out in the divorce court; but the evidence was not sufficiently convincing to secure their complete separation.

The villagers talked, as villagers will continue their gossip, long after the turf had been laid upon the two people mostly concerned.

Madame was fascinated by the news she garnered and pressed her inquiries farther, and all the time that ingenious brain of hers was seeking a recipe as to how the material she had gathered could be cooked into a meal that would be most unpalatable to the man she hated without any reservations – the doctor, who had defied her, had threatened her by inference, and who guessed her ghastly secret.

Her plan took definite shape the day Peace arrived. That he should come into it at all was due to the fortuitous circumstance of his arrival. She gave him the reward she had promised him; generously increased it; found a malignant delight in adding to her kindness by translating one of the letters that he had stolen; and then brought the conversation to Jane.

"I don't like stuck-up people. She's too stuck-up for me," he said. "And she's only a bit of a girl, too. I like women of the world, and they like me. I'm not good-looking, m'lady, but I've got a way with me."

He continued in the same strain, and she did not interrupt him. When she did speak she brought the conversation back to Jane. Anyway, his idea that they should be better friends was very impossible, and for many reasons.

"Like what?" he demanded resentfully.

She told him, and he nearly jumped out of the chair.

For two hours they sat together, talking eagerly. Baumgarten, who looked in once or twice, withdrew as quickly as he appeared, glad to escape from the atmosphere Peace brought with him.

It was past dark when the victoria carried Charles Peace back to Darnall. The carriage always dropped him in a lonely place near the village; he hated this idea, but Madame was adamant. His mind was now completely occupied. The Dysons had moved in; he had had a first glimpse of the lady and approved of her. He found no difficulty in making the acquaintance of the woman and her acid-tongued husband.

Men were always more difficult than women, for men never trusted him, and some women trusted him too much. The acquaintance had become as much of a friendship as the lanky Dyson would permit. The American woman found him ugly but fascinating.

It was a week after his visit that Jane Garden met the little man, and it was a curious fact that she never spoke to Alan of the meeting. She would have passed on, but the man spoke to her, and out of sheer civility she stopped. He had something to say to her, something that could not be said in a public place. He was very respectful, rather sad. She found herself pitying him.

And then he mentioned a name she had not heard for years, and her marrow froze. She had an hour to spare; Alan was away and would not be back until the evening. She went with the ugly man into the new Frith Park which had just opened. And here he told her what he swore he had never told a soul, and as she listened she grew sick at heart, and once would have fainted but for a supreme effort of self-control.

At the gates of the park she left him. He wanted to see her again in a few days, but she shook her head.

"I don't want to see you. I never want to see you again," she said breathlessly. "I hate you – my God, how I hate you now!"

A cab was passing and she hailed it and drove back to Alan's house. He saw how white she was when he came in, and thought she was ill.

"I really do think you ought to have a rest. That job with Madame Stahm must have taken a lot of vitality out of you."

"I'm all right – I'm quite all right," she said.

She spent her evenings in her room, sewing the chintzes she had bought for her new home. To Alan it seemed she had suddenly become a new person, a Jane Garden he did not know, and he was puzzled to explain the change of attitude. He asked her point-blank one morning what the trouble was; she answered him a little shortly, and he decided not to interfere. She certainly had her own troubles, her own life. A little pang of jealousy grew out of this consideration. Did any man form part of her own life? he wondered. But she would have told him: he was sure of that.

Once, when he spoke of Peace, she changed the subject abruptly, almost rudely. He was talking about the woman whose child had been born and whose husband was still nursing a grievance against her, and out of this arose the reference to Peace.

"Please don't talk about him – it is horrible," she said in a low voice, and he saw that the hands that held the needle and chintz were shaking.

He could diagnose this as nerves: it could be nothing else. Trained nurses do not take too prim a view of the ugly things of life. The mystery of her attitude was to remain unsolved for a long time and develop into a greater and more horrible mystery.

She was younger than he had thought, had begun her nursing experiences before she was sixteen.

"I had to work," she explained. "I lived with an aunt who wasn't particularly fond of me, and there were certain other complications."

What they were she did not tell him.

The death of Lamonte brought to Alan a considerable amount of correspondence, and he was glad of her assistance in such odd hours as she could give him, for her French was perfect. Lamonte had relations, who wrote either to him or to the police. For some reason or other the police decided to turn over all the correspondence to Alan as it arrived, and the thing became a little wearisome; the more so as most of the relations seemed interested in only one subject – the amount of money the dead man had left.

She made an admirable secretary; wrote in a beautiful hand. He almost regretted that he had chosen the nurse's role for her. Except for this strange sense of restraint, this invisible barrier which had grown between them, the time which followed was ideal, though he was very little in her society.

He could not remember the time when she had not been an essential factor in his life, someone to think of when he woke, some sure guide to his dreams. He had a trick of paying little compliments, directly or by inference. They used to amuse her in the first days of their acquaintance, and pleased her, too. Now they seemed to worry her, and he either stopped paying them or felt self-consciously foolish when he saw their effect.

Yet she came to him with all her difficulties and by implication emphasised her dependence on him. But always there was that aloofness which distressed him, so that once he asked her bluntly about her health, and, more bluntly still, if he was boring her. Her emphatic "No" to the last question kept him happy for a week.

14

Letters came for her: how or when they were delivered he could not guess. They did not come by post. Once he saw a ragged little messenger leave the front door hurriedly and, entering the house, surprised her reading a note. She was standing by the window, her face in profile, her fine eyebrows bent, and he saw by the rise and fall of her bosom that something had agitated her.

"Anything wrong?" he asked.

Quickly she crumpled the letter in her hand and put it behind her.

"Nothing – nothing," she said.

He could not ask her particulars about her correspondence. A reference to the letter later in the day seemed to cause her distress. She went out in the afternoon and came back looking like death.

"In the name of heaven, what's wrong with you?"

"Nothing." She was almost defiant.

Then came his astonishing discovery. He had been called to a distant case, and was driving back late one afternoon, when Dixon decided to take a short cut through a lane, the road surface of which was bad, but which undoubtedly cut off a long and tiresome angle. At one point of the lane, set back in the hedge, was a gate leading into a field. He was dimly conscious of seeing two people standing by the gate, but not until he was abreast of them did he recognise them. The woman was Jane. The little man, who was leering into her face, was Charles Peace!

His heart nearly stopped beating. For a moment he had a wild inclination to jump from the carriage and go back and demand an explanation, but he checked himself.

She came home three-quarters of an hour after he arrived, and she offered no explanation, nor did he ask for one. He was baffled, bewildered, in some degree horrified. That this girl, refined and delicate, should find in Peace an acceptable companion was unthinkable.

Patiently he waited, day after day, for Jane to take him into her confidence; but apparently she did not think it was necessary. Whether she had seen him he could not guess. She certainly gave no sign, never once by a word betraying the least uneasiness.

Peace! It was incredible. A foul little burglar, a man whose name was a byword even amongst the lower sort... Was there any truth in this story of an ultra-human fascination? He rejected the idea as unbelievable.

Other people had seen them together. One of his patients called him back as he was leaving the house.

"Oh, by the way, that nurse of yours – Miss Garden...the girl who came here for two days...don't you think she ought to be told?"

"Told what?" asked Alan curtly.

"I saw her the other day in Frith Park with a most dreadful little man. I believe he is a well-known character in these parts. And Mrs Hackitt also saw them together on another day. She ought not to do a thing like that."

"I think Nurse Garden is quite capable of looking after herself," said Alan, and offended a wealthy patient almost beyond forgiveness.

There must be a reason for it. Was it something connected with Madame Stahm and her establishment, some secret that Peace had unearthed? The more he thought, the more confused he became.

It hurt him that she did not volunteer some statement about this peculiar friendship of hers. How could she reconcile her vehement declarations that she hated him with these fugitive meetings? She never saw him except by day. Sometimes she would snatch an hour from a case she was nursing to meet him at a convenient but isolated place, and always Alan knew when these meetings had taken place. She was graver, more laconic of speech, less able to concentrate her mind.

Sometimes he thought she was labouring under great mental agony, and once he bluntly suggested that she had something on her mind and that it would be to her advantage to tell him. The suggestion was received coldly, and he realised that if their friendship was to continue he must make no further reference to this amazing acquaintance of hers.

It worried him a great deal, even though there was something impersonal in the friendship she maintained with the disreputable little blackguard. She was so serene, so infinitely sane, and his loyalty to her was such that the commonplace explanation did not enter into his calculations. No intelligent woman could fall under the spell of the little picture-frame maker. He could believe anything but that.

He discovered that even when she did not meet him, Peace dogged her footsteps. He was seen waiting outside houses where she was nursing, and was moved on by the police.

Baldy was puzzled, and came to Alan for an explanation.

"I run the rule over him in the street, but I couldn't find any burglar's tools in his pocket, but there's the fact: he has been watching that house for two days. I think I am entitled to pull him in."

Alan shook his head.

"I shouldn't if I were you."

Baldy looked at him oddly.

"There's no truth in that story – ?" He hesitated.

"What story?" asked Alan.

"That he's hanging around – well, Miss Garden?"

Alan thought for a long time, then said "No," but not very convincingly.

"I'll tell you what I think, Eltham," he said. "This man must know a friend of Miss Garden's, somebody she does not wish to offend. The little devil is using this as an excuse for speaking to her."

"Has he annoyed her at all?" asked Baldy quickly. "I'll put him inside if he has."

"She has not complained," replied Alan. "So far as I know, he has said nothing to offend her."

Sergeant Eltham rubbed his shining head in perplexity.

"I can't understand it – he bought her a present – "

"A what?" said Alan, startled.

"A present – a silver ring with an imitation stone. He bought it all right: one of our plain-clothes men saw him. He bought it for her, and gave it to her that afternoon, and she chucked it into the road. My man saw her throw something away, and after she'd gone Peace was looking for it, but my fellow found it – a silver ring with a glass sapphire."

"I give it up," said Alan.

"It must have given him a pain to buy it, anyway," said Baldy. "All that his lady friends get are the things he pinches and can't sell."

"Miss Garden is not a lady friend," said Alan coldly, "and it is ridiculous to refer to her as such."

It was during this more acute period of anxiety that Alan Mainford renewed an old and not a very welcome association. The renewal was brief, and ended for the moment abruptly.

He had worked through a number of attending patients, and now he struck the little bell on the side of his desk. It was the signal for the next, and, he hoped, his last morning patient.

The man who walked in, fingering nervously the brim of a high-crowned bowler hat, looked the picture of health and embarrassment. He had waited for a long time outside the house before he had dared enter; waited whilst patient after patient had passed into and from the consulting room. And now he obeyed the summons.

"Well, what is the matter with you?" asked Alan pleasantly.

And then he frowned.

"I've seen you somewhere."

"Yes, sir – Carton, sir." The man's eyes never left him.

"Carton? Good Lord! You were my servant in my army days, weren't you?"

"Yes, sir," said Carton, and coughed.

"Wasn't there a question of a watch being lost – my watch, in fact?"

"There was, sir," said Carton very respectfully. "It is the one act of my life that I have never stopped regretting, sir. Yielding to a sudden temptation, and having a sick wife – "

"You weren't married," said Alan promptly, and his visitor shuffled his feet uneasily. He had hoped that Dr Alan Mainford, in his new and engrossing practice, would have forgotten those petty details of a former life.

"When I say 'wife', sir, I mean sister-in-law. I can only tell you, I've never forgotten my debt to you, and some day I'm going to pay you back."

"And in the meantime?" suggested Alan.

Carton coughed again.

"There's a chance of getting a job and going straight, sir," he said. "A gentleman in the north of England wants a parlour-man – he is a titled gentleman."

"In that case he should have two parlour-men," said Alan sardonically. "You haven't come to ask me to give you a good character, have you?"

Carton obviously had.

"This gentleman's very particular, sir. It would make a big difference to me if you could speak for me."

He gave with every confidence the name and address of his future employer. Alan was staggered by the audacity of the request.

"I remember quite a lot about you now. You've been in prison, haven't you?"

The man nodded.

"How many times?"

Mr Carton looked up at the ceiling thoughtfully.

"About twice, sir," he said vaguely.

"Once for leaving the house where you were employed with the lady's jewels?"

"They weren't real jewels, sir," Carton hastened to correct a bad impression. "Most of 'em were imitation. I took them away to show my – my sister-in-law – she was very keen on jewels – and I lost 'em on my way back, and hadn't the nerve to face the missus."

All this very glibly, like a man who had well rehearsed his speech. The young doctor leaned back in his chair, an amused smile in his eyes.

"And now all you want is for me to write to your gentleman and say that you're 'honest, sober and trustworthy'? I'm afraid it can't be done, Carton. I am willing to forgive you the little incident of the watch, which was not very valuable – "

"I only got eight shillings for it," interposed Carton.

"That's too bad! Your respect for me must have dropped to zero! No, it can't be done, Carton. But I'm glad you called to see me. In these days of strain and hysteria it is delightful to meet somebody who has all his nerve! That will do."

Still Carton lingered.

"You don't want a servant yourself, sir?" he suggested.

Alan waved the stem of his pipe towards the door, and Mr Carton, with a courteous little bow, went out, a shabby but undefeated man, for he had a friend in Manchester who, for a small consideration, would prepare the most glowing testimonials, all written in different hands upon headed sheets of notepaper, and with every letter went a guarantee that the alleged writer was either dead or living abroad.

As he crossed the street he was looking round for oncoming traffic when he collided with a little man, who scowled at him and demanded in florid language where he thought he was going. He hardly noticed his offensive acquaintance, the only impression that was left on him being that his collision-partner was repulsively and extremely ugly. They stopped in the middle of the road, at some danger to themselves, to argue responsibility, and were parted by a swift-trotting butcher's cart.

"That's a man I never want to meet again," said Carton, addressing his remarks to the first person he met when he reached the pathway.

If he could have foreseen the future he would have said this with greater fervour.

Alan was in some dilemma. He recalled now every incident of the man leaving him. He was treacherous – an unregenerate thief. Nothing was more certain than that he would get his job with forged references – Dr Mainford recalled the circumstances of Carton's prosecution, and he remembered that forged characters had figured in the evidence,

Yet he was loth, as all decent men are loth, to make life any harder for those who have been under the iron heel of the law. He took up his pen, hesitated for a long time, and then wrote a brief note to the gentleman whose name Carton had given him. He could not let his former servant engage himself in a decent household without being an accessory before the inevitable crime.

It was a thankless task, as he discovered a couple of weeks later, when he received a haughty letter from the employer, saying that he was perfectly satisfied with Carton's references and with Carton himself, and that it was a pity that he (Alan) had allowed his prejudices over "an unfortunate affair" to take such strong expression. Alan wondered exactly what was the unfortunate affair that Carton had represented to his new boss.

He dismissed the matter from his mind, and never saw his ex-butler again until that fatal night when he drove him from Banner Cross to the railway station.

On the day he saw Carton and wrote the letter he received another visitor; and this one was a little more disturbing. He sent in his card: it bore the name of a Leeds agency, though in what particular commodity the agency dealt was not specified. A young, rather confident man, the caller came quickly to the point. Was a Miss Garden staying in the house, and could he tell him anything about her antecedents?

Alan was too taken aback for the moment to reply.

"I don't understand you. What do you mean?"

"Do you know anything of her past?" asked the caller cold-bloodedly.

Alan got up from his chair.

"Who sent you – Madame Stahm?" he demanded wrathfully.

"I merely want to know – "

"Get out!"

He left hurriedly. An inquiry agent!

15

The winter passed; spring came, and the spring of 1876 was a particularly busy one for doctors.

Jane Garden had found her niche. Within a week of furnishing her little home over the stables, Alan had placed her in charge of a serious case in a wealthy family, and thence onwards she hardly spent a week in her little home before she was again sent off on yet another case.

Alan saw her every day, since she was attending his own patients, and in the spring she contrived to spend several Sundays with him, driving through the country.

He saw Madame Stahm very frequently: she was almost a daily visitor to her experimental plant. There were rumours that the new formula she was applying had given successful results, though as yet the product could not be made in commercial quantities. Silver Steel had boldly made an announcement, and had given a date when their manufacture would be on the market; but in neither case had the samples satisfied the experts.

He saw Peace very rarely, heard a little about him from Sergeant Eltham, who, however, seemed less interested in the little man since he and Alan had discussed the odd friendship which Peace was cultivating with Jane Garden.

One blazing hot day in July he saw the little man, dressed in his Sunday best, and with him a woman whom Alan did not remember having seen before. She was young, about twenty-five, fresh-coloured and rather plump. Her face was bold and with no particularly intellectual expression.

It was a Friday afternoon in a country lane, and his attention was first directed to them – he was resting under the shade of a tree whilst his groom fixed a broken piece of harness – when he saw the little man vault a fence with no effort and collect a handful of flowers. They were not difficult to acquire, for Peace had chosen a nursery garden, and presently the irate voice of the owner or foreman demanded angrily what the intruder was at, and a minute afterwards the lawful custodian of the flowers, a slight young man, came running across the field.

"Put those flowers back where you found them!" he demanded.

By this time Peace was on the lawful side of the fence, but the man had jumped it and was confronting him.

"Put them back!"

The florist caught Peace by the collar. In another second he was hurtling through the air, across a fence, which must have been four or five feet high, and fell with a crash into a glass frame on the other side. Alan got down quickly, thinking the man had been killed, but he scrambled up, his face streaming with blood.

"You dirty little brute, why did you do that?" asked Alan furiously.

If ever he saw death, it was in the horribly distorted face of Charles Peace.

"I'll serve you the same."

The woman screamed and grasped him by the arm, but, shaking her off, he leaped at Mainford. This time, however, he had to deal with a trained athlete and a boxer who had won his way into the Indian Army finals. Alan stepped aside and like lightning brought his left to the man's throat. He spluttered, gurgled, almost went on to his knees, but he was beaten. He had no heart except for a winning fight; he was incapable of taking one hard blow. From the frenzied murderer he became, of a sudden, the whining supplicant. The change was startling, more than a little revolting. Even the pink-faced woman by his side stared at him open-mouthed.

"What did you hit me for? I'll have the law on you for this!" he whined. "A big bloke like you hitting a little feller like me!"

But Alan was attending to the dazed young man who had been thrown over the fence. Except for two or three cuts on his face he was unhurt.

"If you take my advice you will charge this man. His name is Charles Peace; he is an ex-convict with three convictions."

Peace heard him and let out a howl of anguish.

"Don't do that, mister! Don't let him do that! I'll pay him for his trouble."

He took a handful of coins from his pocket and pressed two or three into the reluctant hand of the injured man.

"You oughtn't to have told him that, doctor – you really oughtn't. It's throwing my trouble in my face – I don't think it's right!"

"What's not right?" asked the woman.

It was the first time she had spoken. Her voice was a trifle thick; her eyes were glassy. Alan took a very uncharitable view of her condition.

"It's all right, my dear. This gentleman knows me. He's a doctor – one of the greatest doctors in Sheffield. If ever you get ill you send for him!" And then, to Alan, pleadingly: "I'm always saying this about you, doctor, and you go and take my character away because you're a rich man and I'm a poor man. There's no justice – there really isn't – no justice at all."

It occurred to Alan then that this woman knew nothing of his real character, and had probably not heard the unflattering description of her swain. And it appeared that the little man was most anxious that she should not know, for, taking her arm, he hurried her on out of earshot.

"Three quid," said the young man, dabbing his bloodstained face with a handkerchief. "He's got plenty of money – I suppose he's done a burglary."

"Do you know him?"

"Charles Peace? Yes, I know him," said the other. "And he'll know me – I shall carry a mark of his for a year or two. If I'd had an axe I'd have killed him."

"Who is the woman?"

"She's the wife of an engineer. They live next door to one another at Darnall. People say…"

He told Alan what people said, and did not err on the side of charity to Mrs Dyson, as her name proved to be.

"They're as thick as thieves," said the florist. "I'm always meeting 'em together, and other people tell me she goes out with him to music-halls. Her husband's a gentleman, too. What any woman can see in that little fellow…"

He left nothing to the imagination.

Alan went back to the victoria that he had recently bought, and drove on to his next patient. He wasn't greatly interested in Mrs Dyson, or, indeed, in any of the numerous amours of this surprisingly ugly and unspeakably nasty man. For his part he did not ruminate as to what women saw in men. His experience had taught him the futility of any such speculation.

Peace, except in one important particular, had almost passed out of his life. Mrs Stahm had become a confused memory. The dead man, Lamonte, was forgotten, even by the jury that had inquired into his death.

He took Jane to the theatre that night, and in the course of the evening remarked upon the shortness of memory.

"I belong to that period, too," she smiled.

"You aren't forgotten: you're very much in the glowing present," he said quietly, "and you're becoming just a little too dominant for my peace of mind."

She shot one quick glance at him, and he saw her colour come and go, but she made no comment until they were walking home after the theatre.

"Am I really worrying you?" she asked.

"Not a scrap."

"Seriously, I mean. Do you think I ought to – do anything?"

"Yes, I think you ought to marry me."

He tried to be nonchalant, but his voice broke.

She did not answer. He thought she quickened her pace a little.

She could have gone through the house to her own rooms, but she left him at the door, taking the carriage way.

"You're not leaving me like that?" he asked breathlessly, and held her hand. "I love you – you know that."

"Do you love Charles Peace?" she asked in a strained voice.

"Charles Peace? For God's sake, what do you mean?"

He heard her breathing heavily.

"I am his daughter," she said, and, tearing her hand from his, she fled round the corner of the house out of sight.

16

Alan Mainford stood, petrified with amazement. For a second he could not move. He had read the words "rooted to the spot" before, and they had had no significance for him; but now he knew exactly what the imaginative writers had meant.

Recovering his normal activity, he ran after her, flew up the wooden ladder and reached the landing just as she slammed the door.

"Open the door, Jane."

"Go away."

He heard the break in her voice; she was too near to tears for his comfort.

"Open the door or I'll break the lock!"

The key turned, and he went into the darkened room. She had flung herself on the small sofa, her head upon her arms. He gripped her by the shoulders and pulled her upright.

"Now just tell me what you mean about that piece of nonsense. Is that what has been worrying you all this time?"

"I'm his daughter — isn't it terrible? Isn't it horrible!" she sobbed. "I've known it for months."

Now he understood and a great load rolled from his mind.

"Is that why you have been meeting him?"

She nodded.

"Who told you he was your father?"

She would not answer, and he shook her gently.

"Who told you this lie?"

"He did. It's true, my dear — he knows everything. It couldn't be anything but true. He went by the name of Fenner... Auntie always spoke of the ugly man who was my father, taunted me with it. I knew he was with a circus, but I didn't dream..." Her voice broke.

He got from her, sentence by sentence, the story of her youth; of the two parents, who, utterly unsuited to one another, had finally parted; of the scandal; of the abortive divorce case.

"He may have read it."

"He couldn't have read it. He knows the man's nickname – everything."

Alan sat by her side, biting his lips. That the story was a lie he was certain. Who could have primed the little devil with all the details? Then it flashed on him – Madame Stahm.

"Did you ever tell Madame the story of your life?"

"No. She wanted to know all about my parents, but I would never tell her. I remember she was very much annoyed and said that she could easily find out if she was curious enough."

He got up and began to pace the room, his hands in his pockets.

"That's where it's come from – Madame Stahm! She has managed to get the story somehow, and has told this little beast, giving him dates, names, particulars, everything."

She looked up at him.

"You don't think it's true?"

"Of course it isn't true!" he scoffed. "Look at yourself in the mirror and tell me if it's true! Orchids grow on muck-heaps, but they're odd kinds of orchids. I'm going to find out the truth about this."

He called that night on a brother doctor and arranged for him to see his patients. Early in the morning he left for Warwickshire. Jane was not at home when he returned, and he was glad, for he had not finished his investigations. They carried him to Leeds, and to the office of the private inquiry agency which had sent its representative to call upon him.

The agency proved to be a very reticent organisation until Alan threatened to make a police court matter of it.

They had been engaged by a client, a lady. (They were discreet to the point of refusing her name, but Alan could guess that.) They had pursued their inquiries, had interviewed the girl's aunt –

"A difficult woman," said the investigator.

"Very. I interviewed her myself this morning – a cat of cats."

"I'm inclined to agree with you," said the investigator.

From this lady they had learned everything they wanted, coloured a little maliciously. The dead scandal had, so to speak, been wrapped in wet moss and its roots still sprouted.

He got back to Sheffield, picked up the girl at the house where she had been attending an elderly lady, who required a companion rather than a nurse, and in the drive home he told her the result of his inquiries.

"It was a lie from beginning to end. Peace was primed to tell you this foul story, and how like Madame to invent it! I owe her that one. As for Peace, I owe him a very important duty."

She did not ask what it was, nor, when she retired to her lodgings, why he seemed so anxious to get rid of her.

In the hall of Alan Mainford's house was a square, polished board, and, resting on double hooks, were a number of hunting crops. He tried them all, chose one, and ordered the complaining Dixon to bring the victoria to the door.

For three hours he searched various public-houses. It was in Darnall, in a low beer-shop, that he found his quarry and beckoned him out into the street.

Peace was without fear in some respects. He could face the violence of the law and its officers with equanimity. But here he harboured the illusion that it was he who had triumphed and the law which had failed. Now he was face to face with his master, a man physically equal and morally ascendant.

"I want to talk to you, Peace."

They walked along the road in silence, the little man eyeing the hunting crop apprehensively. At a lonely spot Alan stopped.

"Is Miss Jane Garden your daughter?"

"That's no business – " began the man.

"I want the truth from you. If you lie to me, I'll beat the soul out of you – I may even kill you. Is Jane Garden your daughter?"

A sudden silence. Alan stood back; the thong of the whip whistled through the air.

"No!" screamed the little man. "I was kidding her — that's a joke."

"Madame Stahm's joke or yours?"

"I don't know nothing about Madame Stahm."

Then, as the crop came up: "It was the lady's idea…a little joke."

"If it's a joke, laugh, you swine!" snarled Alan, and the lash fell.

With a scream, Peace backed against the hedge. His hand dropped to his right-hand pocket. The pistol was half out when Alan struck again and he fell with a sob to the ground.

"I'll never forgive you for that, Peace!" Alan spoke between his teeth. "You're such an ignorant brute that you don't know how beastly you've been."

"And I'll never forgive you either, master" — the little man's face was white with fury. "No man's ever hit me — twice you've done it. Nobody's done it, nobody's dared do it, not screws or anyone! One of these days I'll kill you for it."

And then Alan, who was as great a psychologist as he was a surgeon, delivered his moral *coup de grace*. He knew this man through and through. If he had not known him, Peace would certainly have killed him in his time.

"Some day," he said slowly, "you will be brought into my surgery, or into the hospital where I operate, and I shall remember your threat."

He had touched the real weakness of the man. Peace fell on his knees and clawed at his arm.

"For God's sake don't say that, master! It's cruel…it's wicked! Supposed I had an accident…got shot…you wouldn't do that? You're a doctor, you mean mercy. Tell me you wouldn't do that!… It'll haunt me, mister. There ain't a braver man than me, not in the whole world, but that's what I'm always frightened of. That's why I never touch a doctor's house. I never stole a penny from a doctor in my life. You wouldn't do it, master! You couldn't be so wicked! The Lord would strike you dead if you did it!"

He was almost sobbing when Alan jerked him to his feet.

"Behave yourself, Peace. And take that blow as quits."

The man jerked his head up and down. He was incapable of speech for a moment. When eventually he did speak, his voice was the old familiar whine.

"That settles it – everything. I'll write to the young lady and tell her."

The letter came to Jane the next morning. It was hand-delivered by a little girl whom Alan recognised as Peace's daughter.

"DERE MISS,

it was a jok i never ment abut been yor farthur i maid it up so fergif mi prisumson and parden yor humbel survint.

"Dere Miss, yor farthur i dunt no nore eard of him it was a jok maid up so plese furgif yor obent servint becars I ony ment a jok.

"Yor servint. and humbel,
"CHAS. PEACE."

The girl read the scrawl and, with Alan's assistance, deciphered it.

"Thank God it was a joke!" she said fervently.

" 'Jok' is the word you want," suggested Alan.

It was on that day that Peace, after a heated exchange with Mr Dyson, ended his tirade with the memorable words: "You don't deserve to have an educated man for your friend!"

17

Mr Arthur Dyson, the neighbour of Mr Peace, was dyspeptic, short-tempered, secretive. It was his misfortune that he suffered from a superiority sense, which made him a little unendurable, and certainly had not popularised him either in the surveyor's office at York or in his new post.

Possibly the superiority was based upon his foreign experience, which is one of the most oppressive forms of vanity. Though he was not a talkative man, there were moments when he would hold forth on the advantage of American institutions over British, or, alternatively, the appalling character of the American people. He was the type of Englishman in whom foreign travel creates new standards for disparagement. He was insular, narrow, rather querulous, but above all, secretive. The people who met him, or who worked with him, knew as little about him as his neighbours, or, for the matter of that, his wife.

He never ceased to regard her as a social inferior, and it was generally believed that he had married beneath him. If he had a hobby at all, it was steel. This was a period when almost every other man that was to be met in Sheffield had the germ of a patent in his head, or sketched on paper; patent processes, patent converters, methods of extracting silicon, methods of tempering, strange, weird and possibly expensive ways of manufacture; and in the little club which he frequented, inventors were as thick as a smoky atmosphere.

He would sit there, pulling at a thin cigar, listening with a knowing smile to the arguments which waged furiously, or be one of the throng which crowded round a table when some triumphant inventor exhibited a model converter that had "come to him" in a flashing moment of inspiration.

Mr Dyson said very little. He could have said a great deal. It gave him a tremendous amount of satisfaction to know just how much he could say if he so willed. He could tell the stupid engineers, ironmasters and chemists something that would strike them dumb with amazement. He could produce from its hiding-place a phial of pinky-white crystals that would revolutionise the steel industry. And in good time he would.

For the moment he was rather uncertain as to his legal position. He was a cautious man, with a powerful respect for the law. He was all for respectability, desiring the good opinions of his fellows, and this was probably his greatest weakness. For few people are respected by anybody, and honesty is a negative quality. He was regarded as a safe man, quiet and well spoken. His acquaintances said of him that he was "quite the gentleman", which, indeed, he was.

His home life was a continuous strain. His wife, twenty years his junior, was twenty degrees lower in the social scale. He had, he told himself, been deceived by the apparent social equality of all Americans, and had not a sufficient acquaintance with the country and its customs to differentiate between the grades of society which were so subtly but surely separated in the 'seventies.

If he had lived fifty years later he would have occupied a new detached villa, for which he would have paid by instalments. He would have been a member of a golf club, and owned a small car. But the gradations of English society in the 'seventies recognised only two classes: the upper and the lower. The lower middle class was slowly emerging from its parent stem and had not yet split into its multitude of branches and twigs.

It irritated him that he should live, because of his limited means, in a poor-class neighbourhood, the tenant of a cheap house, and have as his neighbours common and illiterate working men. Victoria Terrace epitomised a social dead level. That he should have next door but one – happily separated by empty premises – a horrible little man who followed the trade of picture-frame maker and had, by all accounts, a most unwholesome past, was a source of irritation. He resented Mr Peace; he bitterly resented his wife's friendship with him. Intermittently he hated the ugly little man who came sidling in at tea-time to have a clean cup set for him. Worst of all, Peace was obviously trying to ingratiate himself into Mr Dyson's good graces.

He was foul; kept secreted in a pocket a greasy packet of postcards which somebody had brought from Paris. Judged by a later standard, they were no more than indelicate, but the prim male in Mr Dyson was revolted by the frills and the nudes and the leering smiles of his neighbour as he exhibited them.

"I can't understand how you have that man in the house – faugh!" he said, and opened the window ostentatiously.

Mr Peace had paid one of his evening calls.

"He's cute," said Mrs Dyson, "and a gentleman," she added. "I wish I could say the same of you."

"Gentleman – huh!"

Mr Dyson put on his carpet slippers and his worn smoking jacket, and took down the meerschaum pipe which he kept on the mantelshelf, and which was reaching a stage of ripe brownness.

"I like him; he's very clever; and when a man's clever you can forgive anything," said the woman. "A clever man doesn't depend on weekly wages. He'll always earn big money – and spend it."

Dyson looked at her with a cold and unfriendly eye.

"Do you get enough to eat, woman?" he asked.

"Just enough," she retorted, "and I earn it. I'm a hired help, but I get no wages, and I've got the job for life!"

"You can go when you're tired of it," he said loftily.

"I'll go just when I want to go" – she did not raise her voice – "I'm a slave here. You never take me out; I haven't had a dress for six months."

"Ask Peace to buy you a dress."

It was an unfortunate remark. He dodged just in time, and the saucer crashed into splinters on the wall behind his head. In an instant he was on his feet.

"One of these days I'll give you a beating that you won't forget!" he stormed.

She went out of the room and slammed the door behind her, and was gone a long time. Half an hour passed; he put down the book he was reading and went out into the garden behind. His wife was leaning on the separating wall, talking to the abominable little man. Peace had a big, green parrot perched upon his forefinger, and she was laughing loudly at its antics. He called to her; she barely turned her head in his direction. Mrs Dyson could be very trying.

Peace fascinated her. His repulsive ugliness was almost an attraction. He was a mine of information (mainly wrong) on all sorts of subjects, about which the average man had no knowledge. He could sing; he was an excellent mimic; he could do things with his face that held her in an almost hypnotic stupor. He could recite long scenes from Shakespeare, play tunes of his own composition. One afternoon Mr Dyson returned home early and found his wife sitting on the sofa, listening raptly to a violin obbligato performed on a fiddle with one string. Even he was held by the wild melody, and did not interrupt. When the tune was finished and Peace was smirking his acknowledgments of her ecstatic praise, the storm broke.

"Get out of here before I throw you out!" He gripped the little man by the arm. Peace very gently pried the fingers loose without an effort.

It was the first exhibition he had given the long man of his amazing strength, and Mr Dyson was impressed, and his manner became milder. Perhaps he thought that the quality of the little man's music raised him from his lowliness, brought him nearer to the exalted plane on which moved an engineer – a qualified professional man. He was quite affable the next night, and of his own free will invited Peace in to tea. His surrender set a disastrous example. When Mrs Dyson announced her intention, a little defiantly, of going to Sheffield to see some pictures at a gallery with her neighbour, he did not demur. Thereafter the trips were made without any notification to him.

He was pleased, too, with the almost reverent way the little man had framed some photographs of his. He told an acquaintance: "This man Peace is not so bad. He's very common, of course, but he's rather amusing."

The man who finds vulgarity amusing takes two steps down.

She came back occasionally from these trips a little incoherent of speech and flushed of face, too ready at the first hint of reproof to pick up the thing nearest to her hand and throw it at the tall man. Except from the annoying hurt to his dignity, he was glad to see her go out, because he was a great dreamer.

He would go into his bedroom, lock the door, and, opening a bottom drawer, take out a blue octagonal bottle of liniment, corked and sealed. It was not exactly what it seemed. By pulling, the whole base of the bottle came away, and in its centre was a small white phial, also corked and sealed, full of little crystals which rattled musically when the phial was shaken.

He used to muse on this, turning it over and over in his hand, dreaming of a palatial London house, carriages and horses, and a box at the opera. He had other dreams: of a wasted man who died in Cleveland, telling his story with feverish and disconcerting rapidity. Mr Dyson had learned his French from the dying man. The exercises of his youth, the confusion of irregular verbs, had suddenly become a language, so that he could follow the story that Eckhardt told, could even understand the intricate processes which he described.

Eckhardt had taken a great liking to Mr Dyson, had probably mistaken his dull silences for wisdom. It had been a fascinating page of life for Mr Dyson. The golden gates of romance had come ajar and he had had a peep at shattering visions. In this little phial was all the glamour of buried treasure hunts, of hidden goldfields, without any of the fatigue and expense of the seeking.

In his dreams Mrs Dyson had no part. She was a chattel, a difficult servant, and no friend. If he ever wanted to take that step he could divorce her. She was degrading him by her association with a man like Peace... But Peace was quite amusing. An ugly little beast, but amusing. Some days he loathed the man, would hardly speak to him in the street, would brush past him with long strides and a gruff "I haven't any time."

There were scenes in the Dyson household; oppositions of quivering fury; dramatic gestures; a sprinkling of bad language; much broken crockery. He threw a hammer at her and bruised her shoulder. For a week afterwards he had his meals out, and never drank a cup of tea until he had poured out a little in a saucer for the cat, for Mrs Dyson had talked darkly of prussic acid as a solution to her married misery. And he gathered that she had no intention of committing suicide.

Dyson was proceeding slowly to the realisation of his dreams. He had visited Mr Wertheimer, a slim, volatile man who did most of his talking with his hands; so full of energy that he ran where he could have walked, and leapt where he could have run. A clever man, without that divine spark of genius essential to complete success. Mr Dyson used to spend evenings in the little cottage built within the walls of the Silver Steel factory and talk of Eckhardt, who had once been a personal friend and a daily companion of Wertheimer's. And whenever the little Frenchman led the conversation in a dangerous direction, Mr Dyson would temporise.

He released his information cautiously, item by item. They had known one another for three months before Wertheimer had even a hint that the dead man had discussed the formula with his visitor.

Eckhardt never had a chance of proving his crystals. He was taken ill before the new crucibles were laid down; and, of course, he had no money – not a dollar. The men who intended financing him were ruined in the war – they were on the Confederacy side. Step by step he roused Wertheimer's interest to fever pitch, and then one day he revealed the fact that Eckhardt's secret was in his hands.

"He has made the steel! Look at that!"

From his pocket he took a thin strip of steel that had the appearance of silver. Wertheimer seized it excitedly and carried it to the light.

"You have tested it? It is good?" he almost shouted, bending the strip backwards and forwards. "You will give me this, that I may test it – ?"

Dyson shook his head.

"No fear," he said. He almost snatched the strip from the reluctant hand of his host. "I am not a fool. You could analyse that. No, that stays with me."

Thenceforward began a haggling over terms. Wertheimer did not speak for a week. Mr Dyson sat in his lonely sitting-room with a pencil and paper, working out terms that would be advantageous to himself.

Peace was a being transfigured in these days; wore his best suit almost every day, and a flower in his buttonhole; was shaved by a barber and had his shoes polished by a public boot-black. He was in love and exalted in his passion. He also had his dreams: he would take Mrs Dyson to Manchester, open a magnificent shop for her, spending as much as a hundred pounds on stock. Owning a shop was, for Peace, the banner of respectability. He had opened many, legitimately and illegitimately; had plans in his head for an eating-house. This probably followed a successful burglary of a Sheffield provision store, the perpetrator of which was never discovered.

("Peace," said Baldy Eltham emphatically, "though it's a new lay with him. Two cases of butter, four hams and a side of bacon. How he got 'em away is a mystery to me. There was no money in the desk, and he couldn't open the safe.")

18

Madame Stahm had employed the Leeds inquiry agents for many other purposes. The list of her suspects now covered two sheets of paper. She had traced not only the associates but the servants of the traitor Eckhardt. Apparently the man had worked at Birmingham for a year before he went to America, and she was obsessed with the notion that one of these was privy to the very secret she was striving to unearth. Moreover, she had succeeded in insinuating an agent of hers into the Silver Steel works, and from him received bi-weekly reports.

They were very comforting to Madame. She expressed her jubilation to her secretary.

"Wertheimer has failed. Yet I have an idea that the formula has been in his hands and that he hasn't had the sense to understand it. This girl of his in Manchester has studied science. Their correspondence has become more and more vital, and I would like so much to know what he has told her."

"You can't make a second attempt," suggested Baumgarten.

"Why not?" she demanded. "The girl's father is a diamond dealer. The police hardly noticed the loss of the letters; they thought the burglar was after a packet of stones which was in the house. They say that he was disturbed, and think that he took the letters under the impression that amongst them was the packet of diamonds. Why shouldn't he try again? There would be nothing in the house of any value, so there would be no extra guard. I must know what this man is writing to her."

Baumgarten bit off the end of a cigar and lit it.

"We have not seen our dear Charles for quite a long time. Has he made any report about the Dysons?"

A glint of laughter came into the hard eyes of Madame Stahm.

"Not yet. He is making no progress at all, except in the wrong direction. He has fallen in love with Madame Dyson."

Baumgarten leaned back in his chair and laughed softly.

"The rat!" he said. "Has it become serious?"

"As serious as it can become. They write each other letters, they meet secretly, the husband is jealous, our Charles is boastful, but I have learned nothing of Eckhardt which is of importance."

Baumgarten sharpened a pencil with maddening deliberation.

"If the husband is jealous does that seem to you very promising, my friend? Is it not from the husband all information must be obtained? And if he is antagonising Herr Dyson, he seems to be defeating our ends. Does that occur to you?"

"I don't know," she said. "Peace has been through their house while they were away; he has examined all their papers, and could find nothing directly or indirectly connected with Eckhardt and his experiments."

"Perhaps there is nothing to discover. Who knows?"

That Peace was madly in love, not for the first time in his life, was ludicrously true. That he should choose the man who had flogged him as the recipient of his confidences seemed amazingly impossible.

He came into Alan's surgery about eight o'clock one night, when the last of the patients attending had gone. Alan's first inclination was to kick him out, but the little man, with his ingratiating smile, his cheerful buoyancy and his staggering friendliness, carried too many moral guns.

"I want to see you, doctor. You've always been a good friend of mine" (Alan almost reeled under this shocking accusation) "and I'm in trouble. I always say 'Go to a doctor if you're in trouble, not to a parson.' Doctors are men of the world, parsons know all about heaven and hell and sim'lar fancies, but they know nowt about life."

Alan pointed to a chair.

"Sit down, you unspeakable little blackguard," he said, and Peace grinned and obeyed.

Apparently he was tickled by this method of address, for, when it soaked into his mind, he rocked with silent laughter for fully a minute. When he had recovered: "It's about a fancy matter. As a matter of fact, it's a lady. She's one of the most lovely women I've ever seen, or you've ever seen, doctor. There ain't a woman in England, not at Queen Victoria's court or on the theatrical stage, that can hold a candle to her. And she's gone off her head about me."

"You mean she's mad? I can well understand that," said Alan, wilfully dense.

"She loves me and I love her; but her husband can't stand me."

"That is remarkable," said Alan.

Sarcasm was wasted on Peace. He was entirely devoid of any sense of humour, and it struck Alan afterwards that if he had grown mirthful over the gross insult he had offered him when he came into the surgery, it was because he had regarded the description of himself as being grotesquely wide of the mark and overstated.

"This lady – and she is a lady, bred and born – "

"Is she the woman I saw you with?" interrupted Alan brutally. "The woman who was slightly the worse for drink?"

"She drinks very little," said Peace gravely, "and only then for pains in her inside, so you might say it's medicine. You can't deny, doctor, that she's got beauty and grace."

"I do deny it rather emphatically," said Alan. "But don't let that arrest the smooth flow of your ecstasies."

"I don't know what that means," said Peace, a little shortly, "but there she is. And me and her don't know what to do. We thought of running away to America, where she comes from – Cleveland, Ohio: it's near New York."

"And leaving her husband?"

Peace nodded.

"And leaving your wife?"

"She'd be better off without me," said Mr Peace comfortably. "I'm only a lot of trouble to her. She'd be happier in the workhouse."

The cold-blooded relegation of his responsibility to the ratepayers took Alan's breath away.

"I've given up thieving and burglaring," Peace went on. "I've seen the error of my ways, doctor. I lay awake at night, thinking 'Suppose I died in my sin?'"

He said this impressively. Alan could supply an immediate rejoinder.

"I expect the police are worrying about your *not* dying in your sins! Well, what do you want me to do?"

"I want you to lend me a hundred pounds to pay me fare to America – me and my love," said Peace, and the effrontery of it left Alan helpless.

"Have you asked Madame Stahm?" he demanded.

Peace shook his head.

"I want another hundred pounds from her."

Alan eyed him steadily. He was no longer finding the interview funny.

"I suggest an easy way of getting a hundred pounds," he said. "Mr Wertheimer offers that amount for any information that will lead to the arrest of the people who kidnapped and killed the man Lamonte."

Peace stared at him blankly.

"Never heard of him."

"You helped to kidnap him. I'm not suggesting that you killed him, but you'll be an accessory before the fact, Peace, if we ever find the murderer. I suggest to you that you see Mr Wertheimer, claim the reward, suffer a few years' imprisonment, and come out and live a virtuous life – in America, for preference."

Peace shook his head.

"I've never heard of the man. I wouldn't hurt a fly meself. You won't lend me the money? I thought you wouldn't."

"How right you were!" chuckled Alan. "Is that all you want to see me about?"

"That's all."

Peace put on his old cap and shuffled out of the surgery without any adieu.

Why had he come at all? Not to borrow money. He could not have had a hope of being successful. And if he hadn't come to borrow money, what was the reason for this visit? The psychologist in Alan Mainford examined the situation and found understanding. This little man was genuinely in love. All the extravagant claims he made for Mrs Dyson he believed and reaffirmed. It so obsessed him that he had to talk about it. When events were on his mind he felt impelled to translate them into words for the benefit of an audience, sympathetic or unsympathetic. He was so much in love with this dreary, commonplace woman that he resented the commission that Madame Stahm sent to him, even though it carried a reward greater than any she had ever paid him before – that very hundred pounds which would transport him to a land where his record was not known.

He met Baumgarten at the rendezvous and complained.

"The Manchester police are after me like a bird after seed," he grumbled. "I dare not stick my nose there. I'm watched day and night. The government know that I'm one of the most dangerous and cleverest criminals in England."

"Are you afraid that whilst you're away somebody will steal your lady love?" asked Baumgarten tactlessly, and Peace turned on him in a fury.

"Nobody could ever take a lady away from me!" he stormed. "If you think you can, try it! They worship the ground I walk on. I'll smash your face in if you say they don't! You've never been doted on – you don't know what it's like. Women dote on me, and I'm a gentleman to them always!"

Baumgarten reported to his employer.

"This man is getting dangerous. Let me meet him one night and put him out... I could kill him so easily, and it would be fun!"

19

Peace went to Manchester by a new route. He travelled by carrier's cart to Leeds, a long and a tiresome journey which occupied the greater part of the day. Avoiding the main stations, he picked up a slow train, travelled through the night, and reached Liverpool in the early morning. He came from Liverpool by an express that stopped at one station, and stepped out at Manchester Central under the very eyes of the watchful detectives without being recognised.

They saw only an old sailor man who, in place of one hand, showed a stump and a steel hook. He had a seafaring cap on the back of his head and a growth of grey beard. As he crossed the station, labouring under the weight of a big, white kit-bag, nobody could have imagined that he was anything but what he appeared – one of the hands of a ship that had been paid off at Liverpool. His face was stained a dark brown, as though by a tropical sun, though in reality he owed his rich brownness to the well-applied matrix of a walnut, rubbed on his face between Liverpool and his destination.

Hiring a cab, he drove to a new address, one that he had never used before, and that evening set forth on what was to be the first serious adventure of his life.

Police Constable Cock, who patrolled a beat at Whalley Range, was a man with many enemies. He was, as has been said, officious, and, to a certain class, offensive. Zeal in the performance of his duty had brought him into conflict with the large class which lives on the edge of a criminal career.

There were three brothers who lived in a little hut in a nursery garden; steady men, except when one of them was in drink. Cock, who patrolled near their dwelling place, was their *bête noir*. He had had them in court, and they in turn had offered the usual threats as to what would happen to an officious police constable if he continued to stick his nose into their business.

Of a truth, their business was honest. They were hard-working men, who tied lettuces and picked raspberries in the fields, and went to bed early and rose with the dawn. Of their existence Peace had no knowledge.

He was not concerned with private feuds that night when he dropped over a back wall and made his way to the house that he had burgled before. He had only one desire, and that was to get back to Darnall and to the woman who had enslaved him and who was now showing a distressing coolness.

It was an August night, rather cool. Rain had fallen, and that was all to the good, for it emptied the streets of possible witnesses by the time the moon "came out". The house from the back was in darkness. He saw no light in the kitchen, but when he made an attempt to force the door, as he had done on a previous occasion, he found it was bolted, and had recourse to the pantry window, that never-failing avenue to illicit gains.

He had an extraordinary memory for detail, observed unerringly that the grandfather clock had been moved from one side of the passage to the other, and that the stairs, which on his previous visit had had a red carpet, were now covered with a carpet of a greenish hue.

The girl's bedroom was locked, but that presented no difficulty. In five minutes he was in the room, and by the shaded light which a candle lantern cast had cleared the bureau of correspondence.

There was no interruption; he closed the door behind him, went quickly down the stairs, unbolted the back door and let himself out. Very cautiously he came to the front of the house, walking on the grass to avoid the noisy gravel. Although he could see or hear nothing, and there was no apparent danger, he moved stealthily from one cover to another.

There was, it appeared, justification for this, for presently he heard voices, and, peeping over the hedge, saw two policemen and a civilian talking together three houses down the street, and on the opposite side of the road. He saw one of the policemen go into a garden, presumably to test the door. There was no time to be lost; he vaulted over the wall.

As he did so he saw a policeman crossing the road to meet him, and increased his pace. He heard the scrunch of heavy boots, and a hand gripped him and pulled him round.

"I thought so!" said an exultant voice. "You're the little dog that gave me a punch on the jaw!"

Peace wrenched back, trying to free himself. The policeman was groping for his whistle. Exerting all his strength, he tore himself away. But the man was at his heels. Peace spun round with a snarl. Before him he saw the drab vision of Dartmoor, the loss of liberty, the loss of the woman...obliteration...a life sentence.

His revolver came up. There was a crashing report...another. The policeman staggered. Leaping over the wall, Peace ran quickly round a house, crossed a fence at the back, over a field. He had no remorse, no compunction. He had shot a natural enemy, killed him perhaps, and it did not disturb his night's sleep.

He was back in Sheffield by the following afternoon, having taken a circuitous route. But the real cause of his delay was his efforts to get rid of the walnut stains on his face. In this he was partly successful – Sergeant Eltham saw him in town and noticed nothing peculiar about him.

There was no search for Peace, and for a good reason. When he opened the newspaper that evening he read that three brothers named Harbron had been arrested for the crime and would be charged with murder. The news promised a novel and not unpleasing experience.

"I am going up to Manchester to hear that trial," he said.

Life was becoming a little difficult for him. Madame Stahm was more and more exacting; but her chief offence lay in her vanished interest in Peace the musician. No longer did she call him from his bed to soothe her nerves. Once he had taken his fiddle with him, and had been expressly asked not to play. He was cut to the quick, was almost in tears when he left that grim house.

Mrs Dyson, too, was hurting him, had grown conscious of her power and was avoiding him, giving as an excuse the jealousy of her husband. Peace had tried to make friends with him, had waylaid him in odd places, forced his attentions upon the thin man, and had been rebuffed rudely. And when he had tried to speak to this bold, pink-faced woman she had met his advances coldly, and her studied politeness developed into recriminations. She could storm like a fish-wife, akimbo, wagging her head in her fury.

"How dare you tell my husband you'll take him out and show him the sights!" she demanded shrilly. "My husband is a gentleman!"

"Ain't I a gentleman?" demanded the little man, tremulous with rage.

"He'll be a rich gentleman, too. He could buy Darnall lock, stock and barrel. He'll be worth millions..."

Peace was desperate. Out came that snub-nosed revolver of his; his face was working convulsively, his lips flecked with foam. He had the appearance of a savage dog of an uncertain breed. They screamed at one another like two furies before she went in and slammed the door behind her.

He was losing ground, becoming unimportant. It worried him, set him gnawing his knuckles in the little kitchen which he had turned into a workroom. Not once did he think of the dead policeman and three agonised men awaiting trial for their lives for the crime he had committed. If he read about them, as he did in the newspapers, he took an impersonal interest in the event, and found the satisfaction which is only to be had by the man who has exclusive knowledge, and knows all outside conjectures to be hopelessly wrong.

He had read of the inquest and the account of the police court proceedings, had noticed certain discrepancies which he felt like rectifying. One witness said he saw a dirty little tramp near the scene of the murder. Peace was furious, knowing that it was he who had been seen. But these were the merest sidelights of interest: he concentrated his attention upon the woman who had loved him, spent his nights prowling round the house, peering into windows, overlooking the couple as they sat at their meal, hurtling notes at her, some of which never reached their objective.

He did everything he could to bring her back to him. The heart of the man was wrung with grief in those days. He set his parrot and his canaries on the wall, where she could see them; left in her path significant souvenirs of their secret rendezvous; and when he learned that she was preparing to move away he grew frenzied, attacked the husband in the street and threatened him. The dyspeptic Mr Dyson, in genuine fear of his life, applied for a warrant. When Baldy came to serve it, his quarry, warned in advance, had gone. It was Madame Stahm who offered him seclusion and sanctuary.

But one night spent in that big house was enough for Peace. He came back to his old haunts secretly. He saw the woman go out and dogged her footsteps, watched the preparations for their departure and decided to trail them.

One night Mrs Dyson went out and left by train for an unknown destination. Peace came back like a lost soul to the house she had left. He was watching it, brooding on it from a secluded hiding-place, when a cab drove up and a man alighted. Evidently he instructed the cabman to wait farther up the road. He talked to the man for a while, and in the light of the lamp Peace recognised the visitor. Wertheimer!

He became suddenly the bond slave of Madame Stahm, and for once pleasure accorded with duty, for Wertheimer went straight to the Dysons' house and was instantly admitted by a servant, who had evidently been waiting for the arrival of the cab.

A slight mist was rising. If it grew thicker it would be to the advantage of the little man. He slipped round the back of the house and made a brief survey of the situation. The kitchen door was unlocked. The Dysons had an occasional servant, but she was a daily girl.

Slipping off his shoes, he walked into the kitchen, opened the door carefully and listened. He heard the murmur of voices in the front room. To all appearance from the front of the house this room was in darkness. He discovered later that the heavy curtains had been drawn across the windows. The door of the drawing-room was closed and he heard Wertheimer's excited voice: "… Proof, my friend, proof… Always you are telling me, but never you give me proof."

"Wait a minute!"

He heard the high-pitched voice of Dyson and his step as he crossed the room.

Peace had time to shrink under the stair, when the door opened and the man came out. If he went to the kitchen and turned his head he could not fail to see the intruder. Fortunately, he went upstairs, was gone a few minutes, returned again and closed the door behind him, a little carelessly, for the catch did not fasten, and after a while the door moved slightly ajar. Peace crept nearer.

Through this narrow aperture he saw the two men. The room itself was in disorder; the pictures had been taken down in preparation for the Dysons' departure to another house. They sat at the bare table, and the long man, who towered grotesquely above his companion, held in his hand a large phial which was heavily sealed and bore a white label. It contained something which rattled metallically when he shook it.

"Now, I'm telling you," said Dyson. He had a slight American accent. "Eckhardt gave me this a week before he died."

"Why didn't you say so before?" demanded the agitated voice of Wertheimer.

"I wasn't going to show my hand. I made you an offer – you have to trust me – "

"I trust nobody," said Wertheimer, "nobody, nobody! Why should I? She has taken my men, and she has killed them – I know. Am I a fool? Am I stupid? Do I not see? I can trust nobody. If you had told me you had the crystals – "

"I told you yesterday."

"May I have the bottle?" demanded Wertheimer.

Peace saw the tall man draw the phial back.

"No, you can't. I'd look foolish if I let you have the phial. All you'd have to do would be to analyse it, and where should I be? I can give you all the information you want – temperatures, everything. He told me that before he died and I made a note of it, here!" He tapped his narrow forehead.

Wertheimer was half convinced. He looked hungrily at the little bottle which contained all that he had sought for so many years. The crystals were agglomerate, he guessed. There would be half a dozen or more chemical elements that must be separated.

"You have tried to sell to Madame Stahm?"

"I won't deal with her." Dyson's voice was raised haughtily. "Eckhardt told me about her, and I promised him. I'm the sort of man that never breaks a promise. There's my price, Mr Wertheimer: I want sixty thousand pounds cash, which I'll undertake to put in a bank and not touch. I'll also undertake that if this process does not give you what you want, the money shall be refunded. I can't say fairer than that."

Sixty thousand pounds! Peace gasped. Sixty thousand…! His head swam at the colossal figure. That bottle was worth all that money! Beads of sweat broke out on his forehead as the significance of this conversation slowly began to dawn upon him. He made up his mind quickly. If Wertheimer agreed and carried the bottle away with him, he would take it. If the bottle remained in the house he would take it. Madame Stahm must know.

Dyson crossed the room to close the door. Peace shrank back down the passage and waited in the kitchen, listening to the murmur of voices. There was no need to take any risk. When the door opened, somebody would say something which would tell him all he wanted to know. He had not long to wait: the parlour door opened again, and he heard Wertheimer's voice: "…not so much money at the bank, but it is procurable. You will see me on Saturday, when I shall arrange."

So the phial was to remain in the house.

Peace slipped out through the kitchen door and regained his place of observation at the front of the house. He saw Wertheimer come out and drive away, and ten minutes after the front door opened and Dyson, in a heavy ulster, came out and walked swiftly in the direction that his visitor had taken.

Peace waited till he was out of sight and worked his way to the back of the house. But now the kitchen door was closed and bolted. With the agility of a monkey he swung himself up to the top of the kitchen, pushed up a sash and was in the house and the Dysons' bedroom in a few minutes.

He was handicapped by having made no preparations for a search. There was a street lamp which afforded a certain amount of light. He dared not put a match to a candle for fear Dyson came back or somebody saw him. He began his search of the untidy bedroom in the half dark, groping beneath pillows, under mattresses, in drawers and cupboards, fumbling through pockets and finding nothing.

None of the drawers was locked; that was an ominous sign. Would the long man have taken the bottle with him? It seemed possible. Indeed, it amounted to a certainty, he decided.

He crept out of the house the way he had come, closed the window noiselessly behind him, and dropped from the kitchen roof to the ground.

Where had Dyson gone? He was not a man who went abroad at night, though he was a member of a political club. All that night Peace hung about, waiting for the tall man's return. When he came, and Peace saw his companion, he knew that for the night no attempt could be made. Walking by Dyson's side, and looking absurdly small, was the bearded Baldy. He was talking loudly. Peace heard his name mentioned as he melted into the darkness.

It was nearly two o'clock in the morning when he pulled the rusty bell at Brinley Hall. He had had a long and tiring walk; he was hungry; jealousy and cupidity had intensified his natural ferocity. Baumgarten, a man of keen mental perceptions, sensed the mood of the man when he admitted him, and did not attempt to be facetious.

"Madame is in bed."

"Then Madame had better get up," said Peace loudly. "And I want some food and a quart of beer."

Peter Baumgarten was more intrigued than annoyed. He showed his visitor into a small dining-room and, ringing the bell for a servant, gave orders for a meal to be served.

"What brings you out so late tonight, Mr Peace?"

" 'Mr Peace', eh?" sneered the little man. "That's not the way you talked to me the last time I was here. Are you going to wake the old girl?"

"Madame Stahm has been informed that you're here. If she wishes to see you she will see you."

They brought in a folding table and opened it before the uncouth figure who sat huddled in a chair. Baumgarten went to his desk; this was his own bureau.

"I've got something private to tell her. She knows me. I don't come out here in the middle of the night for nowt."

He was in his ugliest temper. Baumgarten had never seen him in such a mood before, and wondered what would be the effect one upon the other of this truculent little man and Madame Stahm. All day long she had been moody, difficult to deal with. She had had a fit of hysteria following Baumgarten's very sane revelation that already she had spent more money in pursuing the phantom steel than she could hope to recover in her lifetime.

Whilst he was pondering this matter she swept into the room. Usually she was careful about her appearance, fussed over her toilette for hours. The very fact that she came into the room wearing her oldest dressing-gown was in itself a danger signal.

"What do you want?" she demanded of Peace.

He glowered up at her, his jaws munching.

"Do you think you can come here when you wish, little murderer?"

He thought of a dozen retorts, but offered the only one that was likely to produce a sensational reaction.

"That Dyson has got a bottle of crystals that he's selling to Wertheimer for sixty thousand pounds."

There was a dead silence.

"Crystals? What do you mean?"

Her voice and her manner changed instantly.

"Now, little man, don't be cross with me. I do not like to be wakened up in the middle of the night. What crystals?"

He enjoyed his sensation.

"A fellow gave them to him in America – Eck – something."

"Eckhardt!"

Baumgarten and the woman spoke together. Peace nodded.

"That's what the long fellow said. Eckhardt lived with him."

"I know that," said Madame Stahm. "He is offering them for sixty thousand pounds...has he sold the crystals to Wertheimer?"

"No, he hasn't," said Peace. "Wertheimer ain't got the money. After they'd both gone out I got into the house and searched the bedroom, but there was nothing there; no drawers locked, or cupboards or trunks or anything. I didn't lose any time, me lady. When I heard what they were talking about, said I to meself: 'That bottle goes to Madame Stahm.' "

She leaned over and patted his hand, her face beaming.

"Good man! And you got them?"

"No, I keep telling you I didn't get them," he growled. "This fellow must ha' had 'em with him. I waited till he came back, but Baldy was with him, and Baldy carries a shooter."

She said something very quickly to Baumgarten in Russian, and he replied in the same language.

"Now tell me everything, my dear little friend – every word."

Peace had one remarkable gift: his memory was stenographic. What he told his attentive audience now was a faithful record of the conversation he had overheard, adding nothing, subtracting nothing. The woman pinched her lower lip, deep in thought, her eyes fixed upon the carpet.

"He had it all the time, then," she said slowly, "waiting for the moment. That is why he has been negotiating with Wertheimer. He would not come here because Eckhardt made him promise – Eckhardt is a devil, a beast!"

Baumgarten said something else in Russian and she nodded.

"You can get him? You can watch him day and night."

"No, I can't," growled Peace. "There's a warrant out for me. I dare not go near the place. If I could get them to withdraw that it would be easy."

Evidently she knew about the warrant. There must have been something in the newspapers about it.

"You are a little fool to threaten people and to produce your ridiculous revolver in public. You are too free with that revolver. Some day it will bring you to the gallows."

He was in no mood to be told his faults. Rather, he desired a little praise for his enterprise and acumen. He said as much.

"Of course you have been wonderful," she soothed him. "But that bottle of crystals, my friend, that we must have."

Again Baumgarten spoke in Russian, and she replied at some length.

"Very good," she said. "You can stay here, my little dear. I will have a bed made for you, and you shall go out again and find me the bottle and the crystals, and you shall be a rich man."

Peace lay in a bed of unparalleled luxury that night, but he did not sleep. Where had Dyson hidden the phial? He was almost certain that the man had not taken it out with him, that it was still somewhere in that room, in a place easy of access. What had he seen in the room? In one of the drawers he had found an octagonal bottle of liniment; it was securely corked and sealed, a bottle of a popular remedy which could be bought at the chemist's and obviously had not been opened. He had found a set of surveyors' drawing instruments, an old tobacco jar. There could be no panels in the wall; the room was papered and the walls were of the thinness one expects in that class of house. Behind the pictures? Or in the box mattress?

No, it was somewhere where he could slip it away in an instant, recover it in an instant. He had not been upstairs more than a minute. He had followed Wertheimer out of the house in almost as short a space of time, and even then he had had leisure to lock and bolt the back door.

Peace tossed from side to side all through the night, long after dawn came, thinking over and revisualising every object he had seen in the room, and an idea began to take definite shape in his mind — he resolved to put his theory to the test that night.

He had many friends in Darnall, friends he met frequently, who gave him information as to the activities of the police. One of these he had charged to see Dyson and bring them to withdraw the charge against him.

To say that his neighbours were ignorant of his true character is paying small tribute to their intelligence. Mr Dyson might suspect, but surely the shrewd Mrs Dyson knew. Peace was a boaster, a man who could not keep that glib tongue of his from wagging. Mrs Dyson, in fact, had no doubt as to the truth about the man long before the break came.

Peace managed to convey word to a crony and met him in a field. He gave detailed instructions to the man, who was all too willing to be his agent. At eleven o'clock that night, when most of the shops were closed, there came a knock at the Dysons' door and the tall man answered it. He recognised the neighbour.

"Well, what do you want?"

He was a man superior to his environment and never lost sight of the fact.

The caller told a glib story. One of his children had been taken ill, and he wanted to know if they had any Selby's Liniment in the house.

"No, we haven't," said Dyson brusquely, and shut the door in the caller's face.

That ruffled man went in search of Peace and told him, and Charles Peace grinned. Now he knew that his guess had been a shrewd one. The bottle contained no liniment, was not even a bottle in the strict sense of the word. There was an aperture in its base, into which a smaller phial might fit. He had seen such things used by people who smuggled narcotics from the Continent. That was where the precious crystals were.

When he went to sleep it was broad daylight, but he slept long and soundly, for he had the contented mind of one who had overcome great difficulties.

20

There came to Alan Mainford's surgery that day, at the usual visiting hour, an abnormally tall man. He had the superior manner of one who desired to be regarded as an equal, and Alan had too large an acquaintance with the type to look upon him as being in any way singular.

His complaint was a prosaic one; a fish-bone had lodged in his attenuated throat, and if he had been enduring a major operation without the employment of anaesthetics he could not have made a greater fuss. Lying on a couch, which his long legs overlapped, he demanded caution, care, particulars of the instruments to be used, the amount of pain to be inflicted, the danger to be faced, the possibilities of complications and after-effects – all this preliminary to the insertion of a mirror and forceps. When the actual extraction began he writhed, gripped Alan's arm, almost swallowed the mirror. Finally Alan went in search of Jane Garden. She was in her room, enjoying a day's rest.

"I've got two yards of childhood on my sofa. He's got a fish-bone in his throat. Will you come and help me? Perhaps your presence will shame him into behaving like a grown-up man."

She put down her book and followed him down the wooden steps into the yard. But her presence had little effect upon the patient, except to increase his alarm, when she was introduced as "Nurse Garden".

"My God, is it as bad as that?" he asked, hollowly.

"Do you think you ought to see another surgeon, doctor?"

"I've brought this lady here," said Alan wearily, "in the hope that you'll be so heartily ashamed of making a fuss in a woman's presence that you'll let me do this simple little job – it isn't even an operation."

It was a quarter of an hour before he grabbed the end of the bone and brought it to light.

"Thank God that's over!" said the visitor, mopping his brow. "Dyson's my name. I'm an engineer up at the LNE. I'm not used to English surgeons; I've been in America for some time. The surgery is more up-to-date there."

"Do they swallow fish-bones in America too?" asked Alan innocently.

"I don't know whether they swallow fish-bones," said the other stiffly, "but they know how to take them out. What is your fee?"

"I shall charge you nothing," said Alan; "the experience has been worth the money."

His visitor evidently had little sense of humour. He also had no regular medical attendant, he confessed. What was very apparent was that he had been very frightened and very much shaken by this little inconvenience. Alan bade him sit down for a little while before he went out, and brought him a brandy and soda. Under the influence of the stimulant he relaxed, and though he was not usually a talkative man, and his pomposity was a little irritating, he became quite interesting on the habits and customs of the native-born American.

"In Cleveland I had a wonderful home. It's quite different here. A slum, sir, with the most dreadful people for neighbours. There is no accommodation in Sheffield for a gentleman of limited means: he must either herd with the swine or go out into the country, which is extremely inconvenient, although naturally I should have a free pass over the railway. Are you interested in steel?"

Alan was not interested in steel.

"I have a slight interest in a patent converter," began Mr Dyson.

Alan laughed.

"It's difficult to meet anybody in Sheffield who hasn't a slight interest in a patent converter," he said. "You can't get into the Patent

Office for the crowd. Everybody in Sheffield is inventing something, if it's only an excuse for not paying their doctors."

"If – " began Dyson, his hand moving towards his pocket.

"That was a tactless remark, but I am not your doctor; and it is notorious that the good Samaritan had no pay for his service. All the bad Samaritans, one presumes, charge double."

He had Mr Dyson at sea here.

Just as he was going, the tall man – he must have stood six feet six in height – asked casually: "I suppose you wouldn't know – no, of course, you wouldn't."

"I wouldn't know a converter from a crucible, if that's what you were going to ask me."

"No, I was not," said Mr Dyson testily. "You've told me you know nothing about steel – that is sufficient. The man I was going to mention is a person called Peace."

"What – Charles Peace?" Alan's eyebrows rose.

"Do you know him?"

"In a sense I know him," smiled Alan. "I had the satisfaction of horsewhipping him the other day, and on a previous occasion I had the great pleasure of knocking him down in the presence of his fair but inebriated lady friend."

Dyson blinked at this.

"You knocked him down? Was that about…?" He gave a date, and Alan, considering, nodded.

"Did he throw a man over the fence into a glass frame?"

"Oh! You saw it, too, did you?" asked Alan.

"No, sir," said Mr Dyson. He had become suddenly very stiff. "The lady – um – was not his lady friend, as you call it; she was – um – my wife." He coughed.

Alan was momentarily embarrassed.

"When you say she was – um – inebriated – "

"I mean, of course, that she was overcome by the heat," said Alan.

The tall man considered this for a long time, staring gloomily at the carpet.

"She is a good wife, but a little – um – wilful. It is a great mistake to marry, as it were, beneath one. Classes should not mix. I am moving my home in consequence. It is – um – very unfortunate."

He paused again. Alan was at a loss for words, excuses, pleasing lies. He also maintained a silence which had in it the quality of discretion.

"But she was not inebriated. Good morning."

"An extraordinary man," said Jane, when he rejoined her in the sitting-room.

"A friend of a friend of Peace, he said, but not, I gather, a personal friend of Peace. Mr Dyson – I've got an idea I've heard about him. He's so tall he had to have a special desk built for him."

21

In the evening business took Peace to Banner Cross, and here he had a shock. Almost the first person he saw when he reached that suburb was Mr Dyson. There was no mistaking that lanky man; he towered above all other pedestrians. Mrs Dyson was trotting at his side, a subdued but rather dignified Mrs Dyson, conscious of her coming wealth and position, fearfully anxious perhaps to end a friendship which was proving as dangerous as it was distasteful.

They turned abruptly and went into a house. The "To Let" signs were still pasted on the windows. This was where they were moving, then. Peace noted the house, and, making his way back to the region of Darnall, met his wife and made secret arrangements for moving his home to Hull. Obviously he could no longer stay in that neighbourhood unless the warrant against him was withdrawn.

The Dysons' house at Darnall was dark, untenanted. Somebody told him that the moving had not begun. He went round to the back, found the kitchen window open and got inside. The furniture was packed up ready for removal. The bed in the front room had been taken to pieces, and was a disordered litter of iron laths and rolled mattresses. He saw that the dressing-table had been moved, and his heart sank. Pulling open drawer after drawer, his fears were realised; the contents had been taken out. The bottle was probably in Dyson's pocket at that moment.

If he could see the woman, have a few words with her, his quest might be simplified. But he dared not show his face in daylight – not in Darnall.

He slept in the town that night and was at Banner Cross early in the morning. He even went into the house to reconnoitre before the furniture van arrived. After a few hours it came. Mr Dyson had a day off from the office, arriving genteelly by cab. Peace waited till the man had gone in, then made his bold move. The woman heard her name called and turned with a frightened start.

"What are you doing here?" she quavered. "You wicked man…don't you know there's a warrant out for you?"

"There'll be a warrant out for you, me lady," he said unpleasantly. "I want you to help me – get him to go to the police and withdraw that summons."

She looked round fearfully; her husband was not in sight, but there were curious spectators, some of whom must have recognised Peace. She had made a solemn vow to her husband that she would never see the man again.

"I can't; he wouldn't do it."

"Suppose I show him the letters?"

Her eyes opened wide.

"Have you got them? You said you burnt them!"

Peace grinned.

"It doesn't matter what I said, I've got them all right. Suppose I show him those little notes that the grocer's boy brought, eh? That'll make him sit up! And you too. See me tonight."

"I can't," she said desperately. "Be reasonable, Charles."

"Don't call me Charles; my name's Mr Peace," he said bitterly. "After all I've done for you, the music I've played for you, the things I've told you, the money I've spent on you!"

"We're going away tonight," she said quickly. "Come back in a week's time. Our living-room is at the back. If you whistle I'll hear you."

"What are you going away for?" he asked suspiciously.

"We're going to London. Mr Dyson has a holiday."

Should he tell her about the bottle? The idea occurred to him but was instantly rejected. In her present mood she would certainly betray him, and Dyson would find some other hiding-place.

She was terrified now lest her husband should see her, and almost pushed him away just before Dyson came to the door to look for her.

"Who was that man?"

He was a little short-sighted and had not recognised Peace.

"The milkman," she said glibly. "He wanted to know if he could supply us with butter and eggs."

Whether she was telling the truth about going away for her holiday, Peace did not trouble to investigate. His curiosity was calling him to Manchester. The trial of the Harbron brothers was to start on the following Tuesday. Mr Peace promised himself a new sensation. It was characteristic of him that when he arrived in Manchester, though he was unchallenged at the station, he should go immediately to the Central Police Office and report his presence.

"I'm up here on business, sir," he said to the inspector.

"What business?" asked that sceptical official.

Peace told the truth.

"Want to go into court and hear the trial?" said the amazed inspector. "Don't you get enough experience out of your own trials, Peace – we've had you here twice, haven't we?"

"Yes, sir, twice for a sixer. I was innocent, but I bear no malice. One thing they *do* teach you in prison, sir, is Christian charity. I'm a different man now, sir – I'd rather have me right hand cut off than take a penny that didn't belong to me."

"Where's your harp, angel?" asked the brutal cynic. "No, I'm afraid I can't get you a ticket for the public gallery: you'll have to take your place and get admission with the others. You'll be doing a little burglary, I suppose, to pass the long winter evenings?"

Peace smiled sadly.

"In the evenings," he said simply, "I knit!"

Which was true. Most of the socks he wore were of his own manufacture.

The inspector had something facetious to say about fancy needlework, but he was in a good humour and that was everything.

Peace watched the opening of the trial with professional interest. He knew all the routine of it, though he had never seen a murder trial before or noticed that the Clerk of the Court used the phrase with which the trial opened.

"Gentlemen of the jury, the prisoner whom you have in charge pleads not guilty and puts himself on God and his country."

He wondered if he, when he stood in exactly the same place as the two anxious-looking men were standing (one had been discharged), would put himself on God and his country. He rather liked the phrase and repeated it to himself. Yet…

Suppose a man were an atheist? They'd no right to bring religion into it without a prisoner's permission. And suppose he were a foreigner, how about his country then? Peace invariably argued matters like this.

The men in the dock interested him: big, ungainly fellows, obviously distressed by their position. He was curious to know what circumstances had brought them there. It was a great lark, sitting up in the gallery, elbows on the ledge, chin resting on the back of his mittened hands, watching two men being tried for a murder which he had committed! He felt no compunction, no pity, no uneasy stirring of conscience. He was impatient to know how the police had pieced together this charge against them. Lies, of course – the police always lied. They were never happy unless they were getting some poor bloke into quod. But what kind of lies?

He sat immobile whilst the opening counsel eulogised the devotion and patriotism of the dead policeman. How did the prisoners come into it? He learned very soon. There had been a police court case against them; they had threatened the dead man in the hearing of landladies and barmaids and casual drinkers at the pub which they frequented. They were poor men: two of three brothers, who lived in a hut planted in the middle of a fruit garden owned by a nurseryman. Nobody had seen them shoot the man, but there were the footprints.

A pompous and completely self-satisfied inspector produced the boots. Peace knew that thousands of men were wearing boots of a similar pattern, with exactly the same number of nails, but the jury were impressed. He was highly dramatic, this police inspector; described his deductions, how he rushed into the hut where the prisoners were sleeping, how, with great prescience, and before he knew anything about the footprints, he had taken the prisoners' boots away; and the jury were more impressed.

The judge was nervous; a new man to Peace, obviously inexperienced. He had not even the courage of other people's convictions, for he vacillated, disagreed with both counsel in turn, and offered conclusions which were acceptable to neither.

Day after day Peace listened, until there arrived the fatal moment when the black cap was spread on the judge's head, and, in sober terms, he sent one of the brothers to the scaffold and one to freedom.

"I don't believe he done it."

The member of the public who offered this opinion to his fellow occupant of the public gallery was Mr Charles Peace.

"I think," said the man to whom he addressed the remark, "they all ought to have been hung – all three of 'em. There's too many Irish in Manchester."

He was a typical member of the great proletariat.

Peace was very impressed and moved, for he had never seen a murder trial before. The inspector, who happened to be in the court, met him as he emerged and asked him his impressions.

"I don't think he done it, sir," said Peace again.

"Can you suggest who did?" asked the other sarcastically. "You wouldn't like to say that you did it, would you?"

Peace shook his head.

"Human life is sacred to me, sir," he said. "I've never hurt a fly."

"I'd like to hear what the flies say about that before I believe you," said the officer.

Which, as Peace said, was ridiculous, for flies can't talk, unless their buzzing is a language.

22

His stay in Manchester had not been unprofitable. There were others who were less fortunate. The man who had sat next to him on the first day confessed to him over a pot of beer and some bread and cheese that he was on his beam-ends. He was a very respectable-looking man, smooth-faced, deferential, nicely spoken. He had been a butler in a noble family at St Anne's. Butler-like, he put this interpretation upon his employment. He had, in fact, been a parlour-man to a wealthy Liverpool shipbroker, who, in some mysterious fashion, and for services which were rather obscure, had received the honour of knighthood. He had left because he couldn't stand her ladyship.

All this he said over the first lunch. At the second Peace heard more of the truth. The handyman had left in a hurry, and his exit had been accelerated by the toe of the broker's boot. There was a little silver missing, not enough to justify a prosecution. There was a weeping housemaid and a furious mother to be appeased. The broker knight very generously said that the girl could come back and resume her employment after it was all over.

Peace had no patience with liars, and, once he had discovered a discrepancy, was not satisfied until he had the stark truth. But he liked the man; he was well spoken, a gentleman; more of a gentleman than Mr Dyson. He might be extremely useful. Peace pigeon-holed him for future reference, asked questions about the house, the quantity and quality of the silver, the method of safeguarding the household treasures. Was there a dog? The pantry window, now – did it have all those silly bars in front of it? All of which the ex-servant answered to Peace's satisfaction, but added information which was less entertaining.

"The governor's a great pistol shot," he said. "The walls of the library are covered with prizes – a left-handed shooter. I've seen him hit a sixpence when it was tossed in the air. He's got seven revolvers in the gun-room, all of them presented to him…"

Peace changed the subject and lost all interest in the broker knight and his indubitable treasures.

It was on his advice that Carton – that was the name he gave – came with him to Sheffield.

"I know Sheffield – I used to work for a gentleman."

"He must have come to Sheffield when I wasn't there," said Peace sarcastically.

Until this moment Peace had been very reticent, had spoken scarcely at all of himself. On the journey, warming to the companionship and sympathy of his new-found friend, he told the story of his life, his loves, and some of his adventures. He explained his importance, hinted at wealthy friends; but always the subject came back to the chatelaine of a newly rented house in Banner Cross.

"I've only got to lift me finger and she'd leave her husband tomorrow. She's always saying 'Charles, take me away.' Wants me to open a shop in Liverpool. A lady, mind you. There ain't a prettier girl in England."

"This girl I was telling you about – " began the ex-butler.

"It's funny how women dote on me," Peace went on. "There was a girl in Hull that used to follow me about the streets like a dog. I had to stop her. I said: 'It's not ladylike.' When I got up in the morning she'd be sitting on the step, waiting for me to open the door. She was one of the most beautiful creatures you ever saw; rather a stout girl with red hair. I never did like thin women."

"This girl I was telling you about – " the butler began again.

"I've broke up more homes than any man you could name," said Peace. "I've never wanted to – I'm a God-fearing man. There's a woman up in Manchester who committed suicide because I wouldn't talk to her – as pretty as a picture, she was, and her husband was a titled gentleman. There's a ladyship down in Sheffield that cries if I don't go and see her."

"This girl I was talking about – " said the butler for the third and last time.

"It's something in a man," said Peace. "It's not his looks or his age or his height, it's his spirit."

"I daresay," said the butler, relapsing into baffled silence.

When Peace reached the house of call where messages were left for him, he received an urgent summons to attend upon his wealthy employer. He had only five minutes to reach the place where the victoria was waiting, but he might have been more leisurely if he had foreseen the slowness of that drive. A heavy fog had settled on the countryside, and the horses moved at a walking pace almost throughout the whole of the journey.

He did not go to the Hall. Half-way from Sheffield a big cottage stood back from the road. To Peace's knowledge it had been unoccupied for four years and was reputedly haunted, since its previous owner had hanged himself in an outhouse. Before this habitation the victoria stopped.

"The lady's in there," said the coachman, speaking with some difficulty, for he had a very slight knowledge of the English language.

Peace got down grumbling, opened the gate, walked down the flagged path and knocked at the door. It was Baumgarten who admitted him.

"You're late, my friend," he said, and closed the door.

Then, taking the little man almost affectionately by the arm, he led him into a large front room, which smelt musty and was only half furnished.

"Madame Stahm will be down in a little time," he said. "She has taken this cottage to be nearer to the works. Also" – he looked Peace straight in the eyes "to make a home for a little friend of ours who may find it convenient to be a long time absent from Sheffield."

"Me, do you mean?" asked Peace in surprise.

Baumgarten nodded.

"We have heard of your sufferings and the trouble you have had with the police, my poor friend."

His sympathy was entirely spurious, but Peace, for all his peculiar perceptions, was impervious to sarcasm, and seldom recognised it. On the other hand, he was ready to accept even oblique tributes to his importance.

"Madame bought the house for a few hundred pounds. There are provisions here; these will save you the trouble and risk of going to the shops. If you could think of a man who would act as servant here without exciting the suspicion of the police, that would make it easier."

"Don't talk to me about servants," said Peace, roughly. "What's the lay? You mean I've got to stay here till things blow over? Suppose the police came?"

"This is the last place in the world they would think of searching."

The little man looked around uneasily.

"I don't see through all this gammon," he said. "The police warrant is nothing. I'm going to get the lady to withdraw the summons. What can they charge me with? Nothing!"

"The police warrant is unimportant," said Baumgarten. "What follows may be another matter. We are prepared for all emergencies. Above this floor" – he pointed upwards – "is a little attic. Nobody would dream there was an attic there at all. You might hide there for years and nobody would suspect. If you had a friend who could act as servant it would be all the easier – I am thinking only of your convenience."

The nimble mind of Peace went immediately to his newest acquaintance – Carton, the ex-butler. But such a man could only be trusted to a limited degree; to what extent must he be taken into his confidence?

"What do you want me to do – is it the bottle? That's easy. I'll do that job any night, and I'll defy the best copper in Sheffield to say it was me. I don't want a servant for that, do I?"

There was a rustle of silk skirts in the hall.

"Here is Madame," said Baumgarten.

She came in, radiant, both hands outstretched. Peace had never received such a welcome in his life, and was embarrassed.

"My little friend, you don't know how we have wanted you! Have you brought your fiddle? No? That will do some other time. Sit down. Do you like your new home?"

The words gave him a new interest in the cottage – a proprietorial interest that was novel and pleasing.

He looked around him. He had never occupied such a house as this. It was too big, too much fresh air in it perhaps, and for this reason the prospect of settling in an establishment of this size was not particularly alluring.

Also, his mentality was such that he could only appreciate that which was hardest to come by. He could spend a night stealing trumpery articles of jewellery and find a great contentment in exaggerating their value, deceiving nobody but himself. The gift horse became almost automatically a thing of flaws.

"My wife wouldn't like it – "

"Oh, la! Your wife! Do I ever speak of your wife, little friend? To me you are singular; you have no bonds or chains. This is for you alone."

She turned to Baumgarten.

"Did you tell him?"

He shook his head.

"Only that this would be a good place to hide."

"But why he should hide?"

"No," he said shortly.

She sat down opposite Peace and leaned towards him, dropping her voice.

"Those crystals you spoke of, they are life and death to me! I must have them, you understand? Yes, yes, I know you are so clever that you would take them from under his nose and nobody would be the wiser. But you must *take* them – you understand? You must go to every length."

"What's that?" asked Peace, puzzled.

"You must, if necessary, kill him," she said calmly, "but that bottle must be put in my hands before the end of the week. Also, this man has a small piece of steel. That also I must have."

She leaned back.

"For this I shall pay you two thousand pounds," she said.

Two thousand pounds! The little man's head reeled. To him the limit of extreme wealth was a hundred. He had never possessed as much at any one moment, though he had stolen property of twenty times the value. "Two thousand sovereigns in a bag – almost as much as you can carry, little man. That is the price I will pay. This small house" – she made a gesture of contempt – "that also you can have; it is of no value to me. There must be no ifs or buts or whys or whens. By Saturday those crystals must be had. Listen, my ugly dear; there is a man in Sheffield, a bad man, a fool. On Saturday he will have money to buy these things, and we shall lose them. You remember the factory where you found poor Lamonte – alas! he is dead."

"I didn't kill him," said Peace quickly. "I hit him a clip on the jaw, but that didn't do him any harm."

"Let us forget that. You remember the place?"

He nodded.

"I know Wertheimer's place. You want me to go there?"

She shook her head.

"Not yet. It may be necessary. I may want you to go over that wall. But if you're clever and quick it will not be necessary."

He rolled his ugly little head from side to side.

"I'll get that bottle for you – tomorrow, perhaps. They've moved their house – the Dysons."

"Yes, I know that. They have gone to Banner Cross. At the moment he is not attending at his office – this man Dyson. He is waiting whilst Wertheimer arranges the money. He never goes out of the house, but spends his time in his room, where he has a double-barrelled shot-gun."

"How do you know this, ma'am?" demanded Peace in amazement.

"Do not let us talk about how I know, or why I know," she said impatiently. "That is the truth. At all costs you must get what I want.

142

Tonight you must go out and make inquiries – only to inquire; you must not do anything premature."

He sought an explanation. "Premature" was a foreign word.

"Before the right time, I mean. And the right time is not tonight. Have you a friend you can trust?"

Peace hesitated. He trusted nobody. Carton was down on his luck, and it tickled his vanity to be in the position of a patron who could offer him work. He, Charles Peace, with a butler! He chuckled at the picture he conjectured.

"All right, your ladyship. I might as well stay here now, I suppose?"

"There is food in the house – biscuits, canned meat, flour, everything. You can live here even with the house shut. But then the police would search it. It is very necessary you should have a servant."

The mention of the servant reminded him that he would have to return to Sheffield. It was a long walk, but walking would be almost as quick a method as driving on a night like this. At the same time, locomotion might be a difficulty, and he made a tentative suggestion to Baumgarten, and to his surprise, though the scheme entailed considerable outlay, it was accepted.

23

After Madame Stahm and Baumgarten had departed he set out alone, carrying a candle lamp, and picked up Carton at an agreed rendezvous. To him he put the plan and an offer of employment. The wages he could not specify.

"I don't care what they are," said the ex-servant, "so long as I get food and lodging. I haven't enough to pay for either."

Peace left him, after arranging that they should meet later. Going on to Banner Cross, he reconnoitred the position. There was no light in the darkened house, but, creeping close to the window, he listened and heard voices, both raised in acrimony. What they said he could not distinguish. Then apparently Mr Dyson did not spend all his nights in his own room, and he would hardly carry a shot-gun round the house.

He examined the fastening of the kitchen window and made a survey of other means of entry. Satisfied, he went back to the town, joined his chilly companion and with him trudged out to their new home.

"There won't be much walking," said Peace. "I'll be having my own carriage and pair next week – mark my words!"

On the way the ex-butler became more expansive, unreeling yet another length of his picturesque past. He had been in prison at Strangeways for obtaining a berth with forged references; he had also been in Chatham and Maidstone prisons.

"You're a low character, then?" said Peace virtuously.

The man said he liked Chatham Prison, and added inconsequently that he was a Kentish man.

It was difficult to believe that this smooth-faced, nice-spoken gentleman who walked by Mr Peace's side was an ex-convict, a gaol-bird. Peace was a little shocked and more than a little relieved. On the way he outlined his plans. He was doing some work of a very secret and important character. It was quite honest, but the police wouldn't like it, and so it might be necessary for him to lie up in the cottage for a few days.

"You'll be there, looking after the place, to answer the door and say that the owner hasn't moved in yet. If you sell me I'll shoot you stone dead."

"I've always been honourable in dealing with any friends who trusted me!" said Mr Carton indignantly.

"Perhaps you never had any friends who trusted you," said Peace, and was painfully near the mark.

He would be useful as a cover on the night when Peace made his attempt. He had already conceived alternative plans, one of which he was sure would be successful.

In the afternoon be gave his "servant" further details and Mr Carton realised that the secret mission in which he was to assist had all the appearance of a vulgar burglary.

Peace could draw a plan remarkably well, and he reduced the topography of Banner Cross to paper.

"Here's the house, and there's the field opposite, where you'll stay and watch out. If you see a slop, you whistle. I'll get to you, whatever happens, and give you the bottle. You stick it in your pocket and make your way back to the cottage. If I'm caught and searched, there'll be nothing on me, see?"

"What bottle? A beer bottle?" asked Carton, mystified.

Peace eyed this disturber of his romantic dreams with some malignity.

"A medicine bottle about so big. And don't ask questions. People who work for me ain't expected to ask questions. And don't try to shop me. I killed a feller once – he shopped me. The police don't know that."

He loaded his revolver with great deliberation under the awed eyes of his assistant.

"You're not going to use that, are you?" said the man, in alarm. He had all the normal criminal's horror of firearms. Peace took his perturbation as a compliment.

"I keep it in case of accidents. If I go up, I go up for life – I'd sooner be hung. That's why the police are frightened of me; that's why they never tackle me! Go down to Scotland Yard and see my record; you'll see on it 'Dangerous; carries firearms' – that's me. When I'm in prison it's 'Mr Peace this' and 'Mr Peace that'. Even the screws daren't offend me. I escaped once.* I tell you, it makes a few screws tremble in their shoes when they hear Charlie Peace is inside – "

"I've heard about you," said the man respectfully.

"Of course you have! I've done two sixers and a four. I've been in every prison in England. They don't keep me long, they like to push me off to another governor. I give too much trouble. I've heard screws say: 'You have him, I don't want him!' "

"It's the same with me," said Carton, in a moment of reckless emulation, but this self-testimony to his bad qualities was coldly received.

"Don't talk so much about yourself," snarled Peace. "I hate a chap who's always boasting!"

He was reconciled to his new home, and had shown the man over the house with all the aplomb of a proprietor. Also he had inspected the windows and found them good. There were folding shutters, and, in addition, the curtains which covered them were heavy and light-proof. Over the front door was a transparent circular fanlight, which Peace, curiously enough, called a transom, a word generally used in America to describe that form of illumination. He had never been to America, but had probably got the word from a fellow convict during his sojourn in Dartmoor.

* This is partially true. He succeeded in getting out of his cell, but not from the prison building.

146

There were no curtains to this, and he spent an evening making it impossible for light to shine through.

Every window in the house was covered. An inspection of the attic, which was to be his place of refuge in case of danger, revealed that it was admirably approached through what looked to be a cupboard in one corner of the upper room. From here a flight of stairs led to the attic proper. It had no window, but in the roof was a circular skylight which could be raised or lowered, and was not visible from the road. A hinged wooden lid, which could be buttoned or bolted, covered this from the inside, presumably as a protection against burglars, but providentially from Peace's point of view, since he could have a light in his oddly shaped apartment.

There was plenty of space. A bed had already been erected; the mattresses and blankets lay on the ground. For some reason or other it had received recent attention from the former owner of the cottage. The walls had been newly papered, and he found carpenters' tools here, which he appropriated. The hammer and nails, which were subsequently found, were on a shelf too high for him to detect.

He spent some time arranging the entrance to the lower bedroom so that it had the appearance of a cupboard, and he was again fortunate, for he found in one of the bedrooms a number of old dresses that had been left behind by the previous occupant. These he hung on strings behind the door at the foot of the stairs, so that when the door was opened it had all the appearance of being a very ordinary clothes closet, and the illusion could, he saw, be heightened.

He took a rough measurement, went out into the kitchen and came back carrying the coal-cellar door. It fitted exactly, and he propped it up against the wall for use in an emergency.

Carton made tea and they discussed their plans for the night. Peace was something of a general; he had certainly the gift of direction; and though Carton was apparently a stupid man, he could repeat instructions without a flaw after an hour's tuition.

"But I don't understand what's in that bottle. Is it drugs?"

"It's a curio," said Peace, "worth nothing to anybody but the owner. I wouldn't pinch it, but this man's given me a lot of trouble.

He's a fellow that had a warrant out for me. It's highly valuable, but you couldn't sell it – and you're getting a twenty-pun' note for the job."

Carton was impressed.

"You're not going to take a shooter, are you?"

"Mind your own business," growled the other. "I'm taking you, and if you're a shooter I'm a Dutchman!"

He had his own private affairs to set in order. His family did not worry him very much, for he had moved them into Hull, where an eating-house had been opened for them. Hannah, his wife, had to be financed through some circuitous channel which would betray neither his identity nor his location. He sent two five-pound notes by post, enclosed in a half sheet of paper, "From a true friend." Hannah would know him by this strange title.

The bank notes came from the pocket-book of a wealthy-looking man who had come on to the platform at Manchester to see off some relations. Evidently one was his daughter, going on a holiday or to school. When he took out his pocket-book with a flourish, extracted a crinkly note and handed it to the girl, Peace made a mental note. He went along the platform to get a paper, and was reading it as he passed the prosperous owner of the pocket-book. So absorbed was Peace in his reading that he ran into the gentleman. He apologised humbly – the owner did not miss the money until he was home again. Peace had slipped the pocket-case into Carton's pocket until they had passed the station barrier, when he retrieved it – all without the knowledge of his companion.

The numbers of the notes had probably been taken and circulated – that would be bad luck for Hannah. But, anyway, she hadn't pinched them, and "From a true friend" was surely an alibi?

He had a daughter, but this young lady did not occupy any considerable portion of his thoughts, no more, indeed, than did his lady wife. He could have wished that he had entirely obliterated Mrs Dyson, but she persisted. She had given him some quality that he had never known before. There was a fragrance and a beauty in her association that had been foreign to him, and the thought that he was losing her was his only sorrow.

Yet he was a dreamer of dreams, could visualise himself returning at some distant day, immensely wealthy, respected by his fellow citizens, riding perhaps in the mayor's carriage, and exchanging jokes with good-natured inspectors of police who had been mere constables in his day. Perhaps giving a dinner at the Grand. Though the constables might age into portly officers, Mrs Dyson and he remained the same, in these visions of his, though she was perhaps a little more etherealised. She would ride by his side, holding his hand in hers, as she did that day when they drove out into the country for the first time together. A clammy hand, hers, but it was the kind of hand that Peace could not imagine on any lesser woman. She had qualities the thought of which made him shiver. He hoped he would see her tonight, that she would listen to one last appeal.

Just before they left the cottage an idea struck him, and, excusing himself, he went back to the room where he was to sleep that night, shut the door, and, kneeling reverently by the bed, said his prayers. God and Mrs Dyson became oddly associated in that confused supplication. Peace felt all the better for his spiritual efforts.

He had a collection of prayers, written down on little sheets of paper, which he claimed he had composed, but which were obviously memorised from innumerable prison church services. Once he said he was called upon to preach to his fellow prisoners, but he never repeated that assertion.

He stopped to drink a little weak brandy and water, and stepped out into the mirk, where his shivering companion was waiting. It was not cold enough to justify the teeth-chattering of Carton.

For a long time they walked in silence, then Carton spoke nervously.

"I suppose there's no danger tonight?"

"Depends on what you call danger," said Peace tartly. "What are you worrying about? Nobody's going to touch you – you're not going into the house to meet a man with a double-barrelled gun, the same as I am. You're not going to risk your life, as I've done hundreds of times, and only got fourpence-ha'penny for me trouble, which happened to me in Durby, and in a house you'd think was full of money – fourpence-ha'penny!"

"I'll bet you laughed!" said Carton.

Peace scowled at him.

"Why should a man laugh when he expects hundreds of pounds and only gets fourpence-ha'penny?" he demanded angrily, and there was logic in his wrath.

Carton did not understand him, and was already under the spell of terror that the man exercised. He wished he had never "taken up" with this dangerous creature, that he had tried a new trick of making money that he had worked out when he was last in prison. It was too late now. A straight-out burglary – the thought made him cold. Inside jobs he understood, but to go in from outside, to explore a strange house where people were sleeping that might wake – that was a nightmare.

And the shooter...

Suppose Peace used the revolver, that would be hanging dues for everybody. He had sat through the Manchester trial and had seen the black cap go on... He broke into a cold perspiration.

24

Two thousand pounds! That was the golden vision that swam before the little man as he trudged through the drizzle. Two thousand pounds! An incredible sum. There were lords in the land who hadn't that much. He was going to get it, Dyson or no Dyson.

His confederate would perhaps take the punishment. He did not like Carton, he decided. He was a coward, full of complaints. One concession he made to him. As they reached the outskirts of the town he allowed his companion to take a 'bus directly to Banner Cross. Peace could not be seen in Sheffield; he must go by a more circuitous route to avoid the unpleasant possibility of meeting a policeman.

Before they parted he gave very elaborate instructions as to where they were to meet. Peace had his own plan. The first thing he must do was to establish the reason for his return – his personal feud against Dyson must be his excuse. He hoped he would see somebody who knew him, so that he could discuss that aspect. If he could get the small bottle without being detected, there must be a good reason for his being in the neighbourhood. If the worst came to the worst, the police warrant would bring him no more than six months' hard labour, and he could do that on his head. But that must be his excuse.

There would have been no necessity to explain to the neighbours in Darnall why he was returning. The Dyson affair was common property. Women stood at their doors and shook their heads when she passed, and looked at one another with meaning glances when she was near. She was a terrible example of a so-called lady, for all respectable women to study as one studies the habits of unpleasant insects.

Two thousand pounds! Suppose you put two thousand sovereigns in a row, how far would they reach? Over a thousand inches…twenty-six yards. He stopped under a lamp-post in a deserted lane and paced off twenty-six yards. It wasn't as far as he thought, but still, it was far enough.

That night Dr Alan Mainford had an interesting experience. There arrived with dinner a letter from an irate but apologetic baronet broker. He was irate for a very excellent reason, apologetic because, as he wrote:

"I'm afraid I was a little rude to you when you wrote warning me about Carton. He seemed such an excellent servant, and I thought you were a little bit uncharitable, the more so since I hadn't written to you for a reference. My agent tells me that it was he who wrote. Carton let out your name by accident as having employed him, and seemed so anxious to impress him that you had gone abroad. The man is a dreadful blackguard…"

"Is that letter very amusing?"

Jane had snatched a few hours to dine with him.

"Well, it is in a way," he said. "I had a servant when I was in the army, a terrible rascal, and in a fit of mental aberration he gave my name as a reference to this man's agent – after I had warned him not to do so." He tapped the letter. "I wrote and told the innocent employer all about him and got kicked for my pains. I hadn't heard about the beggar since then, but I'll bet he doesn't give my name as reference in his next place!"

"In ordinary circumstances you wouldn't hear of him again," she said, "but you'll probably see him in a day or two. Those things always happen."

She was a true prophet. Alan was called out immediately after dinner to attend a patient who had had a relapse. He could do very little, and when that little was done he walked home – he had sent the victoria away under the impression that his stay would be a long one.

The streets were thronged with people, in spite of the fact that the night was raw and distinctly unpleasant. Most of the shops were open, and although it wanted six weeks to Christmas, the shopping season had begun.

He stepped aside to allow three long-skirted girls with linked arms to sweep along the narrow pavement, and as he recovered the sidewalk he came face to face with the one man in the world he did not expect to see. Carton's jaw dropped.

"Why, why, Captain – " he said.

"You infernal villain!" said Alan good-humouredly. "What are you doing in this town?"

"I left me last job, sir," said Carton glibly. "Couldn't get on with the people. Her ladyship used to drink, sir – "

"First you rob them, then you libel them. Are you working here?"

"Yes, sir; I've got a good job to go to. I hope, sir, you'll let bygones be bygones. Some day I'll pay you back for that watch. It's a funny thing, sir, I passed your house about ten minutes ago, saw the brass plate on the railings and wondered if I'd call. I've always said, sir, you were one of the kindest men I've ever had to deal with – "

Alan motioned him past with a jerk of his head. The meeting tickled him, a point for Jane Garden the seer.

When Alan reached home he found a letter waiting for him. It was written in a clerkly hand which he did not recognise, and was couched a little more pompously than most letters are. It was addressed from Banner Cross Terrace, Eccleshall Road, and ran:

"SIR,
"You may recall the circumstance of meeting me when I called at your establishment with a bone in my throat, which you, sir, with the skill peculiar to the English medical man, removed both expeditiously and painlessly.

"I am living now at the above address, and I should be happy if you would at the first moment available to your good self make it your business to call upon me with reference to a distressing disorder of the mind. Business and domestic troubles have tended to disturb my mental equilibrium, and I think it would be wise of me if I took time by the forelock and anticipated a serious breakdown rather than enlisted your skill to remedy its consequences.

"Your obedient servant,
ARTHUR DYSON."

Arthur Dyson? The name was familiar, but Alan could not place him for the moment. And then he remembered the tall man and the fish bone. He read the letter again; it was perfectly punctuated, pedantic and self-important. He looked at his watch; it was seven o'clock. He had dined early; in fact, his dinner always had something of the character of a high tea when Jane slipped away from her duties to take the meal with him. Invariably she had to return early in the evening to attend her patient. He sent a message to Dixon, who complained bitterly to the stable boy, his assistant, that this man had no hours, no systems, none of the comfortable values of the old doctor.

To Dixon Dr Mainford was always "the new man", though he had been in practice for two or three years. Not that Dixon disliked him he had complained as persistently of the peculiar habits of the old doctor, and had compared them unfavourably in turn with an earlier employer.

He climbed into his heavy coat, jammed his top hat down on his head, and brought the victoria round to the door.

There was no reason in the world why Alan should go out that night, for Dyson was not an important patient, not even a patient at all. But, remembering him, he was interested in the long man; the type rather fascinated Alan Mainford.

Two patients unexpectedly arrived, and it was half-past seven before he stepped into the victoria with a pleasant sense of anticipation, and never dreaming that he was driving straight to the heart of squalid tragedy.

25

A greengrocer's cart brought Peace the greater part of his journey. He was a great beggar of lifts, always giving his great age as his excuse. Though he was but forty-four, he could pass for sixty-seven, and had successfully imposed upon prison officers in this way.

The assumption of age gave him great advantages. People were sorry for him; tradesmen would place their carts at his disposal; in prison he was given the lighter tasks, though he was stronger than any of the ruffians that occupied the wards. He could always obtain admission to the prison hospital. The pity he excited was one of his strongest assets.

He arrived at Banner Cross before his companion and loafed around in the hope of finding somebody he knew. The rain had cleared and it was a moonlit night, which did not particularly please him. He peeped into the Banner Cross Hotel, a public-house that stood on the corner of the block where the Dysons' house was situated, but saw no familiar face.

He was hoping for two things: first, that he would see Mrs Dyson and enlist her help; secondly, that he would find somebody who knew him to whom he could supply a motive for his visit.

He had been there half an hour when he saw, on the opposite side of the road, the hesitant figure of Carton, and crossed to speak to him. He pointed at some gardens behind a low wall.

"You stay there. If you see me coming out of that house and walk away quietly, you go back to the cottage. But if I run, I'll come over this wall; you can either pretend you're one of the public chasing me, or you can walk down the road, get into a 'bus and go back to Sheffield. If you lose the bottle I give you – I'll follow you wherever you go and cut your throat – d'ye hear me?"

The man's teeth were chattering again.

"It doesn't look like a place for a burglary," he said.

"Never mind what it looks like," said Peace roughly. "You understand what I've told you?"

"There's a man over there...under the lamp-post," shivered Carton.

"I'll look after him. When I've got his back turned to you, nip over."

He crossed to where the man was standing beneath the lamp. He was a stranger to Peace, but evidently belonged to the neighbourhood.

"Looking for anybody, mate?" he asked.

"Yes," said Peace, "I'm looking for some friends of mine. They've moved in to a house about here. Know any strange people who've come here lately?"

The man didn't.

"A lady – a great friend of mine."

Peace took some letters and photographs from his pocket and handed them to the man. It was crudely done, but the purpose was defeated, for the stranger could not read. Peace looked over his shoulder: Carton had taken advantage of the stranger's attention being held and disappeared.

"That's what I've come here for – to find her," he said; "he shan't have her – I'll shoot her first."

He found little difficulty in working up his enthusiasm for Mrs Dyson, and the semblance of a man broken by jealousy.

But the man, apparently, had no interest in love affairs, and with a muttered excuse turned and walked away.

There was no sign of Mrs Dyson. Peace drew nearer to the house. He looked for a light upstairs; there was none. By the side of the house ran a passage, on the left-hand side of which were some outhouses. Softly he passed through the alleyway to the back of the premises, and saw a light in one of the upstairs rooms. A figure was moving. He recognised Mrs Dyson, and his heart thumped.

There was one signal he always gave — he gave it now. Twice he whistled softly. The second time she heard it, for he saw her turn with a start towards the window and peer out into the darkness. She might have seen him in the moonlight. The light went out. She was coming downstairs.

He would have to wait for hours, till they were all asleep, unless —

He heard the sound of her clogged feet on the pathway, and then out of the darkness she came, and he sensed her antagonism before she spoke.

"What do you want?" she asked shrilly. "There's a warrant out for you — you know that. How dare you come here!"

"Drop your voice, will tha?" he growled. "I want you to get him to withdraw that warrant. I want to be friends with you both."

"Friends with you!" she cried contemptuously. "My husband's a gentleman; he wouldn't dream of knowing scum like you. You know what he wrote to you — he means it."

Peace always carried the little card that had been flung so contemptuously over the garden wall when he was at Darnall. He carried it now.

"Charles Peace is requested not to interfere with my family."

"Listen, Kate — "

"Don't call me Kate. I'm Mrs Dyson."

"Listen — and keep your mouth shut, or I'll strangle you!"

She shrank back with a little scream as he advanced towards her.

"Help me, and I'll make a lady of you; give you everything you want. I've got thousands of pounds coming to me. Get your husband to withdraw the warrant: that's why I've come here. I've come here for no other reason. If anybody sees you here, that's what I've come for. I don't want to show you up, but I will, me lady. I've got letters from you that'd look fine if they was read in court."

She heard the back door open, and raised her voice for the benefit of her invisible audience.

"I don't want to see you, I don't want to know you. You're not fit for my husband to wipe his boots on. You're a low, common – "

His hand went out and gripped her. It was a fatal mistake, for she screamed.

"Who's that?"

A voice came from the darkness. Dyson! Peace flung her off and turned to fly, but the long-legged man caught him and gripped him by the collar. He had the advantage of height. Peace struck blindly at him, and the two men went rolling together on the ground; fighting like a fury to throw off the weight of the man, Peace reached for his revolver.

"Stand back!"

He had wriggled free, but his assailant came on.

The crack of the first explosion sounded thunderously. The man stumbled and fell. Peace fired again and fled.

He had one thought – the bottle. He doubled back to the house, along the passage and through the door; in a few seconds he was in the bedroom. Pulling open the drawers, he saw the liniment bottle in the second, fumbled with its base, then, with a croak of joy, slipped out the phial it contained and dropped it into his pocket.

He came out into the street, saw men running, and, flying across the road, leapt the wall. Carton was waiting for him.

"What was that I heard – a shot? You didn't shoot anybody?" he whispered. "Oh, my God! You didn't kill anybody?"

"Take this!"

Peace thrust the bottle into the man's pocket.

"Get back over the wall – nobody will see you. Go straight to the cottage and wait for me. Remember what I told you, Carton."

In another instant he had disappeared into the darkness.

Carton ran in the shadow of the wall through the garden before he came through a gateway into the road. It was well for him that he did this, for the flight of the murderer had been observed. A police whistle was blowing. What had happened?

Carton crossed to the public-house and drank a stiff brandy. Men came in and out with the news. A man had been killed – shot dead.

"I've seen him myself. He's laying up there in a back yard…go and have a look."

Fortified by the brandy, Carton followed the advice. Killed – murdered! The horror of it appalled him; the danger turned his blood to water. He made his way through dark passages, guided by the stream of men and women who had been attracted by the shooting, and found himself in a back yard. There it was – a lank, sprawling figure. From the house came the screams of an hysterical woman. Somebody said "Peace – Charlie Peace." Mrs Dyson had screamed his name.

A policeman was already there, making elaborate notes which he was never afterwards to decipher. The book in his hand was shaking, and there on the ground was Arthur Dyson, ludicrously dead.

A surgeon came and made an examination. The policeman, recovering from his dumb inertia, ordered the crowd to disperse, but there was no authority in his voice, and Carton lingered on, held to the spot by a gallows complex.

Then he heard a voice and turned with a start. It was Alan Mainford; he was talking to the surgeon, and frowning down at the limp figure stretched on the earth, a dark pool near his head, his face mercifully hidden from Carton. He heard Alan ask: "When did it happen?" and a dozen voices volunteered.

The surgeon looked up sharply.

"Can't you get all these people away?" he asked the policeman, and only then were the morbid onlookers dispersed.

Outside Carton saw a victoria standing by the side of the road, and guessed it was Alan's. He waited, too. The instructions of Peace were forgotten, or, if remembered, voided by the horror he had seen with his own eyes. Go back to the cottage…? To be killed perhaps…savage little beast. No, Carton could not face that. To stay in a lone house with him, miles from everywhere, at his mercy, or face inquiring detectives and pretend to be at his ease. Stealing spoons and forks, indulging in more pleasant villainies, a forged character or two – that was nothing. This was murder. He had seen the dead man and the blood, and heard his wife's maniacal laughter.

He put his hand in his pocket, touched the bottle and drew out his hand quickly. People who passed him were talking about Charles Peace. They all knew him; every man had seen him. They were eager to discover or invent an acquaintance with this celebrity.

"A little fellow about so high," said one man. "He used to work with me in the Millsands Mill...that's where he hurt his leg...a lame little fellow, but you'd hardly notice it."

What a celebrity the man was! Carton could have said something, if he could have spoken a word. But his mouth was dry. He went back into the Banner Cross Hotel and had another drink, swallowing it down quickly for fear Alan went away without his seeing him. What he could say to him he did not know, but Alan was a gentleman and an officer, and Carton had served seven years in the army and had acquired the habit of faith in military authority. Officers were still godlike to him, and Alan had been an officer – only a medical officer, it is true, but still an officer, whom one had to salute and before whom one stood to attention.

What was he to say to him? He did not know. He would just wait till he came out and then say – something.

Three police officers arrived in a trap, the horse in a muck sweat. The policeman who drove him got down and covered him with a rug. Carton watched, fascinated. The men who came by that cart would think nothing of taking him, putting handcuffs on his hands and driving him off to the police station, discussing their private affairs, and, leaving him in a cell, go home to their wives as though nothing had happened. It was just their ordinary business. And the screws would come in one morning, followed by a bearded man, who would shake hands with him, and say: "I'm very sorry I've got to do this, and I hope you don't bear any ill will." Marwood always said the same thing to all condemned prisoners, and if they asked him whether the rope would hurt he used to say: "I'll make it easy for you."

Suppose he didn't make it easy for them? There was no opportunity for reproaching him.

Carton's mouth was dry again. He had to hold his chin to keep his teeth from dancing against one another.

Then he saw Alan come out, and impulsively went towards him.

"Oh, sir!" he said.

Alan looked round and stared at the man.

"You again?" he said. "What the devil are you doing here?"

Carton tried to speak.

"I've got some relations here," he managed to stammer at last. "Ain't it awful, sir?"

"Did you hear anything – the shots fired?"

"No, sir; I was along the road," lied Carton. "I've got to get back to Sheffield now…to the station."

"Don't let me detain you," said Alan. And then: "Have you got your fare back? There'll be a 'bus along in a minute."

The man shook his head.

"Get up with Dixon – I'll drop you."

He slipped and scrambled up to the seat beside the driver. Dixon, perched in the middle, moved his box a little to the right, eyed the shivering man with no particular liking, and did not offer him a share of the apron.

All the way back to Sheffield the man was living with murder and the scaffold and bearded Marwood. Every minute Marwood was shaking hands with him, and saying how sorry he was, and hoping he would forgive him his unpleasant duty.

Near the station the victoria drew up, and the man, weak-kneed, got to the ground somehow and made his desperate appeal.

"I want to get to London, sir. I've got no money. I've no right to ask you, but, as God's my judge, I'm going to go straight. I know just where this life is taking me."

He was sincere. Alan realised that the sight of the murdered man had affected him terribly. He took a golden coin out of his pocket.

"Goodbye, sovereign," he said flippantly. "You know my address, if you're honest."

The man took the pound and quavered his thanks. Then a thought struck him. He took the bottle out of his pocket.

"I found this, sir…in the road. I think somebody dropped it."

Alan took the phial and examined the contents casually.

"It doesn't look particularly valuable. I should throw it away."

"No, sir, I'd keep it. I'm sure it's valuable." Carton was strangely agitated. "Perhaps somebody will miss the bottle and advertise… I found it on the road – in the gutter."

He took off his hat and ran in the direction of the station. Alan Mainford did not see him again for a long time.

When he got home he put the phial at the back of a shelf in his poison cupboard and forgot it.

26

Peace reached the cottage in the early hours of the morning. The clouds which had gathered at midnight had cleared again, and it was as bright as day. Twice he had to hide behind a hedge to avoid detection by a mounted police patrol. Two o'clock was striking – he heard a church clock which must have been miles away in the still morning air – when he unlocked the door of the cottage and went in.

The place was a pit of gloom; there was neither light nor sound in the house. Peace growled under his breath. Carton had not come back. He had probably passed him on the way. A man like that would be frightened of his own shadow and would hide at the sound of every footfall. He wouldn't dare play false. Peace had considerable faith in his own frightening qualities.

He lay down on his bed in the dark, waiting for his companion's return. He wondered if he had hurt Dyson. He wouldn't have shot him at all if the man had left him alone, if that woman hadn't screamed. He was finished with Mrs Dyson. She was a bad woman, unworthy of him. He had been wasting his time with her.

He was half dozing when he heard a sound which brought him to his feet – a key being stealthily inserted in the front door. He went swiftly into the passage, revolver in hand. He saw a figure silhouetted against the moonlight, and it was not Carton.

"What do you want? Stand or I'll fire!"

"All right, all right!"

It was Baumgarten's voice.

"Put up your pistol, my friend. You've done enough shooting tonight."

"Have you heard?" asked Peace eagerly.

"All Sheffield has heard," said Baumgarten dryly. "Why did you kill him?"

Peace gaped at him in the darkness.

"Kill him? Is he dead?"

"Yes. Come somewhere where we can put on a light."

"You can put it on anywhere in the house," said Peace, struck a match on his trousers, and, lifting off a glass chimney, lit a paraffin lamp.

Baumgarten looked old and tired. He was wearing riding breeches and gaiters, and carried a whip in his hand.

"Is your horse outside?" asked Peace, in alarm.

"Don't be a fool – no, I've tied him up in the orchard at the back. Why did you kill him?"

"I had to," said Peace doggedly. "I didn't want to, but he grabbed at me and I had to shoot."

Baumgarten fingered his chin thoughtfully.

"You've got the crystals?" And, when Peace nodded, his eyes lit up. "Are you sure?" he asked eagerly. "Let me see them."

"I haven't got 'em with me. A friend is bringing them on – the man who was working with me. I didn't want to have them in my pocket and be caught with them."

Baumgarten stood, slapping his gaitered leg gently with the whip, his lower lip protruding, his brows knit.

"Can you trust this man? Why didn't you bring them here yourself?"

For the first time doubt came to Peace. Had he made a mistake?

"He wouldn't dare play with me. He's a frightened rat and – "

"If he's a frightened rat he will not come back here. Murder is a serious thing, my friend."

"So's other things!" growled Peace. "So's keeping a foreigner locked up in a cell and beating him to death! Don't you go telling me what's serious – or I'll tell you something!"

Baumgarten winced at that; his nerves were getting a little frayed. Just now he was looking longingly at an avenue which led to his pleasant villa at Interlaken.

"Yes, I suppose so. I will wait for the man to come."

"Have you brought the money?"

"No," said Baumgarten, and Peace knew that he lied.

But the little man was fair: he was not entitled to the money till the goods were delivered. They waited an hour – two hours. By this time Peace was patently uneasy.

"I'll go now," said Baumgarten, getting up and stretching himself.

He had paid two visits to the orchard to see that his horse had not shaken off the rug he had thrown over it.

"I'd better get home before daylight. You stay here; keep all the doors locked; a policeman sometimes comes in to try them – and the windows. It doesn't matter about the shutters being closed."

He rode off soon after. Peace heard the clip-clop of the horse's hooves for a long time.

He was in no mood for sleep. He must know what had happened to Carton. Would the man have betrayed his hiding-place? If he had, the police would have been here by now. All through the day he waited, not daring to show himself abroad.

They would be scouring the countryside for him, and his description would be circulated. That would not be the first time he had been wanted urgently, but never for so important an offence.

Only one man came near the house. He saw two mounted policemen riding abreast, coming along the road. They stopped before the cottage and one dismounted, opened the gate and came in. Peace heard him trying the door and the windows. Apparently he went all round the house before he came back and, joining his companion, mounted and rode off.

The little man had a big carpet bag in which he kept his belongings, and when he had learned that he had to make this his headquarters he had asked Baumgarten to arrange for it to be brought to the cottage. He found it in the attic, and, opening it, made a selection.

It was no exaggeration to say that Peace was a master of disguise, in spite of the unpromising basis upon which he had to work, for it seemed impossible that a face so marked, so out of the ordinary, could be changed. Again he had recourse to his walnut disguise; he stained his face and hands a deep, sunburnt brown, and brushed carefully into his hair some of the contents of a little bottle containing a dark solution. Shaving himself carefully, he put on a beard almost hair by hair, and with such meticulous care that the operation took him more than two hours. A pair of blue trousers, a blue jersey, bearing in red letters the name of a steam packet, almost completed his disguise.

One artistic etcetera remained. Removing his left shoe, he drew on a second and third sock, and over these he wound a calico bandage. When this was done, he produced from the bag a crutch. It was made in three pieces and screwed together.

This time he would not take the iron hook. People in Sheffield knew that too well. The coldness of the weather excused the woollen gloves. The crutch and the bandaged foot hid his one detectable affliction – his lame leg.

In the dusk he stepped out of the house, his crutch under his arm. Whilst nobody was in sight he could walk, and for this purpose he had provided himself with a carpet slipper, ordinarily three sizes too large for him. This he took off and concealed in his pocket whenever a cart or a pedestrian came into sight.

He reached a cross-roads and waited for a likely conveyance. It came in the shape of a milk-cart, carrying two full churns into the town. The crutch and the bandaged foot were his passport, and he reached the very centre of Sheffield without the least discomfort. It would be more difficult getting back.

The first thing he saw, as he stumped along the street, his crutch under his arm, was a small crowd gathered before a hoarding on which a man was pasting a bill. He stopped and read:

MURDER

One Hundred Pounds Reward.

"Whereas on the 29th of November Mr Arthur Dyson, CE, was murdered at Banner Cross, Sheffield, having been shot in the head in the presence of his wife by Charles Peace, who escaped in the darkness of the night, and is still at large, NOTICE is hereby given that a reward of One Hundred Pounds will be paid by Her Majesty's Government to any person other than a person employed in a police office in the United Kingdom who shall give such information and evidence as will lead to the discovery and conviction of the said Charles Peace."

He read it, fascinated. Later, when the bill was amplified as the result of the coroner's verdict, it was so familiar to him that he did not even stop to read it.

His disguise was perfect, but he took no risks, not venturing into any of the public-houses where he expected to find Carton, but contenting himself with a furtive peep into the bar. He went the complete round without finding any indication of the man, and was giving up the search when it occurred to him that he might inquire at the lodgings which Carton had taken on his arrival.

He went to the house and had a shock: the landlord did not recognise him.

"Your brother, is he? Well, all I can tell you is that he's a swindler. Tried to get away without paying his rent, he did! My son's a porter on the station, and he see him get into the London train, and says he to himself: 'I wonder if he's paid the old man his rent?' and with that he goes up to him."

"When was this?" quavered Peace, in the deep voice he had adopted.

"Night before last. Anyway, my son got five shillings out of him."

"Gone to London, has he?" The heart of the little man sank like lead.

"It's my belief," said the landlord, "that he was in with this fellow Charles Peace. I wouldn't be a bit surprised."

"Who is Charles Peace?" asked the bearded little stranger.

"A murderer," said the other emphatically; "and they'll catch him – you mark my words! And Carton too."

Peace ambled down the street, his mind a violent, bubbling sea of hate. Carton had gone away, had he? And taken the bottle. But perhaps he was only scared. He was a frightened cur of a man who would fly in terror, though there was no danger to him. That was the only hope.

In the street he heard his name spoken at every few yards. The town was being scoured; every lodging-house had been raided. Near Fargate he saw Baldy Eltham, looking surprisingly smart in uniform.

To reach home he had to take a cab for part of the way, and there was a long and dreary wait till a carrier's cart came in sight and dropped him at the cross-roads near his new home. The carrier was actually passing the cottage, but Peace asked to be dropped, indicating that he lived in another direction.

There was one relief for him: Carton had not told the police. Peace had an old time-table in his bag, and this he studied. The man must have driven straight from Banner Cross and caught the last train to London. He wouldn't have had time to tell all he knew. That was it! He was frightened; he hadn't Peace's nerve. On this comforting thought the little man fell asleep, without even attempting to remove his disguise.

He improved upon and perfected it the next day. When Baumgarten called towards evening, it completely deceived him. The visitor looked at the little man with a new respect, but he was very grave. Madame had taken a very serious view of the murder, and would not in any case be associated with Peace. He brought fifty pounds in gold. If the crystals arrived, the reward would come in addition.

"There's no sense in me keeping meself locked up here," said Peace. "Nobody would know me. All I want is a little pony cart and a pony. I asked you for that the other day, and you said 'Yes,' but where is it? There's a stable out at the back, and it would save you coming here, too."

It struck Baumgarten as an excellent idea. He promised to bring the matter up again. Without consulting Madame Stahm, he bought a pony, cart and harness and left it outside the cottage that same night.

Peace was almost jubilant. His instructions had been carried out; the cart was loaded with fodder, and he led the pony down the lane by the side of the cottage into the stable he had prepared for him.

Thereafter, farmers and labourers in the neighbourhood became familiar with the sight of the bearded, seafaring man, who drove his pony and cart. When the bearded, seafaring man disappeared, and his place was taken by a groom who wore steel spectacles and a cavalry moustache, they hardly remarked upon it.

The low pony cart served his purpose admirably. It made it impossible to detect his height, and the smartly-fitting livery coat he wore changed his entire appearance.

To the world Charles Peace had disappeared as though the ground had opened and swallowed him. Even more effectively had Carton vanished; no news came from him; he did not reappear in Sheffield. Generally it was believed that he had gone abroad. One theory was that he had left for Hull the same night.

27

Ordinarily Peace did not read the daily newspapers: he reserved his reading for Sundays, and devoured every line that dealt with crime. The police court proceedings, fashionable trials, divorce news — he read them and reread them, gloating over every detail. But now he was an assiduous subscriber to the *Telegraph*. Every item of news concerning the Banner Cross murder he examined and memorised.

A great many of the stories set down were purely apocryphal. He called them lies, and added various adjectives. There was not a word about the crystals: that was a relief, not only to him, but to the troubled people at Brinley Hall. Madame Stahm had her boxes packed ready for flight. Baumgarten had already transferred the greater part of his account to a Swiss bank. As the days progressed and no police inquiries came their way they decided to remain.

The inquest was reported in full, and again there was no mention of the missing phial. Mrs Dyson knew nothing of it. Peace never expected she would, but thought that the man might have had a confidant. He had, but there were excellent reasons why Wertheimer should not mention his negotiations. He could not have raised the money; he had no desire that the world should know that such a valuable secret existed. He himself attended Dyson's funeral, and later that night called on the sorrowing widow. It was easy to discover that she knew very little about her husband's business. She was, in fact, very voluble, since the occasion called for stimulants.

"Do you remember, madam," said Wertheimer, in the first moment they were alone, "what your poor, dear husband did with the little phial of crystals I left with him? I called one evening, you remember, to discuss certain matters with him – possibly you were out; I think you were – and I left him a sample of a new oxide."

She shook her head.

"Don't bother me, mister," she said wearily. "I haven't seen anything. What do they look like?"

He described them.

"Go up to his room and look," she said, and he went up with a bounding heart.

He searched drawers, cupboards and boxes, but found nothing. There was in one of the drawers a curious bottle of liniment, the bottom of which was apparently hollow, but he saw in this no more than an honest attempt by a manufacturer to cheat the purchaser in the matter of quantity.

He was so long and so thorough in his search that she came up to him and demanded irritably whether he expected to stay there for ever.

He followed this up by a visit to Dyson's office. There was a locker there, where he had kept a few personal belongings. His desk had been cleared and the contents put aside; these were available for inspection, and though Wertheimer had no authority his right to examine was not questioned.

He was puzzled and alarmed. Dyson at the last moment might have changed his mind about disposing of the crystals to Madame Stahm. He decided upon taking a bold step; he wrote to that worthy lady, humbly, flatteringly, begging the privilege of an interview. To his surprise and gratification it was granted.

He drove himself out to Brinley Hall one afternoon, prepared for all eventualities. In each pocket he had a loaded derringer. Madame received him graciously, however, cut short all the polite preamble and came down to business. She demanded perfect frankness about his negotiations with Dyson (he was staggered here, for he had never dreamed she knew), and when he gave his confidence he learned in return that the worst had not happened. Dyson had neither offered the crystals nor had she bought them.

They parted excellent friends and potential partners. His treason was forgotten and forgiven. He also had one or two things to forgive, and made no inquiry as to the fate of the lamented Lamonte. It was unfortunate that such things should happen, but such was life.

On his way back he passed a little pony cart driven by a very stiff-looking groom who wore spectacles. He had never before seen a groom wearing spectacles, which practice was essentially the prerogative of the indoor or learned classes.

Another week passed. Peace read the account of the inquest both in the daily and the weekly newspapers. He learned that he had been seen in London and at Portsmouth, and that a man answering to his description had been arrested in Newcastle.

"Every limping man is a suspect," said the newspaper.

Charles Peace was grateful for the hint.

The pony cart enabled him to travel far afield. He went to Mansfield one day, put his horse up at a livery stable and journeyed on to London. He had to find another bolt-hole. Besides which, his family were in trouble with the eating-house at Hull, and he must bring them to a new nest.

He spent three days in London, a bearded seaman with a bandaged foot, and finally decided to take a house in Peckham. It was a two-storeyed villa in a poor neighbourhood, but it was distinctly better than any house he had ever occupied. It had bow windows, and there was a certain touch of respectability in the steps which led to the front door, and in the area and basement. He paid a month's rent down. The house, he said, was for his nephew and his sister-in-law, who were arriving from Wales.

By the time he had finished negotiations, his wife and family had left Hull secretly and apparently unnoticed. Police methods in 1876 were loose and inadequate. Nobody seemed to bother about Mrs Peace and her plans, though it was certain that sooner or later a careful watch on her would bring the observers to the much-wanted Charles.

Peace had plenty of money. In the course of a brief meeting with his wife in London he gave her sufficient to furnish the house, and insisted that one article of furniture should be a piano.

Returning to Mansfield, he retrieved his pony and trap and drove back to the cottage. That was the first of many excursions. The image of Mrs Dyson had eclipsed an earlier love. With the disappearance of the faithless Kate, the tender memories of an older attachment came back to the little man, and he sought out the lady, whose name was Thompson.

The excitement over the murder had died down. He was getting tired of his country life, and had made up his mind to drive by easy stages to London, when a letter came to him. He found it thrust under the front door when he returned from a visit to Sheffield. It bore the London postmark and was addressed to "Mr Gray", the name by which he had decided to be known when he took possession of the cottage.

He turned it over and over in his hand. It was not in his wife's writing or in his daughter's, and yet the postmark was "London, SE". He tore open the flap and took out a single sheet of paper. There was no address on the top, and it began abruptly:

"I haven't told a soul, but I can't stand things like that. I'm doing well now and am going straight. I gave the bottle to Dr Mainford. He lives in Sheffield. He was in the army with me. I said I'd found it in the road."

That was all — but it was enough to make the little man grow in stature. The deep, dog eyes sparkled with life. Alan Mainford — that puppy! There was going to be a lark here. He grew almost young at the thought of adventure. Charles Peace, wanted for murder in Sheffield, would go into Sheffield and do another job right under the nose of the police. Nobody else would dare do it, only Charlie Peace. Or perhaps he wouldn't have to "do" the house at all. Suppose he tried one of his little tricks — the sort of trick that only Charles Peace could think of and have the nerve to carry out.

He cogitated on the matter, strolling up and down beneath the bare, wind-blown branches of the little orchard at the back of the cottage, stroking the beard that wasn't his.

Alan Mainford returned from his early visits one morning and learned from his housekeeper that an elderly gentleman had called on a strange errand.

"He said he had lost a phial of valuable chemicals, sir, on the night of the murder at Banner Cross, and that he'd heard you'd found them. Of course I knew nothing about it."

Alan had forgotten all about the phial.

"Good Lord, yes! I remember."

He went to his poison cupboard and fished out the little bottle.

"What sort of a man was he?"

"He looked like a sailor, sir. He had a very bad foot; it was all bandaged up and in a sling. What he said was that the chemicals were the only things that were good for his foot. He said that if you could find them and leave them for him, he'd call tomorrow or send his groom."

"A sailor with a groom sounds a little curious to me. I'd like to see the gentleman. If he calls again you can tell him I have the crystals, and I shall be happy to hand them to him if he will prove his ownership."

A groom with steel spectacles and a cavalry moustache called and received the message without betraying his natural annoyance.

"The gentleman's very ill with a bad foot," he said, with an indignation which was not simulated. "I'm surprised at the doctor keeping my governor's property."

"That's what he says: if the gentleman will call he will hand the bottle over to him."

"He's got it, has he?"

She nodded.

"Yes, I saw it myself," said the garrulous woman. "It's kept in the poison cupboard. So, if your gentleman will call – "

"He'll call, ma'am," said Peace grimly, and drove home with a light heart.

28

He didn't want any more shooting. He certainly did not wish to meet Alan Mainford with no other defence than his fists. But doctors are called out late at nights, and the house would be patently empty and easy.

Yet it was not an easy place to burgle. It stood on a main thoroughfare, with a police station not a hundred yards away. There was traffic of sorts day and night, and at the back of the house a stable building which was apparently doubly occupied. Peace did not know then that Miss Garden had her lodgings there, but he knew that the groom slept over his stables and that a stable boy slept in a loft.

In the middle of the paved yard was an ornamental lamp-post, an eccentricity of the old doctor, and, more eccentrically still, remembering it was a private lamp-post, its gas burner was lit every night and extinguished every morning.

The house was detached; there was no way of gaining access except from the front or the rear. The only windows at the side were out of reach, and a ladder would be instantly detected by the passers by.

Leaving his horse and trap in a neighbouring stable, he watched Alan go out hurriedly one night, carrying a small black bag, and hardly waited until he was out of sight before he attacked the front window. Luck was with him, for there was no pedestrian within a hundred yards. He was inside and had closed the window down within a few seconds.

He found himself in the waiting-room. He had taken a very careful note of the topography, and, crossing the passage noiselessly, reached the small dispensary, a narrow apartment which had been formed by putting up a party wall that cut off a portion of the surgery and consulting-room. He had hardly closed the door behind him when there came a knock at the front door, which was repeated. To his alarm, he heard the housekeeper go along the passage and turn the key. He had counted upon her being asleep.

"Is the doctor in?" asked a well-known voice.

Baldy Eltham!

Peace looked round for a way of escape. The room was at the side of the house. There were no windows, the light being supplied by two powerful gas burners. Nor was there any key or bolt on the inside of the door. His only escape was along the passage and either out of the front door or by the way he had come.

"I'll wait," said Baldy's voice. "My other tooth is aching like the devil. I want the doctor to give me some of that stuff he put in the other night. I could go right in and find it – I know exactly where it is – in the poison cupboard."

The hair on the back of the little man's neck stood up. He drew his revolver from his pocket and clicked round the cylinder.

"The poison cupboard's locked, Mr Eltham," said the housekeeper's voice. "You'll have to wait till the doctor returns. He won't be very long – the baby was born before they sent for him."

The heavy foot of Eltham sounded in the passage. He gripped the handle of the dispensary door, turned it and opened the door a few inches. Peace crouched down near the floor, rested his pistol hand on his knee. He had extra cartridges in his pocket, but he would have no time to reload. He held six in his left hand in case… One slipped and fell to the floor. It made a clatter which the man outside must hear.

"Well, perhaps I'd better wait."

The door slammed and his voice retreated – but not far enough. He had gone into the snuggery, which was no more than a big recess behind the stairs. Peace pulled his lantern from under his coat, turned the slide and examined the room quickly.

That must be the poison cupboard – the white one. He tried it! It was locked. And here he had another shock: the cupboard was made of steel, and the lock was really a lock. To force it open would not be a very difficult task, but it would be a noisy job, and a little too risky.

He was considering what to do when he heard a key in the street door lock, a light step in the passage, and Alan's voice.

"A false alarm. The other doctor was there before me. Hullo, Baldy! What's the matter with you?"

"Toothache, doctor."

"We'll settle that," said Alan's voice.

It was now or never. Pulling the door open quickly, Peace stepped into the passage. The doctor had not come into sight. Noiselessly he opened the front door and slipped out, leaving it ajar.

"What the deuce is that?" said Alan.

He had caught one glimpse of the vanishing figure.

"What's wrong?" asked Baldy.

Alan ran to the door, pulled it open and stepped into the street. There was no sign of the intruder.

"Somebody was in the house. Have you been into the dispensary?" He saw the open door.

"I haven't been in, but I opened and shut the door."

"Are you sure you left it shut?"

"I'll swear to it with a prayer-book in each hand," said Baldy.

Alan went in and lit the gas. Nothing had been moved or disturbed. With a final glance round he was turning out the gas, when a bright object on the floor caught his eye. Stooping, he picked it up.

"Here's a pin-fire cartridge."

Baldy almost snatched it from his hand and examined it carefully.

"Pin-fire?" he said slowly. "A revolver cartridge, of the same calibre as the bullet that killed Arthur Dyson. You know the name of the man who was in here, don't you? If you don't, I'll tell you — it was Charles Peace."

29

The police kept their secret well. None of the general public knew that the presence of Peace in Sheffield was as much as suspected. The search that was made of the town was thorough; it was also futile. Before dawn every questionable resort, every common lodging-house, every one of his old haunts had been combed and sifted.

Baldy came to breakfast, weary-eyed, baffled. Every railway station for twenty miles in every direction was being picketed and watched.

"The nerve of the fellow, to come back here! And to think I nearly went into that dispensary! He couldn't have got out."

"And you mightn't have got out either, except on a stretcher," said Alan. "On the whole I'm glad you changed your mind about going in."

"Why did he come here?" asked the sergeant. "There's nothing to steal."

"Don't be rude, Baldy. Why shouldn't my house be burgled? It's simply full of valuable property. Seriously, I've got over a thousand pounds' worth of old silver in the house, and it must have seemed easy to him. My theory is that he watched until I went out last night, got in through the waiting-room window – if you look you'll see where it's been forced up – heard your knock at the door, and nipped into the dispensary."

"Why the dispensary?" asked Baldy, and Alan groaned.

"Because it was the only place he could go. The door is exactly opposite the waiting-room door. It is the last place he would have chosen. There is no way out except by the door."

"What nerve!" said Baldy, with reluctant admiration. "To come back to Sheffield – "

"Has he ever been away?" asked Alan quietly.

"He's away now," said the sergeant, "but he'll be lucky to get right away! He won't put his nose in Sheffield for many a day."

But here he was wrong.

Alan did not for one moment connect the phial of crystals with this unpleasant visitation. The caller who wanted to retrieve his property passed out of his mind. Two or three days later, Jane Garden came home for a long rest. She had been continuously working almost since the day this strange partnership had been formed. Christmas was approaching, and she planned a visit to the south coast.

"Why not follow the example of your late employer and see some white snow and blue skies?"

"What do you mean?" she asked.

"Madame Stahm has departed for Switzerland, lock, stock and barrel, with all her personal staff, her Mr Baumgarten, her furniture, hangings and tapestries. In fact, the Hall is for sale."

She hardly credited the news.

"Madame will leave nothing behind in England," he went on, "but some forty thousand pounds which she has foolishly spent in her fruitless attempts to make a new kind of steel. She will also leave a bad impression and a disconsolate minstrel boy. Mr Charles Peace never had such an appreciative audience."

The rumour was that she had formed some sort of business alliance with her arch-enemy, Wertheimer. At any rate, they had been seen together at one of the leading lawyers' offices three times in a week, and it was accepted that a working arrangement had been signed, sealed and delivered.

"And I think she's wise. She had some sort of connection with that little beast. Possibly he knows a little too much about her, and she is wise to go before he's arrested and opens his mouth."

He told her of the midnight intruder, and was frank about it.

"I'm telling you," he said, "because, if I didn't, our dear housekeeper would make a song about it. That woman ought to have been a reporter: she can keep nothing to herself."

Jane was staggered when she heard the story.

"Here? Peace? Alan, it's impossible!"

"I should have thought so, but it isn't. He'll not come here again, so you can sleep sound at nights!"

He might not believe that Peace had left Sheffield. He was dangerously confident that the little man would not repeat his foray, but here he underrated the audacity of one who boasted that he believed in God and the devil and feared neither.

Two mornings after the burglary an unexpected visitor called upon Dr Mainford, and on seeing him Alan almost gasped.

"What are you doing here?" he asked.

Carton grinned.

"I came up to bring down one of our young gentlemen who goes to school near here, sir," he said. "I thought I'd call in and pay you the money I owe you."

He took a sovereign from his pocket and put it on the table.

"An unexpected windfall for me – I hope you got it fairly, Carton?"

"I'm going straight, sir. All old lags say that, but I'm telling the truth. I've got a good job, and I've told the governor all about my past. It took a bit of courage, but I did it."

"Good luck to you! And keep the sovereign as a souvenir of our unpleasant acquaintance!"

The man shook his head with a smile.

"No, thank you, sir; I've always looked forward to the day when I'd pay you back."

There was a note of anxiety in his tone when he asked: "Has anything more been heard about Peace?"

Alan was almost inclined to tell him of his recent experience, but thought better of it.

"He hasn't been caught."

"People think he's in London," said the man in a troubled voice. "I hope he isn't. Not that I'm likely to meet him – I live on the outskirts. That was a lesson to me."

"Were you with him that night?" asked Alan quietly, and when Carton did not answer he thought it wise not to press the question.

He was saying goodbye to the man when a thought occurred to him.

"You remember that bottle of chemicals you left with me? I wish you'd take it away. I'm afraid I shall lose it, and I'd like to hand the responsibility on to you – not that there's very much responsibility attached to it."

The man shifted awkwardly, cleared his throat.

"If it's a bother, sir, I'll take it."

He had often wondered whether the doctor had thrown the phial into the dustbin. Alan unlocked the poison cupboard, took out the bottle and brought it from the dispensary.

"Here you are," he said.

Carton took it gingerly and dropped it into his pocket. The very motion brought back a too poignant memory of another occasion when someone else had given him that bottle to dispose of.

Jane came in just before the man went, and Alan told her the story of the phial, but it had no special significance for her.

When he had gone, she chatted about her patient, and, as a thought struck her: "I saw such an odd-looking man, a groom, today. He was driving a pony cart. A queer-looking man with steel spectacles and a moustache."

"What did he do that was odd?"

"He looked at me," she said, and he laughed uproariously.

"That wasn't odd, it was the most perfectly natural thing to do. I look at you – I'm never tired of looking at you. Where did this terrible happening occur?"

"Outside Mrs Elford's house. I had a feeling he was following me in the pony cart, but probably he was only waiting for somebody. It looked rather like a doctor's trap, but I've never seen the man before.

It was his eyes that were so strange; it may have been my imagination, but they seemed to glare at me."

"To look at you is praiseworthy; to glare at you is unpardonable. Find me this groom and I'll poison him," said Alan. "I think I know the pony cart – I've seen it several times. Sometimes it's driven by the groom, and sometimes by a rather nice old gentleman in a square felt hat. I'll look out for him and tell him not to glare. By the way, I was wrong when I told you that Madame Stahm had gone – she did not leave until yesterday morning. Apparently she has been staying in a Sheffield hotel for a week."

30

The first intimation received by Peace that his patroness was departing had come with the arrival of Baumgarten in the red dusk of a wintry evening. Peace listened incredulously.

"She's going away?" And then, with righteous indignation: "What about me?"

"To be exact, she has gone away," said Baumgarten. "She crossed the Channel yesterday, and I am leaving this afternoon. Madame is not well; she is very unhappy; she has lost money, and people who might have helped her have been stupid. It was stupid to trust a man you had not met till a week before; it was stupid to shoot when you might have threatened."

"What about me?" demanded Peace again. It was easy to act the wrathful, ill-used man. "After all I've done and the risks I took! I wouldn't have taken 'em for anybody else in the world."

Baumgarton sat down at the discoloured table – it had once been white, but Peace was an untidy eater – and laid down a heavy leather wallet, opened it and poured out a stream of shining gold.

"There is a hundred pounds there. Recover for us the crystals, and there will be two thousand in addition. Have you a good memory, my friend?"

Peace nodded.

"You know Madame's name and how it is spelt? Yes, I remember, you do. You know my name and how it is spelt? Add the two names together. Madame and I are to be married. Remember, Madame

183

Stahm-Baumgarten, and our address will be the National Bank, Berne. Write it down, commit it to memory, and destroy the paper."

"I never forget anything," said Peace. "I've only got to read a scene in Shakespeare twice and get the words in me head, and I never forget it."

"A letter will find Madame, or, better still, a telegram. If you find the crystals, send a telegraphic message, telling me where I can meet you, and I will be with you in twenty-four hours. If you do not find them" – he shrugged – "this is the end." He waved his hand to the shining heap on the table. "And now, I will go."

"I hope you have a pleasant journey, sir," said Peace, and held out his hand, but Mr Baumgarten apparently did not see it.

Peace gathered up the gold, counted it and adjusted it in ten little heaps, and then in five larger heaps, and then balanced the hundred coins one on top of the other, finally wrapping them in paper so that they made rouleaux of twenty each. These he secreted in various odd pockets and belts.

In a sense the departure of Madame Stahm was a relief. He intended leaving the cottage and putting it into the hands of an agent to sell. It would be worth three or four hundred pounds. He drove into Sheffield, interviewed an estate agent, who was most agreeable to carrying out his instructions.

"You can either sell it or mortgage it," he said. "If you will let me have the title deeds, I will see what is the best arrangement."

It was on the tip of the little man's tongue to say that he had no title deeds, but instinct told him that that would be a false move on his part. He searched the house for them, thinking they were left behind, and resolved to write to Madame Stahm to supply the missing documents. She had given him the cottage – Baumgarten had said so. A gentleman's word ought to be his bond.

He would stay at the cottage a little longer, for he had not given up his quest. Though Alan was unaware of the fact, Peace haunted the house, gaining an extensive knowledge of the doctor's movements.

He found another interest – the presence of Jane Garden. He could put only one construction upon the friendship between Alan and the girl, because he knew no other variety of friendship. That whipper-snapper must be very fond of her, he mused; and who wouldn't be? She wasn't as fine a creature as Mrs Dyson. He thought she was rather namby-pamby, and namby-pambyness in a woman cancelled out most of her attractions. But she was a good-looker, a high-stepper – and a lady. That factor had an irresistible appeal to Peace. He worshipped gentility.

If the truth be told, he had been none too pleased with the impish role which Madame Stahm had assigned to him on a certain occasion. His vanity rebelled against the suggestion that he was old enough to be the father of any woman of attractive age and appearance, and he was almost glad when the deception had been revealed.

Yet, for all her beauty, Jane Garden had something of a neutral quality in his mind. His gross daydreams took baser shapes. Her rare and delicate beauty was beyond his appreciation, for he progressed by comparisons. Kate Dyson was prettier than Thompson; Thompson was prettier than that girl in Hull. Between the most ravishing beauty in his drab life and Jane Garden was an unbridgeable gulf.

But she had a rare figure and good teeth. Peace, who had few serviceable teeth, set great store by this gift of nature. She lived in a little house over the stable. At first he could not believe that any man who called himself a gentleman could allow a lady to live over a stable like a common groom; but apparently she did not feel the disgrace of it. She would have been surprised and alarmed to know how often those dog-like eyes of Charles Peace watched her running up the wooden steps to her room in the course of the next few weeks.

There was a small walled enclosure where stable refuse was thrown. Peace found this a convenient hiding-place one night, when Alan and the girl went out together. It offered no great opportunity to the little man, for the housekeeper had been nervous since the burglary, and had brought in a stalwart nephew to keep her company when she was in the place alone.

Dixon also was out. It was a boisterous night. Creeping from his hiding-place, Peace took the long pole which hung on one of the stable walls under a protecting ledge, and extinguished the lamp, replacing the pole where he had found it. He was curious to see what kind of a hovel the girl had for a home, and, passing swiftly up the steps, he tried the door, and, when that failed him, a narrow window which was within reach. He clambered into a room, pulled down the dark blinds and lit a candle end. He was surprised to discover how cosy and pleasant it was, and continued his leisurely inspection.

There was a possibility that he might find something to his advantage, but there was nothing in either of the two rooms that it would have paid him to take away, even if it had been wise to do so.

He extinguished his candle end, pulled up the blinds and let himself out of the door. As he crossed the yard he could see through the kitchen window the faint light of the room where the housekeeper and her nephew were sitting. But the place was too small to burgle whilst anybody was awake inside.

He tried the flanking wall of the house, hoping for an inspiration. The roof was no use. This was going to be a very difficult job. He was meditating upon ways and means when he saw the victoria pulling up at the house, and hastened to his hiding-place. Usually Alan and the girl went indoors, but tonight they walked around through the gateway into the yard.

"Hullo!" he heard Alan say. "The light's blown out. One minute – I'll light it for you."

He walked across the yard, found the lighter's pole, and, after several attempts, set light to the methylated wick at the end, and, pushing up the governing tap, relit the lamp.

"There's always that profession for me if medicine fails," he said, as he hung up the pole. "Are you sure you won't have supper?"

"No, I'm going to bed – I'm tired."

Alan glanced up at the stable building.

"Dixon won't be back till late. I hate leaving you there alone. If anything happened to you, Jane, I think I'd go raving mad."

She laughed softly.

"What can happen to me except a good night's sleep?"

"I wish to heavens they'd find this man. He's getting a little on my nerves."

"You mean Peace?"

"Yes."

She laughed again.

"How silly of you! He wouldn't hurt me."

"He'd cut the throat of his own mother if it served him," said Alan.

The hidden man smirked as at a compliment.

"Good night!"

He heard a kiss, and her light feet on the steps. It was funny that they should part with a kiss, like two people who were only just courting.

He caught a glimpse of her on the landing at the top, waving her hand, and heard the door close. That house would never be burgled, he told himself as he drove homeward. The young doctor was too wide, and it was dangerous. He'd probably have a gun or a pistol in the house – bound to have, he being an old army man. And there in that house was a fortune – that was the maddening thing about it. If he could only lay his hands on that phial! If he only had a friend there! If he could get round the housekeeper, or have a talk with the girl! He only wanted a chance of meeting her and talking her over. Women would do anything for him.

Peace had no doubt at all about his powers of fascination. His mind went back again and again to the girl and Alan. Sloppy, that's what it was. Going on like two school kids. He couldn't understand it. If "anything happened" to her, Alan had said…

His lips curled, then suddenly drooped. A splendid idea dawned in his brain – a wonderful idea. It was one of the grandest ideas he had ever had. He almost shouted for joy as he whipped up the pony into a gallop, and he pottered about the house for the greater part of the night, singing, in his not unpleasant falsetto, a song which he himself had written and composed. It was called: "If the Angels Should Take Me Away", and it was about heaven and mothers and lonely lovers.

This was to be a job after his own heart, a job that required planning and timing and rehearsing.

He snatched a few hours' sleep, and prepared the house for certain contingencies; fed and groomed his pony, and washed down the trap with water that he drew from a well at the back of the cottage. There was an air of gaiety about the equipage that drove into Sheffield. This time he did not bait the horse, but walked him slowly round and round until he stopped by the side of a dark road within view of Alan's house. He waited half an hour, saw the doctor come out and drive away. Leaving the pony unattended, he walked across the road, and, taking a letter from his pocket, slipped it into the letter-box, knocked a sharp rat-tat and hurried away.

The housekeeper, who carried the letter to Jane Garden, did not mention the fact that it had been put in the letter-box, although it had been brought by hand. Jane opened the envelope and read the ill-written scrawl.

"If you please, miss, Mrs Elford has been taken very ill again. Can you come at once?

Yours truly,
MARY SMITH."

It looked like a letter that a servant might have written. Mrs Elford had been one of her patients – the last she had attended – and she had left her a picture of robust health. She could not suspect that the little man, who, unknown to her, had been collecting information about her for days, was well aware that she had nursed Mrs Elford.

It was only a short journey; she decided to go on foot. Peace, watching the house, saw her come out and his heart sang within him. Turning the pony, he followed her at a distance, overtaking her just as she was turning into the gate of a house.

"Excuse me, miss!"

She heard the urgent voice and looked round.

"Is that Nurse Garden?"

"Yes," she said, wondering.

"Mrs Elford isn't there. She's gone out into the country, on the Chesterfield Road. I was sent to bring you to her."

Jane hesitated.

"Does the doctor know?" she asked.

"Oh, yes, miss."

Beyond the fact that he had a high, squeaky voice and was a seemingly inoffensive old man with a beard, she scarcely noticed the driver, and got into the trap without further demur. Peace urged on the pony, and she noticed, as a curious fact, that he avoided the main exit from the town, and took a bumpy side road which eventually joined the main road where Sheffield proper ended and the country began.

She was a little puzzled. Mrs Elford was a woman who told her all that she knew, and she had never made any reference to relations who lived outside of Sheffield.

"Who wrote the note?"

"The cook, miss," said the driver.

She asked him one or two questions, and when he again turned off to a side road she thought they were near their destination. What Peace was doing was to avoid the cross-roads where police patrols sometimes met.

"You're going a long way round," she said when they were again on the Derby road.

"The pony don't like traffic, miss. He's a bit shy, so I keep him to the quiet lanes."

They drew up before the cottage, and Peace drove the pony up the side path to the back of the house. He apologised for keeping her waiting while he unharnessed the horse and put him in the stable. This done, he led her back to the front of the house, unlocked the door and flung it open. The place was in darkness.

"Are there no lights?" she asked, and for answer found herself roughly pushed into the passage.

She stumbled and nearly fell. Before she could recover herself the heavy door was closed with a crash, and a voice which struck terror to her soul, said: "You'll have all the lights you want, my girl. Get in there and keep your mouth shut, or you'll be sorry."

31

"Miss Garden has been called away," reported the housekeeper. "Mrs Elford was taken very ill tonight and sent round for her."

Alan stopped himself in the act of hanging up his overcoat. "Mrs Elford ill?" he said incredulously. "Did she send for me?"

"No, sir, the letter was for Miss Garden."

He looked at her blankly.

"But I saw Mrs Elford this afternoon and she was perfectly well."

He went over the case in his mind. Though there was a possibility of a relapse, it was extremely unlikely. He put on his coat and hat again and went out. The house was no great distance from his own, and in ten minutes he was pulling the bell at his patient's residence. Mrs Elford was in the drawing-room, said the maid, evidently surprised to see him.

"Is Nurse Garden here?" he asked.

"Nurse Garden, sir? No. The missus is quite well."

"Let me see her," said Alan sharply.

He was shown into the drawing-room. Mrs Elford was sitting by the fire, a newspaper on her lap.

"No, I didn't send for the nurse, doctor. Why should I? I haven't felt as well for a long time."

"There must be some mistake," he said, and hurried home.

His housekeeper had made mistakes before, but now she was emphatic.

"Where is the letter that came for Miss Garden?"

"It's in her room, I think."

"Let me have the key."

He ran across the yard, flew up the steps, and, opening the door, lit the gas. The letter and envelope were on the table. He took one glance and his heart almost stood still. He knew that writing; Jane should have known it. It was unmistakably the hand of Charles Peace.

"Do you want me, doctor?"

Dixon heard him running down the stairs.

"Yes; harness the bay and put him in the trap."

"Anything wrong, doctor?" Dixon came pattering down to the stables.

"Miss Garden's gone away, and I'm rather worried about her. Send the boy round to Sergeant Eltham's house and tell him I want him urgently. If he can't find him, we'll go to the station."

He returned to the house and closely questioned the frightened woman. She had nothing to tell him, except that she had found the letter in the letter-box and there had been a sharp rat-tat preceding it. She had looked out − this Peace had not noticed − but could see nothing except the lights of a trap on the other side of the road some distance away.

Then there flashed upon the doctor an earlier experience of Jane's: the groom with the steel-rimmed glasses and the pony cart, who had followed her. There was a hundred to one chance that there might be something in this.

Going up to his bedroom, he unlocked a drawer and took out a long-barrelled Service revolver, a relic of his army days. He broke the breech and loaded it. Peace would be an unfortunate man if he met Dr Alan Mainford that night.

Putting the revolver into his overcoat pocket, he came downstairs again. He could guess what had happened. Somebody had picked up the girl near the Elfords' house, in which case he would continue in the same direction she had taken, which was towards the south. Peace would hardly double back through the town, where the trap could be identified and traced.

If Madame Stahm were still in England there might be an explanation for the disappearance. He would have driven straight out to Brinley Hall and searched the place from basement to attic. But the Hall was shut up, its presiding genius had departed.

This could only be the work of Peace.

Baldy Eltham came in half-dressed. He had been sleeping after a day and a night's search for a wanted man. Alan told him the story briefly, and by this time the trap was at the door.

"You'd better call at the Central Station. It's going to be difficult to get any more men out on the job. The reserves are dead beat. You think it was Peace in the pony trap, do you? I've seen the man half a dozen times – wears a sort of dark green livery coat and a top hat with a cockade. I can't see any likeness to him, though. He's a cunning devil, and we know he does disguise himself."

They were only a few minutes at the station and then went back to the road in which Mrs Elford's house stood. They found a policeman who had seen the cart, and remembered seeing the nurse. Jane wore a long veil for a bonnet, and this was flying out behind her when the cart had passed the officer.

"We're on the right track, at any rate. We'll make for the Derby road."

They drove as far as the cross-roads, and here they had a check. Since the general alarm had been sent out for Peace, a mounted officer had been on duty day and night at this point. He had taken careful note of all the traffic, which was not considerable at this time of the night, but he had seen no trap answering the rough description they gave.

It was curious, but quite usual, that although the pony cart had been seen by a dozen different people, no two agreed as to its colour or shape. Baldy thought it was a dark blue; an officer at the station was equally sure it was varnished brown.

"We'll go on as far as Brinley," said Alan, and sent the long-striding bay flying along the hard road.

There were very few habitations, and these he noted as they passed.

"Who lives in that cottage?" He pointed with his whip.

"I don't know. It's been empty some time, then a gentleman took it some months ago – a Mr Gray."

Brinley drew blank, and here they had definite negative news. The place had been under observation by the county constabulary, and the man on duty almost opposite the entrance gates was very definite that nothing had entered or left that night.

"The gates were padlocked anyway, and there's no other way of reaching the house," he said.

Alan stopped at the local inn to water and rest the horse.

It was one o'clock in the morning when they got up into the trap and began their return journey.

32

Peace eyed the girl critically and admiringly. She was pale, but she showed none of the signs of fear he expected. She was looking at him intently, trying to pierce his disguise and reconstruct the evil face she knew.

She saw now how perfectly he had hidden every characteristic feature — except those glowing, animal eyes of his. Those she would have known anywhere in any disguise.

"What are you going to do?" she asked.

"I'm going to keep you here for a day or two, and see if we can persuade that doctor of yours to do me a little favour. Now, listen, miss. I'll do you no harm. I'll swear it on the Bible. I'm a gentleman. You do what I tell you and nowt will come of this. If you don't — well, I can only be hung once!"

There was some relief in this news. She was being held as hostage, then: he had no personal venom against her.

"Remember the time when you and me met, lass?" he asked.

He sat astride a chair, his arms resting on the back, feasting his eyes upon her.

"I said to her ladyship: 'That's a nice nuss you've got,' and I said to her: 'What about me taking her out for a stroll and showing her the sights of Sheffield?' "

She wished he wouldn't look at her so continuously. She turned her own eyes away, hoping to induce a relaxation of his scrutiny, but when she looked again he was still regarding her with that same steadfast, desiring stare.

"The doctor's sweetheart, ain't you? I heard him talking to you the other night. You didn't know I was there, but I was. Charles Peace is everywhere. A hundred pound reward for me, me girl, but they'll never take me. I'm too clever for them. Listen to that!"

He thumped his waistcoat and she heard the dull chink of money.

"The doctor! I could buy him up! Do you know what he did to me? Took a whip to me! And do you know why he did it? Because of my little joke about being your father." He chuckled. Mr Peace was in high spirits.

"What do you want of the doctor?" she asked.

"What do I want of the doctor?" he repeated. "Well, for one thing I want him to give me a little bottle of stuff that he's got in his poison cupboard. I tried to get it the other day."

She opened her eyes wide.

"The phial of chemicals that Carton gave him?"

He nodded eagerly.

"Have you seen it, miss?"

"No," she said. "But the doctor hasn't got it."

He smiled at this.

"Don't you tell me no lies! I know the doctor's got it. I tell you it's in his poison cupboard. I'd have had it, too, if that flat-footed copper hadn't come in."

"He hasn't got it," she insisted. "Carton called two or three days ago, and the doctor gave it to him."

He grinned again.

"That's comic, that is. Carton called, did he? Why, he wouldn't dare put his nose in Sheffield. I'd snuff him out! He knows what Charles Peace is."

"I tell you he called," she insisted desperately. "He came to pay back a sovereign the doctor had lent him to take him out of Sheffield on the night of the Banner Cross murder."

It was strange and terrible to think that she was sitting at that moment *vis à vis* the very murderer, the loathsome little man with a price on his head, and the scaffold looming before him.

Peace was impressed.

"You tell me the truth, my girl, or look out for yourself! If they catch me, I hang, and they can't hang me twice, can they, whatever I do? I could murder you, and they could still only hang me once – if they caught me. Not that I'm going to murder you – don't be frightened, love. You're better-looking than Kate, and you're a lady. I've always been partial to ladies. Now just you tell me about Carton, and don't tell no lies. A lady shouldn't tell no lies."

"He came to see Dr Mainford," she repeated, "to pay him back the money. The doctor drove him from Banner Cross to the station on the night of the murder. But perhaps you know that?"

He didn't know it, but this story fitted in with the remarkable rapidity of Carton's movements, which had enabled him to catch the last train to London.

"The doctor told him he still had the phial, that he was afraid of losing it, and asked him to take it back. He took it back."

"Where does Carton live?"

"I don't know – he's in London somewhere."

He looked at her suspiciously.

"I don't believe it. You're telling me this because you think I'll let you go."

He got up from his chair and, walking across to where she sat by the table, took her chin in his hand and lifted up her face to his.

"You're better-looking than Kate Dyson," he said. "You're a beauty."

The touch of her soft throat set him a-quiver. The dark eyes glowed like dull fire. To show fear now would be fatal: she pushed his hand aside gently.

"Mr Peace, why do you stay in this neighbourhood? You know there's a reward for you, and that the police are looking for you?"

"They don't know I'm here."

She nodded.

"They know. You left one of your cartridges behind in the doctor's dispensary."

He started at this.

"I dropped a cartridge, did I? Yes, I did an' all! Well, anybody might drop a cartridge. Who said it was mine?"

Was she talking too much, she wondered. She must risk that, make him think of his danger, of anything but her.

"Sergeant Eltham said it was the same kind of cartridge that had killed Mr Dyson – they know you're here; they've been searching the town for you. Why don't you go away?"

He grinned at this.

"Searching the town? And where was Charles Peace? Driving through the town as bold as brass! I got a policeman to hold my pony's head tonight – that'll make you laugh. A policeman looking for me, and he held the reins and I gave him sixpence for his trouble. No, nuss, you're staying here. I've got a nice little room for you, right up in the roof; you lay snug there till the morning and then you'll write a letter to the doctor and I'll get it sent to him."

She got up.

"Which is the way?" she said.

A room to herself gave her at any rate a fort to hold, flimsy or strong.

He took up the lighted lamp.

"Go first," he said, and she went ahead of him up the stairs, through the bedroom.

"Open that door."

She thought it was a cupboard, filled with old dresses, and he was flattered.

"I did that. Nobody would think there were stairs there. Push through the dresses, lass, and turn to the right."

She went up before him, stooping her head to avoid contact with the sloping ceiling.

"Here's your room. You stay here quiet."

He could not take his eyes off her.

"I'll leave you the lamp. There's another downstairs. I'll take the key out of that door." He leered at her. "Nobody's going to hurt you, lass, though I'd get no more for it. They can only hang a man once if he commits twenty-six million murders!"

She said nothing, and heard his retreating footsteps with heartfelt thankfulness.

There was a chair, a small washstand and a bed in the room. The water jug had been newly filled. She poured out a glass and, raising it to her lips with a trembling hand, drank eagerly.

The place was stuffy, airless. She looked round for a window, but there was none. Listening at the head of the stairs, she heard him go down to the ground floor. His heavy boots sounded hollowly on the bare boards. There was no time to be lost: she began to draw the bed across the room. The castors squeaked a little, and she paused, listening for some sound from below. She heard a voice singing: it was Peace, and he was singing a hymn!

Desperately she pulled at the bed. It ran readily across the floor, and she clamped the head of it against the closed door. But she knew a strong man could push it aside, and she must find something to keep it in position. The opposite wall was too far away, the articles of furniture too few to jam the door tight.

Searching the room, she found a hammer and a paper of nails lying on a shelf. Workmen had been here, and evidently the tool had been overlooked because of the height of the shelf. Then to her joy she found that the thick shelf was movable, and lifted it down. Fitting one end against the rails at the back of the bed, she began nailing the loose end into the floor. She had never used a hammer before, but her very terror gave her skill. She heard the clatter of feet on the stairs below, and worked frantically.

He was shouting at her, but she did not desist. It was a bungling job. If she had not used twice as many nails as were necessary she would have failed. His fist came hammering at the door.

"What's the row? What are you doing?"

He tried to open the door. The bed moved a fraction of an inch, but the board held in its place.

"Open the door and let me in!" he howled. "I gave you a chance. Now you're going to get what you asked for, my girl."

She waited, breathless, exhausted, leaning on the end of the bed and lending her weight to take the strain he was imposing on the barrier.

"Got the bed here, have you?…"

He poured out a volume of foulest threats. She, who had seen the worst of humanity, had never till then plumbed the depths of its vileness.

Presently he became calm.

"Open the door, miss. Don't be silly – I wouldn't hurt a hair of your head. You can trust old Charles Peace. I've never harmed a lady in my life. Don't get my temper up, miss – it'll be all the worse for you. I'll let you go. Will you open the door?"

"No," she said.

He expected her to scream, to be crying, to be broken by terror. The steadiness of her voice took him aback and to some extent calmed him.

"What's the use of being silly, miss?" he wheedled. "You can't sleep if I'm hammering on the door all night, can you? Put the bed back in its place and I'll let you have the key."

"Put it under the door," she said.

A long pause.

"Here it is, miss. Put your fingers under."

But she was not to be caught.

Another interregnum of silence.

"You don't think I can't get in, do you? Charlie Peace could go through a steel door: he's done it millions of times! I'll have the panels out of that before you can say Jack Robinson, and when I get in, me lady, you'll be sorry you was born."

He went downstairs again, and was gone a long time. He came back, and she heard the rasp of metal cutting wood, and after a while the bright end of a bit showed in one corner of the panel. Then the end of a thin saw thrust through, and as it did she struck it, breaking it off short. He howled his imprecations at her, threw his weight against the door, and for a moment she thought that the barrier would give way.

Again he went down, and was absent for an even longer time. He was searching the house for a hatchet, and when he failed to find one, continued his search in the stable. He found an axe with a rotten handle. It took him some time to improvise a new one with the help of a stable yard broom. Then she heard him coming up, and waited.

"Are you going to open the door?"

She did not answer.

Crash! The panel split under the impact of the axe head.

"Get aside if you don't want to be hurt!" he yelled, and struck again.

Not only the panel but the supporting frame splintered. There was an aperture wide enough for a man to scramble through. Beating down the jagged edges of the wood with the back of the axe, he wriggled through on to the bed.

The beard was gone, though stray hairs still clung to the bristle on his cheeks. Here was Charles Peace in all his ugliness, in all his menace. She could not mistake the message of his eyes, but she stood calmly in the centre of the room waiting for him.

Peace saw a woman subdued, ready for surrender, her hands hanging limply by her side. He never suspected the hammer that the folds of her dress concealed.

"Got you, me lady! You remember what I told you? They can only hang me once. You'll write that letter, and be glad to write that letter. You'll do it because you love me. Women get used to me – they dote on me…worship the ground I walk on."

He was coming towards her stealthily, cat-like, his long fingers curved like the paws of a wild animal.

"I like the looks of you," he went on huskily. "I've never seen a young lady I liked so much…you brought it on yourself…they can only hang me once."

With incredible swiftness she struck, turned sick as she heard the thud of the blow. Peace went down on his knees and sprawled forward on the floor, blood on his temple.

She dropped the hammer and leapt on to the bed. She had seen the cover that hid the skylight, and guessed that there was a window beyond. In a second she was on the bed, unbolted the cover and dropped it. She pushed up the circular window with such force that it fell back on the slates. She must have a light of some kind. The man was moving on the floor. She flew across the room and took the lamp, and, hastily snatching up a chair, planted it insecurely on the bed and mounted.

Peace was rising to his feet. She had not a second to lose. She pushed the lamp high over her head, and with a superhuman effort drew herself up onto the sloping roof. It was terribly steep; she could not possibly keep her foothold and the lamp, she thought. Her shoes slid on the damp tiles, and she kicked them off one by one, and, setting her teeth, scrambled up to the roof ridge.

It was a still night. The lamp flickered but did not go out. Somebody must see her – there must be neighbours.

The dark bulk of the man's head and shoulders came through the broken skylight. He was half mad with rage, and at the sight of him she screamed again and again. He scrambled up after her; his hands had almost grasped her dress when his nailed boots slid on the tiles and, but for their tripping the gutter, he would have fallen to the ground.

She made another attempt. She was screaming now – somebody would hear her. In his rage was terror. The nearest house was a mile away, but there might be somebody passing along the road. Something was coming. She saw two bright lights appear round the bend of the road, heard the beat of horse's hooves and waved the lamp frantically. At that moment Peace reached up and gripped her knee. She kicked herself free, but he grabbed at her ankle.

He made another attempt to reach the roof tree some distance from her, and began working his way along. He had not seen the cart, but suddenly he heard the sound of men's voices, and, looking down, saw the trap at the door and somebody leap out. There was only one thing to do: he slid down the roof towards the back of the house and caught the gutter in his hands. There was a crack; the cast-iron gutter broke, and he dropped into a bush. As he ran round the corner of the house he drew his revolver and fired point-blank at the man who barred him.

It was Baldy, and as he staggered back to avoid the consequences of a second shot, Peace flung past him. He reached the front garden when a pencil of flame leaped from the other corner of the house and a bullet whizzed so close to his face that he thought he had been hit. Screaming with terror and rage, he turned and fired at the second man, and an answering shot came back instantly.

There was only one hope: he dashed through the gate, banging it behind him. The restive horse was prancing at the sound of the shots. Peace was in the driver's seat in a second; the whip flopped down, and the maddened beast leaped forward.

Alan was not concerned about the escape. He was looking anxiously at the dark figure on the roof. The lamp had gone out: it had slipped from her hand and smashed; the fragments were at his feet.

"Is that you, Jane? Are you all right? Can you hold on until I get up?"

"Yes, I'm frightened, but I'm quite all right," came her reassuring voice. "But I can't get back the way I came."

"Is it possible to force the door or the window?"

Baldy, searching at the back of the house, found a ladder that reached to the height of the roof, and ran up. It was a nervous task in the darkness of the night, bringing the girl to earth. She was trembling in every limb; felt physically sick; and sat for ten minutes on the high stone doorstep of the cottage, her head on her hands, whilst Baldy went round and put the pony in the little cart.

By the time he was ready she had recovered.

"I feel I ought to faint. I suppose it's because I'm not what Mr Peace calls a lady."

"You're sure he didn't hurt you?" Alan was beside himself with anxiety.

She smiled.

"That is the one thing I'm quite sure about" she said.

All the way back to Sheffield he was cursing his bad marksmanship.

"The light was bad, and I'm out of practice, I suppose. There is no other excuse."

He would not allow her to go to the stable that night. Peace was quite capable of returning. He sent her up to his own room, and sat up for the rest of the night, waiting for Sergeant Eltham to report.

Alan's trap and his distressed bay had been found abandoned in a field near Mansfield, and the horse was being taken care of locally.

"There goes eighty guineas' worth of good horseflesh," said Alan; "the brute!"

He was not speaking of the horse.

The trains from Mansfield were being watched all down the line. A man answering the description of Peace had been seen near the station, but nobody seemed to have noticed whether he got on the train or not.

All day long false clues abounded, and the usual innocent citizens were placed under arrest or observation. For the second time Peace had entirely vanished. There was some interest when the body of a man was taken out of the Trent, and in many particulars the description tallied with the wanted murderer.

"We've sent a man down to identify him," said Baldy," but bless your heart, it's not Charlie! There's an old saying and a true one – a man who is born to be hanged will never be drowned – "

"I'm so tired of hearing that," said Alan. "He may probably never be arrested, but leave me the hope that he'll get drunk and fall into the canal!"

At the first opportunity he saw Jane Garden alone.

"You are staying in this house permanently, Jane," he said firmly. "And what's more, you're going to figure in the newspaper. 'After a brief honeymoon, Mr and Mrs Alan Mainford returned to their well-known surgery.' "

She smiled faintly at this; then a look of alarm came to her face.

"Do the newspapers know – about last night?"

He shook his head.

"For some reason or other the police are not anxious to advertise the fact that they have had Charles Peace as a close neighbour," he said drily.

33

A letter arrived at Berne, via the National Bank. It was in a strange handwriting, and the composition was more literate than was usual.

DEAR MADAME (it began), I am Charles Peace, who you know served you faithfully and suffered cruelly in your loyal service. Dear Madame, I am in a terrible position owing to the way I have looked after your interests, and I can't get any money because of the title deeds of the cottage. Dear Madame, could you send the title deeds to me in the name of Gray, and I can get them transferred to another gentleman who will pay me well for them, because I am in very sad circumstances and starving to death because of the way I looked after your interests, turning out in the middle of the cold nights to play the fiddle when you was feeling poorly, and all the trouble I got into with the police because of you know who being killed by accident which was not design, which I had no intention of killing the man, because nothing is further from my thoughts than taking human life which is sacred according to the Bible I honour. Dear Madame, if you will send the title deeds to a friend of mine, Mr Thompson, 5 East Terrace, Evelina Road, Peckham, London, he will see that I get justice done to me which I have never had since I was a boy owing to the perjury of the police which as you know are always ready to swear away a man's life for a few shillings. And that nurse turned against me. She is a low woman as you can't deny when I tell you she is carrying on with the doctor and brazen about it. She has sweared my life away and your life away too, and the doctor tried to murder me and the police tried to murder me by firing arms at me which it is against the law for the police to carry firearms and they have kept it quiet or the Government would have had his coat off his back. It's a bad day for England if police carry firearms because they are not trained to use them and all sorts of accidents would happen as you will see from the piece of newspaper I have put in this letter when the Home Secretary said in the Houses of Parliament that the police must not use firearms and it is against public policy. I had to come away from Sheffield for my life and left behind the money which you so humbly gave me, and I am now destitute and starving and God knows what will become of me. But He looketh after the fallen sparrows and comforteth them. If you have Bibles in Switzerland you will see this. God knows how I shall live through today and tomorrow. I am weak with want of food, so, dear Madame, please send me the title deeds before the end of the month because you are my last hope and if the police take me, which they'll be clever to do, I shall have to tell them everything about Mr Lamonte and the goings on at the house which I have seen with my own eyes and can bring witnesses. Is there any justice? No, there is none. Oh, God, who seest thy servant inflicted by thy enemies, lift up thy hand and help thy humble servant.

> Yours obediently and respectfully,
> CHARLES PEACE.
> J THOMPSON.

Mr Peace, remembering in time that, being a foreigner, Madame Stahm was probably a Roman Catholic, had drawn a neat crucifix with emanations.

Madame Stahm read through this epistle, glanced at the newspaper cutting, and handed the letter back to her husband.

"Tell him to go to the devil," she said.

Mr Baumgarten would have addressed himself to this task with considerable pleasure if he had not glanced at the back of the second foolscap sheet and seen the postscript:

DEAR MADAM,
The cristals are safe. The doctor gave them to Carton and I am looking for Carton. You will hear from me by return of post.

C P

"Do you believe him?" asked Baumgarten.

"Do you?" she challenged.

He pursed his lips.

"I don't know. I think I do. Possibly it would be safest to send him a little money — a thousand francs."

She was not especially eager to send money to anybody.

"We haven't heard from the reptile for a year — more than that, Peter. If the crystals could be recovered they would have been in his hands by now."

"Nevertheless, my dear, I should send him a thousand francs," said Baumgarten.

He could afford to be judicial in the matter, because it was not his thousand francs.

Mr Peace received the letter addressed to Mr Thompson, because at the moment he was Mr Thompson. He was not starving: he was eating a large steak in a comfortably furnished room. He had taken kindly to his new life in London, as his wife had been pleasantly complaisant. There was a Mrs Thompson in addition to a Mrs Peace, who called herself Ward. She had appeared out of the blue, a bold throw-back to pre-Dyson days, an especially well-favoured lady in the matter of looks, being blonde and winsome; more to the point, comfortable, in the sense that she and Mrs Peace — the real Mrs Peace, who lived in the basement — were on the friendliest terms.

The little man with the dark face was popular in the neighbourhood; attended a local church; made and mended kites for small boys; manufactured toys of all kinds and distributed them gratuitously. He had a kindly word for everybody. His neighbours said of him that he was quite the gentleman, which had been said before by witnesses who had a better opportunity of testing his gentility.

On the whole he was pleased with himself, though there had been one or two irritating circumstances that had occurred since his arrival in London. For example, the man Harbron, who had been sentenced to death for the murder of Police Constable Cock, had been reprieved by a pusillanimous Home Secretary. By this reprieve he had robbed Peace of a permanent illustration that justice sometimes miscarries. He could cite the case if ever misfortune overtook him; if necessary, plead guilty to the crime to prove his point. He felt that the reprieve robbed him of some importance, and was glad that he had not followed his inclination, which was to go to Manchester when the petition for reprieve was being circulated and put his name to it. He would have done this, because he was quite certain that the petition would produce no effect. Petitions never did. The petitions he had sent to the Home Secretary from Dartmoor, Chatham, Wakefield, a dozen prisons; the heartrending appeals he had made to the official heart, and which probably had never gone beyond the cunning governor of the prison, were proof of this. The world was full of injustice: he used to enlarge on this theme when he had company at No. 5 East Terrace, for he often gave musical evenings and played on a Spanish guitar, to the delight of his guests.

There were people who thought he had once had something to do with the law, he was such an authority on the subject, and this surmise was so near the truth that he never denied it.

They were broadminded people in Peckham; they did not object to the touch of colour in his blood, for how else might he attain to that swarthy complexion? He was not above admitting relationship with African kings. Generally it was believed that he was a much travelled and widely-read man. He was thinner than he had been, wore glasses on occasions, and the deep wolf eyes had acquired a benevolent glint.

People liked Mrs Thompson very much; they did not like the faded Mrs Ward, who was believed to be a poor relation of the Thompsons.

Mrs Thompson was pretty, had fair hair and a good figure. If she had any drawbacks it was her weakness for strong drink. Therein she followed the example of other ladies, whom Peace had known, and who also found consolation and forgetfulness through the same medium.

"Mr Thompson" was an active man. He did a great deal of night work; sometimes left home as late as ten o'clock and did not return till the morning. The number of petty burglaries in New Cross, Lewisham and Camberwell showed an alarming increase. Scarcely a week passed but there was an account of them in the Sunday newspapers.

Peace folded the thousand-franc note with a grunt of satisfaction and put it in his waistcoat pocket.

"What's that?" asked his pretty companion.

"Ask no questions and you'll hear no lies," said Peace.

It was true, as he had said, that he had not lost hope of finding Carton. In point of fact he had seen the traitor, but too late to accost him. It was on London Bridge Station; their two trains stood parallel on either side of one platform. The train in which Peace was moved out first, and as he was passing the last carriage he saw a man, smoking a pipe and reading a newspaper. It was Carton: there was no doubt about it. It was a Woolwich train, he noted, and for a week after he hung about the station in the hope of seeing his sometime partner again. Luck was against him, and though he paid many visits to the station at the same hour, he caught no further glimpse of the villain who, rightly or wrongly, he decided had betrayed him. It was not outside the range of possibility that Carton had also seen him.

He spent quite a lot of time in Woolwich and Greenwich, hoping to pick up his quarry; but Carton had vanished. He was in London, and in south-east London. Peace had infinite faith in his luck. All would come right. He added to the petitions he offered to his Maker one very important item: that he should meet Carton and that Carton should be reasonable.

He had had one or two good hauls at railway stations, absent-mindedly picking up other people's baggage and carrying it away; but he was checked in this new branch of activity when he witnessed a clever arrest for this particular crime, and realised that a special staff of detectives had been turned on to watch the luggage thieves. It was too dangerous, especially in London and in daylight. He went back to the easier business of housebreaking; made one or two coups that were quite valuable, and one or two that proved very troublesome and yielded little profit.

He had established contact with a fair-dealing fence in East Greenwich, but he was too wily a man to be content to dispose of his stolen property through one channel, and he made new connections in places as wide apart as Poplar is from Hammersmith.

Once, returning from an unsuccessful foray in the early hours of the morning, he had been stopped by a policeman and summarily searched in the street. Fortunately, he carried no housebreaking tools. There was an early morning coffee shop in a side street near New Cross, where you could leave a bag and be sure that no prying eyes would search it. His indignation at this outrage against the liberty of the subject expressed itself in a complaint personally presented to the nearest police station. The delinquent officer would have been reprimanded, but Peace generously pleaded for him and excused his zeal on account of his youth.

Thereafter this particular policeman always touched his helmet when Mr Thompson passed. Peace got more satisfaction out of this than he would have done if a gold medal had been pinned on his bosom for spotless integrity.

Sometimes his operations carried him far afield. He liked to indulge in travel, and on a certain Sunday morning he was sniffing the air of Brighton as he strolled leisurely along the front, when a newly-married couple on their honeymoon drove past. The girl turned with a little cry. She couldn't be mistaken.

"What is it, darling?" asked Alan, looking back.

He saw that her face had gone white.

"Aren't you well?"

"No, no. Only I thought I saw somebody I knew – somebody who is dead."

She lied recklessly, for she remembered that spiteful snub-nosed revolver which never left the little man's pocket, and it was the second day of her honeymoon and she wanted life and many bright years with the man who sat at her side.

He had a trick of reading her thoughts, and when they got back to the hotel from their drive: "You saw Peace?" he said, and she nodded. "On the front?"

"Yes, darling. He was walking – I am sure it was he. Don't go and look – please, please!"

"I do not intend joining any more search parties after that little villain," he laughed, "but I think the police should know."

He sent a note round to the inspector, who was at first sceptical, and then, when he had interviewed Jane, very much alive to the possibilities of a capture.

Mr Thompson had not seen the girl and was quite oblivious of the recognition. Later in the afternoon he was having tea in a flamboyant restaurant, when he heard somebody say: "Did you hear that Charles Peace has been seen in Brighton? It's a fact – a bobby told me."

Peace paid his bill and left the restaurant at his leisure. He went back to London via Shoreham and Littlehampton. He was alarmed and worried. Who had recognised him? His curiosity was piqued, and curiosity was a vice in a man who needed no embellishment of his viciousness. It couldn't be an inhabitant of the seaside town, because he had never been there before. It must have been a visitor, and he remembered seeing on the bookstall at the station a visitors' list. He had thought at the time what a joke it would be if somebody had put in "Charles Peace".

A few days later the bookstall clerk at Brighton station received a request for a copy of the visitors' list, two penny stamps being enclosed. Mr Thompson settled himself down to an enjoyable evening, scanning the long columns of names. Presently he found what he wanted: "Mr and Mrs Alan Mainford".

There were two surprises here. He looked up over his glasses at his companion.

"He's made an honest woman of her after all."

"Who?" asked Mrs Thompson.

"A certain party," said Peace. "I used to keep company with her, but she drank too much for me."

So he had married the nurse, and they were the people who had given him away. For all they cared he might have been in a police cell now, facing the certainty of the gallows. A cold rage possessed him. Honeymooning...she probably had to marry him in a hurry. He brooded on this, became an assiduous collector of south coast visitors' lists and located them at Bognor. Peace took an afternoon train, arrived at Bognor after dark, with no especial plan of campaign in his head, but with a general bias towards wickedness.

It was a poky little place, with scarcely any front, and few people were visible, for the sky was overcast and a chill wind blew down from the north-east. He knew their hotel, and he kept watch opposite the entrance, and later in the evening saw them both come out and drive away. He waited till midnight, but they did not return, and he made friends with an outside porter.

"Mr and Mrs Mainford? Oh, they've gone away to London – left two hours ago."

"I didn't see any baggage."

"That went on to the station before them."

Peace trudged in search of a lodging, and on his way threw into the sea the small bottle of vitriol that he had purchased at a local chemist's.

Gloat over him, would they? Laugh at him, sitting in the condemned cell and waiting for Marwood to come in? Everybody knew what Marwood did: it was the talk of the prisons, common gossip. Every man discharged from a convict prison told the same story. There was Marwood, stocky, broad-shouldered, bearded, the dangling straps in one hand and offering the other.

"I am very sorry I have got to do this, but it's my duty and I hope you will forgive me."

And the prisoner saying: "Will it hurt?" and Marwood saying he would make it very comfortable for him.

That was the kind of morning this nurse wanted to give him. His heart was bitter with hate. All the way up to London the next morning he thought out ingenious methods by which they could be brought to ruin. Suppose they had a baby? They were bound to have one some day, and in the morning they'd wake up and find it gone, and a note in the cradle saying: "Charles Peace never forgives." Probably he'd throw it in the river or under a steam-roller, or they might never know what happened to it. He'd give it to gipsies. And you know what gipsies did to children.

He had wasted two good days at a time when the thousand francs were nearly exhausted, and the profits from his evening excursions were abnormally low.

On a Saturday evening he liked to frequent some busy marketing place. His old profession came back to him readily, and his fingers were as nimble as ever they were. He could take a purse out of a woman's back pocket and she'd never know she'd lost it. He made one or two good "gets" – fat purses, crammed with the week's wages, which women had taken out to provide for the week-end marketing. Working women mostly. It was his practice to justify himself, and his main justification was: "This'll teach them a lesson," though what the lesson was he never explained, even to himself.

He was in High Street, Deptford, one night; he had worked Broadway, and had turned into the crowded market street, which looked full of possibilities. He saw a stoutish man walking in front of him, smoking a pipe which he filled from a silver tobacco box, and the tobacco box went into the man's side jacket pocket. It wasn't worth much, but every little helped. Peace passed him, glancing away towards the street and dropped his hand into the other's pocket nonchalantly. His fingers had closed on the box when his wrist was gripped.

"Hi! What's the game?"

He turned and stared at his victim.

"Oh, my God!" said Mr Carton, his jaw dropping.

In a moment Peace had recovered his presence of mind.

"Come down this side street; I want to talk to you," he said.

212

Carton obeyed meekly. He, too, was conscious of that revolver which never left Peace day or night.

He lived in terror of Peace and his ruthlessness; more dangerous now, with the rope hanging over his head.

"That is a very pleasant surprise, I must say."

They had reached a dark, narrow and ill-lit street, and Peace had stopped him against a wooden gate that formed the entrance to a back yard.

"I – I didn't have time to see you," stammered Carton. "Lord! You're changed, Mr Peace. I couldn't believe it was you at first. What have you done with your face?"

"Never mind my face. Where's that bottle?"

Carton licked his dry lips.

"It's like this – " he began.

"Where's that bottle? Don't shilly-shally about. I'm a desperate man, Carton. I'm starving because of you. Where's the bottle?"

"It's up at the house." The man blurted out the truth.

"What house?"

"Where I'm working."

"Where is that?

There was a second's hesitation, which was a second too long.

"In Lewisham."

"You're a liar. What's it doing there?"

"The doctor gave it to me," said the man earnestly. "I didn't want it. I asked him to take charge of it because it was valuable. I might have thrown it away but I wouldn't do a dirty trick like that on you, Mr Peace, so I asked the doctor to look after it, and then when I went up to Sheffield to pay him some money I owed him, he handed it to me back. I knew sooner or later you'd turn up, and I dursn't get rid of it, so I gave it to the governor to mind."

Peace drew a long breath.

"If I did the right thing, do you know what I'd do to you? I'd shoot you right through the heart. If I wasn't a Christian man who never took life, which the Maker of all things giveth to us, I'd kill you, you hound!"

Carton was shaking with terror. He saw a tragic end to an evening which he had hoped would finish more pleasantly, for he had a young lady, contemplated matrimony in three rooms with the use of a kitchen, and all his pleasant dreams were to be wiped out – unless –

"I can get the bottle for you. The governor's away on holiday just now, and I don't exactly know where it's kept; but I swear to you, Mr Peace – "

"My name's not Peace. Don't call me that. Call me Ward. And don't swear – take not the Name in vain, Carton. Was you brought up as a heathen or wasn't you? Where do you live?"

Courage came to Carton with a vision of the fresh-faced girl he was to meet that night.

"I shan't tell you," he said doggedly. "If you want to shoot, start shooting!"

A certain reckless courage came struggling through his fear. His voice grew loud. A man and a woman, passing on the opposite side of the street, turned and stopped in anticipation of a fight – a form of entertainment which costs nothing to see and provides a topic of conversation for a week.

"Shut up, will you!" hissed Peace. "Who's going to shoot you? I'm a reasonable man, and you're a reasonable man. I forgive everybody who's done me harm. When can you get the bottle?"

"In a couple of weeks," said the man sullenly.

"You needn't be afraid of me knowing who your boss is," said Peace. "I could go up and tell him the kind of man you are, all about your low life and the time you've had – "

"And perhaps you'd tell him about yourself?" said Carton, exulting in his new-found courage. "That would do you a fat lot of good, for him to know you was Charlie Peace!"

Mr Peace restrained himself with an effort.

"I tell you I wouldn't go to him and split on you."

"It wouldn't matter if you did," said the other defiantly. "When I took this job I told him everything, except that I'd made friends with a murderer."

Peace winced at this. That any man should be ashamed of his acquaintance with him was an unpardonable affront.

"Where do you live?" he asked again.

"Find out," said the other.

"I'll find out," growled Peace. "There's nothing I couldn't find out. I'll track and trail you wherever you go. I'll search every house in Greenwich" – he was looking at the man – "and Blackheath – ah, that's where you live, my boy! I'll track and trail you there, and I'll never leave you!"

"You can go to hell," said Carton, shook off the detaining hand, and stalked majestically back to the High Street.

34

Peace waited until he had turned the corner, crossed the High Street quickly, and, taking cover behind two stout women who were moving in his direction, kept the man under observation.

There was a possibility – a grave possibility that if Carton was too much terrified he might blab. The man walked on. He had already located his shadow, and took a bold step. A policeman was standing under the railway arch, jotting down notes in his book. Carton walked up to him.

"Excuse me, sir, could you tell me where Evelyn Road is?"

The policeman pointed. The accusing finger moved in the direction of the alarmed spy. Peace turned and walked quickly away. He was taking no chances. Carton might have been pointing him out; on the other hand, he might have been bluffing. Peace had often gone to a policeman to impress somebody who was suspicious of him.

From a safer place of observation he watched. The constable and Carton parted. The ex-butler was moving in his direction. Peace waited in the cover of a side road for his former companion to appear. He waited ten minutes; there was no sign of Carton. But it was too late: the man had slipped into Deptford Road Station in time to catch a Greenwich train.

That was where he lived then – Blackheath! He cursed himself for not having given the man an address to which he could send the crystals. Probably it was true that he couldn't get them. And now, if he found them, how could he pass them on to their lawful owner? That was a mistake: Peace was magnanimous enough to acknowledge it to himself. The next time he met Carton he must adopt another attitude.

For weeks afterwards he haunted Blackheath, always by night; but Carton stayed indoors after dark: he knew that that was the only time his enemy would be abroad. He had spoken the truth: his employer was away in France, and the phial was locked up somewhere perhaps in the safe.

The little man's luck was out. Again he was stopped by the police and this time taken to a police station and searched. It happened in Peckham High Street on a Saturday night. There had been some complaints about pocket-picking, and special plain-clothes officers had been detailed for observation. Peace had time to drop the purses which would have convicted him behind a barrel of meal outside a corn chandler's. When he was arrested he was volubly innocent. He had money, plenty of money, in his pocket, for he had emptied the purses as fast as he had taken them.

There was nobody to identify one sovereign from another, or one hard-earned florin from its neighbour.

"The papers are going to hear about this," said Peace, quivering with indignation as he was escorted to the door. "Here am I, a respectable householder, dragged through the streets by a lot of common coppers and boys hooting at me! How can I go to chapel tomorrow and face my fellow-men and my Maker?"

"It's very unfortunate," said the tactful inspector, "but you must understand, Mr Thompson, that there has been a lot of pocket-picking on Saturday nights in this neighbourhood, and we're here to protect the poor as well as the rich."

"And punish the wrong-doer," said Peace. "That's the text – 'Protect the children of the poor and punish the wrong-doer.'"

The inspector, startled to discover that he had been quoting Scripture with the same unconsciousness as Molière's gentleman spoke prose, offered his personal apologies.

"If you like to make a case, and submit a written statement to me, I will see that it goes forward to the proper quarter," he said. "Our men are only doing what they think is right, and they were under the impression that you behaved in a suspicious manner. The woman said she brushed against you – "

"A common woman like that! I wouldn't even brush against her," said Peace. "I'm a gentleman, as I can prove…"

He went home, bristling with wrath, and arrived at East Terrace in time to hand his wife two sovereigns to do her Saturday's marketing before the shops closed – Sunday morning marketing he would never countenance.

"Mind where you keep that two pounds," he warned her as she went out. "There's a lot of pickpockets down by Rye Lane."

He gave up his night searches for Carton and went out to look by day, choosing Sunday. He sauntered from morning till night up and down the strip of asphalt pavement which fringes Blackheath, and it was on the third Sunday that he found his man. He was walking with a young lady who was beautifully attired, and from their attitude one to the other he gathered that they were something more than friends.

"Old enough to be her father," he muttered.

All the afternoon he dogged them, through Greenwich Park to the Observatory, down the hill to the Naval College, and along to the church gates. Here were eating-houses, where you could buy a good tea with shrimps for sixpence.

He waited patiently until they had satisfied their gross appetites, picked them up when they boarded a horse tram, and followed them through Greenwich to the foot of Blackheath Hill, where they alighted. He had gone up to the top roof of the tramcar, though it was not at all outside weather. He waited till their backs were turned, stepped off the noisy vehicle while it was in motion, and followed them up Blackheath Hill, past a police station with which he was to be better acquainted some day.

At the top of the hill they parted. Carton kissed her, raising his hat in a gentlemanly way as he did so.

"Old enough to be her father," said the disgusted Peace.

She wasn't a bad little piece, either. He had a good look at her as she passed him. He liked the way she walked, and wondered what her name was. Then he turned to follow his quarry, who strolled along, twirling a lah-de-da walking-stick – an elaborate piece of acting on the part of Carton, for, whilst Peace was observing the girl, the ex-butler had recognised him and knew that he had been followed.

He had made acquaintance with a footman at a house in St John's Park. He knew the family were out that day, because he had been invited to tea. It was too late for tea, but not too late to deceive Mr Peace. Unconcerned, he strolled through the gates, mounted the steps and pulled the bell, and, as luck would have it, it was his friend who opened the door to him.

"Hullo! You're late. I thought you weren't coming."

"Do you mind me stepping in? There's a man been following me all the afternoon."

The footman closed the door on him.

"Do you owe him money?" he asked naturally. "Or is he a girl's father or something?

"I owe him a bit of money."

"Come on down in the kitchen," said the footman.

Peace made a note of the address: No. 2 St John's Park. It looked a good house, too – a place you could "do" without a lot of trouble. There were menservants, but they did not matter. It was the woman servants that gave all the trouble, screaming and squawking all over the place.

He came up two nights in succession to reconnoitre the house. Yes, it was easy enough, but where would the bottle be kept, supposing Carton had been speaking the truth? Apparently he himself didn't know. He resolved to get in touch with the man, but that was more easily planned than accomplished. Again he waited on the Sunday, but this time he took another post of observation – the foot of Blackheath Hill. He reasoned, knowing something of his fellow-men, that Carton would reverse his walk and start from the Blackheath Hill end and finish through the park, and he was not wrong.

Carton saw him when he mounted the tram, and, excusing himself to his young lady, climbed up on to the top.

"What are you following me about for?" he demanded truculently.

Peace was unusually mild.

"If I knew where I could write to you, or what name you was going under – "

"Carton is the name I'm going under," said Carton. "It may seem a bit funny to you, a man going under his own name."

"I know where you live, but I'm not going to call on your governor. All I want to know is, speaking as man to man: where does he keep that bottle?"

"It's in the safe, or else it's in one of the drawers of his desk. He's a gentleman in the City – keeps a lot of papers in his desk. They're always locked up. I shouldn't think it's in the safe, because I remember his opening a drawer and putting it in the desk when I gave it to him."

"That's all I want to know," said Peace. "Why the trouble? Why the lack of harmony? I'm not going to ask you for it; I'm not going to wait till this man comes back; I'm just going to take it. It ain't much to ask you to leave the kitchen door unfastened, is it?"

"You can go on asking me," said the exasperated Carton, "till you're blue in the face, till you choke yourself, till you drop dead on this very tram, and then I wouldn't do it. If you want to get into the house, get in, but don't ask me to help you. That's my last word to you."

He got up abruptly and went downstairs. His indignation seemed real. But there was, working at the back of Carton's mind, a counter plan, which involved a supreme act of treachery, though he owed nothing to Peace but considerable disquietude of mind.

He had been promoted to butler at the modest establishment which he managed. It was nearly half a mile away from the house at St John's Park; it was on the same police beat, and as butler and dispenser of culinary favours he was friendly with the policeman, even with the sergeant, who sometimes dropped in to drink a forbidden glass of beer.

The sergeant either dropped in or popped in on Saturday night. There was a subtle distinction between the two acts. On the Monday night a sergeant popped in, which meant that he was not really on duty, and was at liberty to pay a friendly call, and with him Carton discussed the vulnerable character of certain houses on the heath.

"There have been a few burglaries, but none up here," said the sergeant, "or next to none."

To Carton's credit it must be said that he had taken the sergeant and the divisional inspector into his confidence regarding his own past, and the friendliness of the police force may be better understood from this fact.

"You know what I am, sergeant." They were sitting alone in the kitchen, but Carton lowered his voice. "I've been an old lag, but I know a better game. A lot of other old lags don't believe I've turned over a new leaf, and I get to hear things. It's not for me to give away people I've worked on the same landing with, but you're either on the side of the law or you're against it. Correct me if I'm wrong."

"There never was a truer statement," said the sergeant earnestly, and added: "Have you heard anything?"

"I've heard a lot." Carton was very deliberate. "From information received – no names, no pack drill – I've got an idea there's going to be a job done at St John's Park. Number Two is the number, but I can't tell you when."

The sergeant jotted down the information in his notebook.

"I don't want to be brought into this – "

"Naturally," said the sergeant; "and you won't be brought in."

They shook hands solemnly when they parted.

Did Peace have some premonition of coming danger? For the next six months he shunned Blackheath, confining himself to small burglaries in the middle-class districts that surround Dulwich.

He had made a survey of the West End, where at one time he thought good pickings could be found, but had learned, almost at a glance, the insuperable difficulties which confronted a single-handed worker. The place was too well lit; the mewses which form the backs of the big houses were too densely populated. It was impossible to get in with the servants. He confined himself to the "cook-parlourmaid houses" in the vicinity of Lordship Lane. But there was too much electro-plate there, and many of the imposing silver bowls that decorated front drawing-rooms were so thin that you could bend them with your finger. There was a lot of German silver about, too, and German silver is so called because it is not silver and was made in Birmingham.

Always at the back of his mind was that house on Blackheath, which had been rigorously watched and guarded for three months, and which was in a condition of normal unprotection now.

The sergeant was gently reproachful.

"You made me look a bit of a fool, Carton, but I know your intentions were good," he said.

"I tell you I'm right," said Carton, stung to self-defence. "And what's more, sergeant, when you capture this fellow you're going to catch a man that'll make you famous."

"Nobody would make me famous," said the sergeant, who had been long enough in the force to have lost his illusions. "The inspector'll get a bit of the credit, but Scotland Yard will get most of it. You wouldn't like to tell me who it is?"

For one second Carton was tempted to tell the truth, and then he remembered the revolver.

"No, I wouldn't. But I can tell you he's armed – never goes about without a shooter."

The sergeant laughed.

"There's not many of them about, since Charles Peace got out of the country," he said, putting into words the prevalent police delusion.

Carton said nothing. He felt hurt at the inactivity of Peace. Had he lost his nerve, or was he suspicious? This thought made him sweat. He took to meeting his young lady in unusual places, which involved a considerable outlay in railway fares.

Every small man he met in the street was Peace; every noise he heard at night was the stealthy footstep of an armed and resentful burglar. Peace became an obsession to him, kept him awake at night, robbed him of sleep and comfort. His young lady noticed and remarked on the change.

"You're not half as loving as you used to be," she complained, and hinted that there were as good fish in the sea as ever came out, which Carton had known all along.

Relief came unexpectedly, violently. Peace came to Blackheath, with no intention of burgling unless there was a fog, and there was no fog. He decided to make a third reconnaissance of the house. It was very quiet, and he passed into the garden and round to the back of the house without difficulty. He could hear no sound...such an opportunity might never offer again.

He did not realise then that the back of the house was visible from the avenue which connects Blackheath with St John's Park; and, even if he had, the complete quietude of the night – it was nearly two o'clock in the morning – would have encouraged him.

He took a jemmy from his pocket and made an attempt upon a window. It yielded readily and without sound. He found himself in the drawing-room, and, lighting a small dark lantern, his own invention, he made a quick survey of the valuables. There was no sense in devoting all his attention to a search for the crystals.

He took such articles as came to his hand, slipped them into his pocket and made his way to another room, where there was a desk. He had hardly started on this when he heard the sound of voices on the lawn outside. A policeman had seen his light from the avenue, and, summoning a brother constable, was crossing the lawn. Peace saw them and heard the front door bell ring. He thought he could still escape unobserved and, stuffing his jemmy into his trousers' pocket, he jumped to the ground and ran. He misjudged the distance.

The man at the front of the house came round to intercept him. He made a dive at the little man, but Peace fought him off. Turning, he doubled towards the bottom of the garden, the policeman at his heels. Suddenly Peace turned and his hand shot out. He was holding a revolver, clearly seen in the moonlight.

"Keep off, or by God I'll shoot you!" snarled Peace.

The policeman's reply was not heroic.

"You'd better not," he said.

Before the words were out, Peace fired – once, twice, three times. By a miracle the constable was not hit. He leaped at his man, and Peace fired again. With his left hand he struck at the burglar, knocking down the pistol hand with his right. There was a fifth shot: this time it took effect, passing through the policeman's arm. Nevertheless he would not release his grip of his prisoner, and flung him to the earth. The policeman doubled up his arm, gripped the revolver, still strapped to the burglar's wrist, and struck him on the head with the weapon. Then, turning him face down, he held him till assistance came.

Peace was in a fury. He spat venom at his captor, but presently consented to go quietly, and, escorted by three officers, including the wounded man, trotted down Blackheath Hill with his captors.

Carton had heard the shots and had leaped out of bed. One, two, three, he counted, then a fourth, and a fifth, and no more. He was terrified, but he must know the truth. Drawing on his clothes and shoes, he raced out of the house on to the moonlit wilderness of the heath.

If it was Peace! He ran on, breathing strenuously towards St John's Park, and arrived as the prisoner and the three officers came out through the gate. He saw half-clad servants following at a distance and learned the truth.

"An ugly little man. He looked like a nigger... Shot a policeman."

"Dead?" gasped Carton.

"No, he's only wounded. Come along, I'll show you the blood on the grass."

People always seemed to be showing Carton blood on the grass, blood that Peace had shed. He declined the invitation.

Returning to his house, he dressed more completely and walked down to Blackheath Hill, hoping to find an officer he knew. It happened that a friend of his was on duty at the desk, and showed him, with some pride, the revolver with the strap attached. He recognised it instantly as Peace's pistol.

"Would you like to see him?" asked the sergeant. "The inspector has gone up to the house, and if you promise not to let on I'll give you a squint at him."

He took a key and opened a heavy door, and Carton found himself on familiar ground: the corridor of the cells. Stopping before one of the closed doors, the sergeant moved a peep-hole aside and beckoned his companion.

At first the shaking man hardly dared look. At last he summoned up his courage and put his eyes to the observation hole. A man lay on the hard plank, a thin blanket over his legs. There was no doubt about his identity – it was Peace, and he was sleeping as calmly as if he were in his own bed. That in spite of the wounds which lay under the heavy bandages about his head.

Carton tiptoed out into the charge room.

"Never let on I showed him," said the sergeant again. "He's a tough customer. Thank God there are not many like him!"

"What is his name?"

"Ward – that's the name he gave. Usually they are Smiths, but this one's Ward. Ever seen him before?"

It was on the tip of the man's tongue to tell the truth, but such was the terror that Peace inspired that the words would not come. He'd get a long stretch for burglary and would be out of the way for years. Shooting a copper, too – that was serious. Better he went down for that than for the Banner Cross job. Carton might be dragged into that – you never knew what lies Peace would tell.

"Ever seen him before?" asked the sergeant.

"No," said Carton.

He went back to his house, treading on air; up the steep hill, across the heath he swaggered. Going into the kitchen he brewed himself a cup of tea, found notepaper and envelopes and wrote to his young lady.

"Meet me at the usual place on Sunday," ran the letter. "The gentleman I spoke about that I didn't want to see me because he wanted me to marry his daughter, which I would never do, because you're the only true love of my life, has gone away for good."

There were five pages more, one of which was entirely covered with crosses. Carton was nearing fifty, had been the inmate of several prisons, had narrowly escaped penal servitude, but his sentiment endured; and anyway, crosses are almost a relaxation to draw.

35

Peace woke in the morning, blinked round the cell and swung his feet to the ground. John Ward – that was his name. No address. If they wanted to find out where he lived, let 'em find out. That was what they were paid for.

The gaoler brought him in coffee and bread and butter.

"I'm entitled to two ounces of bacon," said Peace, "and I want my rights."

"You've been in before, have you?"

"That's nothing to do with you. I'm entitled to two ounces of bacon – "

"A prisoner on remand is entitled to a little extra," said the gaoler patiently. "But you're not on remand. You'd better wait till tomorrow; you'll be on remand then all right, and you'll be eating government food for a good many years, you old so-and-so."

Peace scowled at him.

"As a bird is known by his note, so is a man by his conversation," he said reproachfully.

The gaoler's reply was unprintable.

The prisoner sipped the weak coffee, munched at the bread and butter and calmly surveyed the situation. There was a solicitor he had consulted in reference to the cottage property. He must communicate with him without delay. Hannah must know and Mrs Thompson, who had enough money to last her for a few months, must surrender a little – all of it if necessary.

Shooting with intent to murder – that was the charge. He might get a seven for that, or perhaps less. It depended on the judge. He hoped this man Hawkins wouldn't try him. Hawkins' reputation ran through the gaols of England. He was inhuman, without even the lesser bowels of compassion. Men like Hawkins made criminals; every criminal agreed on this. He had a dog in court, which he kept under his feet all through a trial, which in itself was unlawful. How could judges expect poor, hard-working people to keep the law if they broke it themselves?

He wrote a note to his solicitor and got it sent off by police messenger; later he made a brief appearance before a magistrate and was remanded.

There was a lot of interest in the case. The court was crowded, more crowded than it had ever been before when he had made an appearance at the bar of justice. He was an important man. How much more important would it be if they knew they had got Charles Peace! But Sheffield was far away, over a hundred and fifty miles. That would have stirred them up a bit – Charles Peace in court! Instead of which he was John Ward, and if he was fullied he'd probably get seven years at the most – five, perhaps – and then he could be ill and be released on ticket.

There was nobody in the police court who recognised him. They hardly would: he was a master of disguises… He wondered if Jane Garden would know him. Then he remembered that she had seen and identified him at Brighton. It must have been the girl: that doctor hadn't brains enough to see something under his nose.

Alan Mainford put down the London newspaper he was reading.

"John Ward!" he said. "That name sounds a little familiar."

Jane Mainford looked round from the chrysanthemums she was arranging.

"Who is John Ward, and what has he been doing?"

"He's been shooting a policeman."

She shivered.

"How dreadful! In Sheffield?"

He saw the look of anxiety in her eyes and laughed.

"No, it's in London. You were thinking of Mr Peace."

He looked up at the ceiling with a perplexed frown.

"I seem to have an idea at the back of my mind that he did call himself Ward at one time. I must ask Baldy when I see him."

"Have they arrested him?" she asked.

"Yes, he was charged on remand yesterday morning at Greenwich. He seems to be a particularly ferocious kind of fellow; in many ways the description tallies with Peace, except that they say this man is half a negro."

She looked at him open-mouthed.

"Half a negro? That's how he was when I saw him at Brighton. His face was so dark when I saw him in full light that I wouldn't have recognised him. It was only because I saw him in profile as the carriage was overtaking him that I knew him."

Alan considered the possibilities.

"Rubbish! It isn't he. I'll never be surprised if the little devil comes back to Sheffield."

"Oh, don't!" she begged, and he was all penitence.

She was very quiet for the rest of the day. In the evening, when they were sitting together, she said: "I'd like to be absolutely sure. He's so much on my mind, Alan. I wake up in the night sometimes, terrified!"

"Peace? Do you mean the man who has been arrested at Blackheath? Well, that is very easily settled. The trial comes on next week. I'll go down to London and see him at the Old Bailey. I know the Associate there."

"I wish you would," she said. "I have a very special reason for not wishing to dream about ugly people."

"That isn't a reason, that's a superstition," he laughed. "But I'll set your mind at ease. I'll see if I can get old Baldy to go down with me."

He looked at his watch, and at that moment there was a knock at the outer door. He was like clockwork, that man. Baldy was very cheerful: he had obtained a committal against a gang of coiners that day, and he was very cock-a-hoop.

"They'll go before Mr Justice What's-his-name, and that means we shan't see 'em for a long time," he said.

"Do you know Ward – John Ward?"

Baldy knew several.

"There's a John Ward who kept that what-do-you-call-it public-house on the Eccleshall Road. There's another John Ward whose father was manager for What's-their -name?"

"I'm talking about a criminal."

Baldy mused on this.

"I've got an idea I've heard it before," he said. And then he slapped his knee. "It's one of the names that Peace used," he said, and husband and wife exchanged glances.

"Read this."

Alan handed him the newspaper. Baldy, adjusting his newly purchased glasses, read slowly to the finish.

"That's not Peace," he said. "He never looked like a negro. If they'd said 'just ugly' it might have been he."

"Mrs Mainford saw him at Brighton. She said he had a dark skin then."

Baldy shook his head.

"No, he's abroad, in Switzerland. Didn't he send me a postcard with an insulting message on it, addressed to 'Baldy, Sheffield Police Force'?"

"Somebody else may have posted it."

"That's impossible," said Sergeant Eltham. "There was a picture of the Alps on it."

"You can even buy those in London."

But the sergeant took the very confident view that Peace had left England by the machinations of some wealthy friend, and that he might no longer be regarded as an active factor in criminal circles.

"Bless your life, Peace has any number of imitators! There was a feller down at Northampton who did everything that Peace did, including disguising himself. There was that man, What's-his-name, at Bristol – the feller who got ten years – you might have sworn he was Peace. They're imitators; they've got no brains."

"I'm going down to London to the trial to make sure, and I'd like you to come along with me."

Baldy, however, did not like London, and excused himself. It was too noisy a place, and he had a personal feud with Scotland Yard over the question of a police reward which had been denied him and wrongly credited to a member of the London detective force.

"If Scotland Yard says he's Peace, you can be sure he's not. If they say he's not Peace, you can take the coroner's warrant down and pinch him."

"Will this man get a heavy sentence?" asked Jane.

"Ten years to life," said Baldy indifferently. "Shooting a policeman, you know, is not only an offence against the law of the land, but a crime against nature. They ought to hang 'em for it – one of these days they will. By the way, doctor, I've found out who the cottage belongs to – that Swiss woman, Madame Stahm. She put it in the hands of an agent. Peace tried to sell it – did you know that? That fellow!" He shook his head in wonder. "No, we shall never see Peace again. He'll be elected Lord Mayor of Switzerland or something. He'd kid the hair off a baby's head."

36

He voiced an opinion which was pretty general. Mr Peace was preparing for his trial, and the fatal news came to him a week before. It was to be Hawkins! The name did not send shivers down his back, but it aroused him to a pitch of indignation that such men should be appointed to judge and try their fellow-creatures.

By judicious inquiry he discovered the great judge's age – a warder procured the fact from the prison library. Peace had marshalled all his reserves: every penny of money had to go to his defence. Hannah was ordered to sell and sell and sell, to collect debts of dubious authenticity, to borrow money. The main point was that he must be saved. His solicitor, at his own suggestion, briefed a barrister who had just then come into fame.

"Montagu Williams – I don't think I know him," frowned Peace.

He had heard of him at any rate.

His consultation with his lawyer was a memorable one. For a quarter of an hour the speechless barrister sat whilst Peace laid down the system of defence.

"The point you've got to make is this, mister – you've got to say to this judge: 'What? Are you going to send an old man like that to his grave?' – just like that." Peace gave an imitation of sorrowful, pleading anguish.

"I'm afraid I can't say it just like that." Mr Williams's eyes twinkled.

"Well, somehow like that," said Peace. "And another thing is this: if he knows that I'm an old man, he's not going to give me a long stretch. He's going to say: 'Poor old devil! He ain't got long to live, anyway!' Do you see my meaning?"

"I follow your reasoning, yes."

"What you've got to say is this:" – again Peace grew dramatic and declamatory – " 'My Lord, you see before you an old man of sixty-seven, tottering on the verge of the grave' – rub that in! 'He's got no time to live, my Lord and gentlemen of the jury, so why pass a terrible sentence on him? Why not give him a year? He's penitent. I give you my word, gentlemen of the jury, he'll go straight.' "

"That, I'm afraid, I'm not allowed to do," said Mr Williams. "Sixty-seven. Are you sixty-seven?"

"Sixty-eight," said Peace.

He was then approaching his forty-fifth birthday.

"That's the point you've got to make – about me age. Get me a short sentence. What's the good of 'em giving me ten years? I shouldn't live to serve it. Do you see what I mean? You know what Hawkins is – you might touch his heart."

"That's all very well," said counsel, "but what age was the policeman you fired at? Was he so old that it didn't matter if he died or not?"

Peace made an impatient "tchk!"

"You're not on his side, are you? You're on my side. Never mind about the policeman – he's alive and well. I could have killed him seven times over. I'm one of the best shots in the land. But did I? No. When I shot him it was done by accident. He pushed my hand and the pistol went off. Didn't he admit it with his own mouth that he hit me on the head with my own hand and my own pistol?"

Counsel left the consultation-room not very considerably assisted. He had tried his best to bring home to Peace the seriousness of the crime. Peace had harped upon the desirability of a light sentence.

"Never mind whether I'm sixty-eight or not. I'll look ninety when I get into the box."

He tried to dodge the sessions and find a lighter judge; was found in a fit, foaming at the mouth, in his cell. This was a day or two before the trial. The unimaginative prison doctor tested the foam and found it was soap.

"It's the first time he's ever used it for any purpose," said the chief warder unkindly.

Peace came feebly into the dock of the Old Bailey, gazed pathetically at the judge, and was allowed a chair. If he did not look ninety, he looked the years that appeared upon the bill of indictment. His pathetic survey embraced the jury; he looked at them with a dog-like pleading in his eye, and shook his head slightly, as a beggar shakes his head when he is appealing for charity.

"I have never seen such a lousy, uneducated lot in my life," he said to the warder on his left when he sat down. "There's not one of them that can sign his own name, I'll lay!"

His comments on the judge were unprintable in the columns of a family journal. So that was Hawkins – granite-faced, hard-eyed, iron-lipped! What a dog! What an unfeeling hound of a man! It was going to take the mouthpiece all his time to get him off with three. Not less than five, that lawyer said, maybe seven. It'd be an outrage to send an old man of sixty-seven to quod for seven years. He wondered how judges slept in their beds at night, inflicting suffering and pain on their fellow-creatures.

"It's hard to believe, mate," he said *sotto voce* to the warder, indicating with a nod of his head the great judge, "that him and me was produced by the same Maker."

"I expect he thinks so too," said the warder.

"You're all as bad as one another," growled Peace, folded his arms and appeared to fall asleep.

Now and again, when a police witness was giving testimony as to what happened that night on Blackheath, he opened his eyes, shook his head and murmured: "Lies! All lies! They can't speak the truth!" Once his counsel had to rebuke him sharply.

He was not too pleased with Mr Montagu Williams. He didn't seem to be enough on his side, and when it came to the speech for the defence, what a defence it was! He could have done better himself. Messing about with all sorts of fancy ideas instead of getting down to the point that you oughtn't to give a man of sixty-seven a long sentence.

No wonder the jury came back so quickly with its verdict. And yet, did he expect any other than the verdict of "Guilty"? It was hardly likely; but he was a magnificent actor. At the word "Guilty" he staggered, looked, bewildered, from face to face, stepped forward, broken in voice and attitude.

"I haven't been fairly dealt with," he sobbed. "I declare before God that I never had the intention to kill him. All I meant to do was to frighten him, so I could get away. If I'd wanted to kill him I could have done it, but I never did. I really didn't know the pistol was loaded. I hope, my Lord, you'll have mercy on me. I feel that I'm that base and bad that I'm neither fit to live nor die. For I've disgraced myself, for I have disgraced my friends." His voice quavered, "I'm not fit to live among mankind. I'm not fit to meet my God. So, oh, my Lord, I know I'm base and bad to the uttermost, but I know, at the same time, they have painted my case blacker than what it really is. I hope you will take all this into consideration and not pass upon me a sentence of imprisonment which will be the means of causing me to die in prison, where it is very possible I shall not have a chance amongst my associates to prepare myself to meet my God, that I hope I shall meet. So, my Lord, do have mercy upon me!" he wailed, wringing his hands over the edge of the dock at the imperturbable man whose mask of a face never changed. "I beseech you, give me a chance, my Lord, to regain my freedom and you shall not, with the help of my God, have any cause to repent passing a merciful sentence upon me. Oh, my Lord, you yourself do expect mercy from the hands of your great and merciful God. Oh, my Lord, do have mercy upon me, a most wretched miserable man, a man that am not fit to die. I am not fit to live; but with the help of my God I will try to become a good man. I will try to become a man that will be able in the last day to meet my God, my Great Judge, to meet Him and to receive the great reward at His hands for my true repentance. So, oh, my Lord, have mercy upon me, I pray and beseech you. I will say no more; but oh, my Lord, have mercy upon me; my Lord, have mercy upon me!" ★

★ This is an actual verbatim report of that extaordinary outburst from the dock, the most superb piece of acting that has ever been seen in a criminal court.

The judge moved, rested his arms on the desk before him, his cold eyes fixed on Peace. Briefly, mercilessly, he sketched the character of the man before him. He saw the soul of Peace, naked. Not three years, not five years...

"Notwithstanding your age, therefore, I feel I should fail in my duty to the public if I did not pass upon you the extreme sentence of the law for the offence of which you have been convicted, which is that you be sent to penal servitude for the rest of your natural life."

Peace accepted the sentence more calmly than he had taken the verdict. He had shot his last bolt; he could do no more. Natural life! That meant natural life – all the days of his living in prison; no hope of release. It was final – final for all except for Peace.

"There ain't such a sentence," he told the warder on his way to Pentonville. "It's against the law, and I'm sending a letter to Our Gracious Majesty about it."

There was a merciful release for him at hand. As he paraded round the swing on his first morning in Pentonville, he saw a group of police officers and civilians in the centre. Two men walked out, and somebody called him by name, "Ward!" and urged him into the centre of the ring. He came face to face with Alan.

"Do you know this gentleman?" asked somebody.

"Yes," said Peace boldly; "he's the man who tried to poison my wife by giving her arsenic in her beer."

Only the solemnity of the moment checked Alan's laugh.

"Do you know him, doctor?"

"Yes. His name is Charles Peace."

37

That day Hannah, his wife, was privileged to see him at Pentonville. She had not had the opportunity before he was removed from Newgate. He saw her in the usual office, spoke a few commonplaces, of the necessity of raising further money. No king levied tribute upon his subjects more ruthlessly than Peace upon his family. When she was going: "Here," he called, "send a telegraph message to Mrs Mainford."

He gave her the address and made her repeat it.

" 'Mrs Dr Mainford.' Send this telegram the moment you get outside the prison, or I'll never forgive you. This is what you say: 'Deepest sorrow to tell you your husband, Dr Mainford, was run over in the street today and is dead.' "

"Is he?" asked Hannah.

"Never mind about 'is he'!" snarled Peace. "Can you remember that – the address? Send it. Maybe she's going to have a baby."

The telegram never reached Jane, partly because an official of the prison stopped the woman in the lobby and terrified her into promising that such a message should not be sent, and partly because Hannah could never have remembered it; and if she had remembered it she couldn't have sent it, for she could neither read nor write.

Whether she sent it or not was a matter of indifference to Peace, who knew as well as anybody the limitations of her intellectual equipment. He had the satisfaction of devising the shock. There was a certain relief in being Charles Peace again, the famous Charles Peace, the Charles Peace that everybody was talking about and writing about and thinking about. How they'd talk in Sheffield! They'd come from miles to see him. There'd be crowds at the station; they'd have to get the soldiers to keep the court cleared. He wished they had an Assize Court in Sheffield: it robbed him of some of his glory to be transferred to Leeds. Who would be there?

He procured a copy of the inquest proceedings and reread it carefully.

Kate Dyson – she was in America. Would they bring her back? That would cost a lot of money – hundreds of pounds. Fancy spending hundreds of pounds to bring that (whatever she was) from America! It was wasting the public money. In such matters he was a rigid economist.

Carton! He bared his gums at the name. If that man came into court he'd jump over the dock and strangle him. They'd never pry his fingers loose from the traitor's throat. He was pretty strong; he always was powerful in the arm. That would be a sensation if you liked – Charlie Peace strangling a man in court in front of judges and juries and everything.

He knew now the part that Carton had played in trapping him. It wasn't his house at all. His solicitor had asked at the preliminary police court proceedings if there was such a man working for the owner of the house, and had been told "No." By various methods Peace came to learn who his actual employer was. He had sold him, horn, hide and hoof, to the enemy. A man he had befriended, looked after. He went back in his mind to recall the services he had rendered the traitor, but could remember no more than that he had paid his fare from Manchester to Sheffield – or was it half the fare? Anyway, he had helped him.

He could bring Carton into the case, perhaps get him put in the dock with him. He consulted his London solicitors about this, but they shook their heads.

"He has never been mentioned. He could not be arrested on your word."

"Why not?" asked Peace indignantly.

The solicitors were tired of arguing with him.

He passed hours planning vengeance on the ex-butler, and in the face of his shocking perverseness could find excuses for Alan Mainford. After all, Alan Mainford was a gentleman bred and born, whilst Carton was just a (whatever he was).

He spent quite a lot of time in a voluminous correspondence with the Home Office, demanding that certain photographs which he had kept as a pleasant souvenir of his association with Mrs Dyson, and which had been taken from him at Blackheath Road Station, should be restored to him. There were letters, too, if they could be called such; notes she had written to him, all rather cryptic, all having a peculiar significance which, he asserted and she was to deny a little unconvincingly, was discreditable to her honourable name.

Mrs Dyson was enjoying the dignity and honour of a cataclysmic widowhood. She must be brought down to her place. The notes would prove it; the photographs might prove it. Face to face with justice, she might, under pressure, volunteer to prove it.

"The beginning and end of the argument," said his solicitor, "being that if he could prove that she and he had a love affair, then the murder of her husband was the merest trifle."

They did not like Peace at Pentonville. In every sense he was a nasty man, crude, undisciplined, lacking even the rough polish of civilisation. He confounded fear with disgust, and preened himself upon his importance.

He wrote a letter to Alan (the spelling has been rectified):

"DEAR SIR,
I am that wretched and unhappy man, Charles Peace or John Ward, who you know, and which had never done wrong to you but always spoken highly of your merits. Dear Sir, you and your dear wife, who I love as my own child because she's so dear and true as any woman can be, which you're lucky to get her, as I have always said, you know I am under misfortune, that my very life is being sworn away by people who are jealous of me though I've never done anything and am a poor old man of sixty-eight with one foot in the grave, they still persecute me

for righteousness' sake, as it is written in the Bible. So I ask all my friends to rally round me especially those who are not my friends but will take pity upon my helpless state knowing that some day an account will be rendered of them according to their works. Dear Sir and Doctor, be kind, let your noble heart speak, forgive bygones and suchlike misunderstandings. Your word would go a long way to the judge and the gentlemen of the jury (so called) if you could speak for me or send me a few pounds, my wife is starving, I have given her everything I have and she is being hounded by the police as you well know they do if they've got a down on anybody which they have for it's Charles Peace this and Charles Peace that, and never taking the trouble to find out if I did it. Dear Sir Alan Mainford, life is short and time is on the wing, and no man knows what tomorrow bringeth forth, no not one, and if we help our enemies then, dear sir, there is a heavenly crown for us, but if we spit upon our enemies bad luck will follow us hither we go and whither. A few shillings will not hurt you, but especially if you can come and say a few words about how I've always been the first to help others. Oh, dear sir, perhaps you will have a son of your own, please God you may, and what will happen to him, says you, if he's in the same position as Charles Peace (John Ward)? Oh, how terrible that would be for his mother! So do help, for many can help one but one cannot help many.

Your obedient servant,
CHARLES PEACE,
JOHN WARD."

"Do you know," said Alan, "I'm inclined to send the drivelling old devil a ten-pound note?"

"He'd hate you if you sent ten. He'll not forgive you if it isn't a hundred," said Jane quietly, and it was a pretty accurate diagnosis.

A great weight had been lifted from her mind when the identity was established. On his return Alan told her of the message Peace had dictated — the prison authorities had got into touch with him immediately, in case he wanted to prepare his wife. She was not shocked but a little sad.

"Isn't there something in him, some brilliant mind-atom, that might have placed him among the great geniuses of the world? Even in his vileness there is an odd novelty which in a perverse way is charming."

"I'm glad you see it like that," said Alan, astounded.

He saw it like that himself a day or two later, when he heard some private gossip about Peace. Peace had learned that Carton was leaving his employer and was opening a fish shop on Blackheath Hill. The news drove him into paroxysms of jealous fury. From his point of view it was the act of an upstart, venturing into the kingdom reserved for greater men with greater minds. Always to Peace the shopkeeper was the aristocrat of the lower classes. He thought of no finish to the most magnificent of his dreams but that it would end in a magnificent store of which he would be the proprietor. A patron of pretty shop girls, with a new kind of shutters that rolled down and rolled up. He would come to business every morning in a small brougham, drawn by two proud and high-stepping horses. If he ever made any wonderful promise to any woman of his acquaintance, the culminating and crowning argument was that she should be set up in business with a shop of her own.

Carton in a fried fish shop, and married to that young girl in magenta silk! Carton living away from his place of business, in three rooms with the use of the kitchen! It was not to be endured. He spent time that he might have given to his defence, writing a letter to Carton, so vile in tone and expression that it never got beyond the office of the prison censor...

Here he was on his way to Sheffield, wearing convict garb, handcuffs on his wrists; a warder beside him, one in front of him, blinds drawn at every station and let up after the train steamed out. A whole compartment to himself. For many reasons it was not a pleasant journey for the warders.

Pollard, the rising man at the Treasury, was sent down to prosecute. The defence was hastily organised by the shrewdest of local solicitors, who was neither in awe of Pollard nor abashed by the immense character of his task. Whatever discouragement there was, was supplied by the prisoner.

Peace was in his most truculent and arrogant mood. His reception had fizzled out, owing to the earliness of his arrival. It was not even necessary to have soldiers to keep people out of the court, which was, however, uncomfortably crowded. There were no familiar faces to be seen as yet — yes, there was: he saw a veiled woman.

"You wouldn't think she'd have the face to come here," he said to the warder at his side; "the sauce of it!"

They'd brought her all across the Atlantic Ocean, thousands and thousands of miles, from Cleveland, Ohio! She'd better have stayed away. There was a showing up coming for her, if she only knew it. Modesty? She didn't know the meaning of the word. If he was her he'd run a thousand miles rather than stand up in that box and hear the things that she was going to hear, if his solicitor did his duty. He rather suspected all solicitors and counsel: they were too friendly with one another. He had seen the prosecuting counsel and the defending counsel shake hands at the Old Bailey. That wasn't right. They had probably made it up before they came into court, what they were going to say. A nice state of affairs!

There was Baldy, leaning with his back to the wall of the court, eyeing him with a benevolence which would not have been out of place in a rose grower showing a championship exhibit. That's what he was! Charles Peace, the champion of Sheffield.

Peace could never interpret, though he received unerring reactions. He could not put into words Baldy's attitude of mind, but he knew the effect that attitude produced in itself, and could express it.

Who else? The doctor wasn't here, but there was a bench of magistrates, with a stipendiary in the middle. He didn't bother much about this stipendiary; by all accounts there wasn't a great deal to him.

The stipendiary was inclined to have preconceived notions. He was obviously anxious to shift the case from his own court to a superior tribunal. He started by being a little in awe of the Treasury counsel, and ended by being respectful to the solicitor for the defence. He was neither strong nor weak, good nor bad: he was adequate for the occasion. Peace was held on a coroner's warrant, and it was not absolutely necessary that he should come into the magistrate's court at all.

The doctor was not here: Peace made sure of that. Nor the nuss – nor Carton. Carton ought to be sitting up here, and so ought her ladyship, Madame Stahm, and that long-faced foreigner. He wished they'd let him have his fiddle in prison. He wondered, if he asked the magistrate, whether he could get it. But no, that would disturb the other prisoners. Being tried for his life, he ought to have just what he wanted. That was the law.

He listened while his lawyer pleaded for an adjournment, battling with the Treasury counsel, and, if the truth be told, with the stipendiary too. The case was shockingly presented; no amateur could have done worse than the Treasury. The rules of evidence were flagrantly ignored. The magistrate allowed reference to previous charges to be made – the very presence of Peace in the dock, wearing convict's uniform, would have been sufficient, if he had been tried fifty years later, to quash the trial.

There was something farcical about it. Everybody knew he was guilty, and wanted to get to the point where someone in authority would say so. They resented as a waste of time taking any point that might properly be offered in the man's defence. Peace was a little deaf – whether naturally so or conveniently does not matter. He interrupted occasionally, but, generally speaking, his attitude towards the first witnesses was one of indifference. It was when the veiled woman went into the box that he sat up.

Let her show her face, not hide herself so that nobody could tell what she was saying and what she meant. He whispered excitedly to his solicitor, pleaded and gibbered.

Would the lady remove her veil? The lady removed her veil. Peace shook his head. No, she wasn't what she had been. Put her beside Thompson, and what was she? Put her beside that nuss, and she was just a common drab. He felt very superior to her; he had never felt so superior before. He was fighting for his life. As for Mrs Dyson, who had come all these thousands of miles to testify against him, she was fighting for her reputation, which was much more precious to her than anybody's life.

She was very emphatic where she could be, very evasive where she had to be; glossed over extremely awkward questions with a complete loss of memory. Peace her lover? The idea was absurd. She had always looked upon him as rather a vulgar little man, not to be compared with her husband, who was a gentleman in every sense of the word.

There was a wrangle between bench and advocate on the production of letters. The stipendiary, with one eye upon the Treasury, would have none of them. That dogged solicitor would not be denied. He was persistent, unimpressed by this particular majesty of law, thrusting spear-points of logic towards a vacillating bench, which burst a few bubbles and ruffled a few tempers. In the end he had his way.

There were the letters written, said Peace, by the woman to him; appointments made, assignations arranged. She had never written the letters; they were forgeries. Her attitude seemed to say: "Here is a man charged with murder. Why shouldn't he also commit forgery? How can you doubt me, who have never been charged with murder? Forgeries, all of them!"

That she was lying, nobody doubted. That between these two people there had been criminal knowledge, the most callow or the most charitable must believe. The Treasury believed it. Mr Pollard was a little pompous; in a wearisome way, majestic. There had been an earlier passage of arms between him and Peace, and once, when the prisoner interrupted, the Treasury counsel rose in his might and became the legal pedant, explaining to the justices just what they could do. They seemed to know.

Peace went back to London, depressed. The dice were loaded against him; he was not having a fair deal. He hadn't a chance. He told the warders this. The warders agreed.

"Anything to keep the little beast in an amiable mood."

38

He was remanded to Pentonville, for he was still in the custody of the governor of that prison, and would remain so until he was committed to another gaol.

In the intervening period he conceived a great idea. That he should be hanged was little matter. To be buried in gaol – that was an ugly end to a man of affairs. He questioned the chief warder about it. What happened to a man who died in prison? Did his relations have his body?

"Certainly they do," said the chief warder.

"But suppose a man is being tried for murder, and he dies before he's sentenced, do his relations have his body?"

There was a point of law raised here. Offhand, the warder thought they would have the right to claim all that was mortal of him and dispose of it reverently and decently, until the judge uttered the fateful words: "And your body shall afterwards be buried in the prison in which you were last confined."

The fleshly part of him was a responsibility for his relations. Peace split hairs.

"Suppose a man died just before the judge came to that bit – eh? That's a tickler for you! I'll bet nobody's ever thought of that before."

He grew quite animated.

"I've set posers to judges that they couldn't answer. And lawyers – I've got 'em all tied up! Just ask your bloke what he thinks of that."

He was very pleased with himself, that he had set a difficult case. He had forgotten the matter the next morning, having made definite plans for the disposal of his own body. There would be an inquest at the Duke of York, and a quiet, mournful procession to the cemetery. Spectators would take off their hats as it passed, and drop a silent tear. Mothers would bring their children and say: "There goes Charlie Peace. You remember that, my boy, when you grow up."

To have the cause of your death and the state of your mind amicably settled over a pot of ale — that seemed a very attractive proposition. Peace considered the matter from every angle and found it good.

The whining coward in him was too apparent to be true. It belonged to the pageantry of his misfortune, was never revealed, except publicly and within the hearing of reporters. He was too much without fear to be as contemptible as he seemed to be; his whining, his sycophancy, his nauseating supplications were all parts appropriate to the roles he played. Largely they were as mechanical as the beggar's whine or the milkman's howl.

A five-pound note came to him from Sheffield. Alan Mainford made no attempt to disguise the fact that he was the donor, for though he sent no letter, the money was enclosed in a sheet of his notepaper. Peace shed tears and wrote an incoherent letter of thanks. To his wife he also wrote:

> "If you can get up to see this man Mainford, he's a doctor, and you pitch it strong, you might get £50 out of him. Dear wife, if anything happens to me, you go on writing to him about every three months. Remember, dear wife, that the rich must help the poor. Did you sell my violin and have you got the money I told you about? Dear wife, ask Mrs Thompson to see her husband and get some money. And, dear wife, don't go gossiping about my business. I'm not dead yet."

He put a PS to this letter:

> "Don't send the money until you hear I'm fullied." *

---

* Fully committed for trial.

He had reason for this warning. On the morning of the 22nd of January, with handcuffs on his wrists, he was taken from Pentonville Gaol by cab and hurried into a third-class carriage on the milk train, the earliest train. He gave more than ordinary trouble on the journey, exasperating his custodians to the last point of endurance.

Just before the train reached Darnall he asked to have the window down. The warders were not averse. Apparently he had been grumbling, but had quietened down. Their attention was distracted for the briefest space of time, and Peace seized the opportunity. Like a cat he leaped for the narrow opening of the window. The warders spun round just in time to catch him by the ankle. They held him as long as they could, pulling frantically at the communication cord.

The man leaning out of the window strove desperately to get a firmer grip. Peace was lying head downwards, flying rather, spreadeagled away from the train. And then the warders' grip loosened and he fell by the side of the line, turning over and over. They got the train stopped at last and the warders flew back along the rails to where the inert figure lay. That he was dead, neither doubted. One may suppose they were a little relieved, whatever reprimand might come to them.

Peace lay in the snow, unconscious, bleeding from the head. One of his ribs was broken. A slow local train came to a standstill behind the express; they lifted him into the guards' van and covered him with rugs. He missed the big crowd that was waiting for his reappearance; they waited in vain. He lay in a cell, moaning, weeping and cursing. He cursed very hard.

He gave Sheffield another sensation, which brought the stipendiary, his brother magistrates and the Treasury counsel a considerable amount of discomfort. It produced a macabre setting for the second hearing that was in the atmosphere of the crime and the criminal.

No more would he sit in the dock, noisily protesting against reporters sketching his picture. He knew his rights there, could frustrate the *lèse majesté* which expedient journalism practised. Now he came to his own. Enfeebled with age and debility, doubly underlined by the eerie setting of his own misfortune. Dosed with milk and brandy, he appeared to sleep through the night, but denied that he had as much as closed his eyes in slumber.

They brought him out of his cell the next morning for the second hearing. The court was the corridor before his cell at Water Lane Police Station. Candles were lit to illuminate the gloom. The lighting and the composition of the picture was a subject for Hogarth, the central figure being a man swathed in blankets, huddled up in a chair, who said he wished he was dead, and at times appeared to be dying, but was never far from his arrogant self.

"Please don't put your feet on my table," said the stipendiary plaintively.

Here they played out the second scene of the first act, with Mrs Dyson present to deny, to forget and sometimes to affirm with too great heartiness. Some events she could remember to the day, the hour, the minute; other events which, if they had developed, must be discreditable to herself, she could not recall within a year or two, if she could recall them at all.

There was the usual passage between the cold and shivering stipendiary and the razor-sharp solicitor for the defence. Always in the end the stipendiary leaned back in his chair and looked helplessly for sympathy from his colleagues, very few of whom knew what it was all about.

Peace was for calling witnesses then and there. They were prepared to be called. He cared nothing for the routine of preliminary examinations. He wanted justice – that was all he wanted – and he was very cold; he wanted to sit before a fire and take the chill out of himself.

They committed him to take his trial and put him back into the cell. He went, groaning. A few minutes later he called in his solicitor and offered emphatic views about the line his defence should take. He had a retinue that a distinguished person might envy when they removed him to Armley Gaol by easy stages. The prison van must move slowly; he must have a soft mattress beneath him.

That night there were two happy men in Sheffield: a chief warder and a warder from Pentonville Prison, who went back to London alone.

"Thank God they won't hang him in London!" said one, and the other may or may not have said: "Amen!"

"I saw him before he went away," said Baldy. "I don't know whether he's hurt or whether he's acting. In my opinion you couldn't hurt him. You remember Carton? Peace says that it was he who fired the shot and he shielded him. He told me a rigmarole story about some crystals that Carton was trying to get for a foreign woman, and he's given me a long list of burglaries that he has committed. By 'he' I mean Carton He said Carton put him up to abducting your lady – "

"By 'he' you mean Peace. I gather he doesn't like Carton. He'll have some difficulty in bringing him into it."

"That's what I say," said Baldy. "Carton isn't a Sheffield man anyway, and you wouldn't kill a rat on Peace's evidence."

Alan leaned back in his chair.

"I don't know. I suppose it's all right. The man's a murderer, a most unscrupulous little beast, but, of course, he won't get a fair trial. The jury will go into the box with the express intention of hanging him; they'll know every detail of his career; and when the judge asks them to disabuse their minds of what they've heard before, he might as well be asking them to forget that they've a pain in the stomach, if they have one. The only evidence against the man is Mrs Dyson's. There's nobody else. And Mrs Dyson is admittedly a – well, a prevaricator. Any lawyer could prove that. She's another on whose evidence you wouldn't hang a rabbit!"

Baldy listened in amazement.

"If ever a man deserved death – " he began.

"Yes, yes, I know," nodded Alan. "And if ever a bottle deserved to be kicked into oblivion as a public nuisance, it is one filled with asafoetida. It was designed to hold whatever was put into it – an Eastern scent, rare wine, slime from a stagnant pool. Have you ever thought what might have happened to Peace if somebody had taken him by the ear and led him out of the circumstances where he looked after the animals, and sent him to a school, put him in a dentist's chair and saw to his teeth, whacked him when he didn't clean his hands, and gradually instilled into him the healthy education that I had? Do you realise what he would have been?"

That was indeed a little beyond Baldy, who was accustomed to dealing with facts and stark realities.

"There it is," said Alan. "He'll go up before a judge, posture and whine, strike attitudes, and the end of it all will be that he will hang by the neck until he's dead, and that will be the last of him. Nothing can save him. There's no doubt, no mercy, no hope. But you couldn't convict him, strictly on the evidence. It's his word against Mrs Dyson's – that and no more. The other evidence hardly counts. And who can believe her? Who would believe her on the facts as stated? And they do not require more than superficial examination. Yet on her word Peace will die – rightly, as it happens; wrongly from the strict point of view of equity."

Alan's ears should have burnt. At that very moment Peace was talking to a warder who was attending him.

"There's people I've helped," he groaned. "I've given away hundreds. There's a woman in Switzerland that owes me two thousand – a foreigner. Down in Sheffield there's a doctor called Mainford who wouldn't be anywhere if it wasn't for me. I got him the house he lives in; he wouldn't have known his missus, only I introduced 'em. She used to go down on her knees an' ask me to take her away, but I wouldn't. Nuss Garden she was – a whipper-snapper. But now I'm down she don't know me! That's gratitude, because I'm old and poor and helpless – mind my head, you clumsy lout!"

He wrote letters. Caesar was no more assiduous in correspondence than Peace. They were weird-looking letters, scrawled, ill-spelt, full of phrases that had neither beginning nor end. Taken as entities, they were objective. Always he required something, and what that something was he never left any doubt in the mind of the person to whom they were addressed.

He wrote to his wife, a letter full of instructions for raising money, and signed himself her affectionate and unhappy husband. Almost by the same post he wrote to his lady friend, the blonde, vivacious Mrs Thompson, and begged her not to forget the love they had for one another. He signed it "Your ever true lover till death". Was it by accident that he put his own name and followed it with the name he had borne when they lived under the same roof?

39

Leeds Assizes opened on the 30th of January, 1879, and the grand jury voted a bill of indictment against Charles Peace, *alias* John Ward, joiner or carver or gilder. They put his age as forty-seven. This saved his counsel from a lot of unnecessary instructions.

Here was Charles Peace, on the last grand lap of his course. A man of tremendous importance, all eyes focused on him.

Carton got a holiday, came up to Leeds with the greatest assurance, secured admission to the court, and at the last moment funked it, not daring to meet the accusing eye of the joiner or carver or gilder, who stood indicted in that he did kill and slay Arthur Dyson by shooting at him with a revolver. He sneaked out of court, and, finding an eating-house, ordered his breakfast, for he had been travelling the greater part of the night. When he attempted to get a place in the public gallery later in the day he was told that the court was full. He was not sorry.

Though the weather was bitterly cold, and powdery snow had fallen, there was an immense crowd about the Town Hall. It was rumoured that Peace would be brought to Armley Gaol under a strong escort of hussars, that an attempt would be made to rescue him. By whom was never suggested. He had no friends; he was no leader of desperate gangs; in all the thousands that filled the court or looked around it, there was not one but was impatient to see the end of the trial come and Peace stand up to take his medicine.

How would he take it? What would he say? Would he whine, grovel, as he did at the Old Bailey? Would he hurl imprecations at the witnesses, defy the judge? That was the only thing that mattered – the end of it. Not the bald result, but the spectacle it might afford.

Nobody spoke a word for him. There were joking admirers, who knew nothing about him, or had any cause for admiration. He was dead and damned too, if public opinion could control the hereafter.

"If, when I saw him in the yard at Pentonville," said Alan, "I had walked up to him and said 'You are Charles Peace' and shot him dead, that would have been a logical and praiseworthy disposal of the matter."

Alan snatched a day to witness part of the trial, but did not stay long. It was imperative that he should be within call in Sheffield. He tried to keep the subject from Jane, but she discussed it very calmly.

"He'll die before his time – that is all. There is nothing really tragic in that. The tragedy is his life, but of that he is probably quite unconscious. Don't worry, darling. I'll even read an account of the execution and not be hurt by it."

"I won't test your philosophy," said Alan.

The judge was a new man to Peace – Lopes.

"Never heard of him."

He was better than Hawkins. Anybody was better than Hawkins. Suppose there was a verdict of guilty and they scragged him? That'd be a smack in the eye for Hawkins, who wanted him to live in prison all his life and die there.

He was more comfortable about his new counsel: a gentleman, every inch of him. The junior counsel was another gentleman. And he didn't mind the Treasury man, who put the case fairly – up to a point. Of course, it was his job to make it hot for the prisoner: that was what he was paid for. Peace prided himself upon being a sensible man. He didn't put it like that fellow Pollard put it, but he brought up the escape, which had nothing to do with the business. When Lockwood got up and told him off and the judge approved, Peace felt that he was getting his money's worth.

The same old dreary procession of witnesses. He was expecting Mrs Dyson to be called last. He sat up in the windsor chair, and observed with interest when her name was called early on in the proceedings. There she was, as brazen as ever. She was getting fatter, too. He eyed her critically. Really, it was a wonder the woman wasn't struck dead. And they wouldn't let her be asked questions about the letters; that was an injustice – he boiled at it. Some legal quibble, one of those lawyer tricks. The letters hadn't been handed in, so they couldn't be talked about. Of all the injustices!

He depended on those letters and photographs. Mrs Dyson was "couldn't remembering" all over again. How she twisted and turned, and how that memory of hers turned blank at a snap of the finger! She couldn't remember when she moved to Darnall. Peace laughed aloud. Nobody took any notice of him. It might have been 1875 or '76 or '74 or '73.

"I cannot tell... I cannot tell."

Peace wanted to stand up and shout at her, ask her if she'd been drinking again, if she remembered that night at the Duke of York.

But that Lockwood got over her artfulness. He managed to get the letters in somehow. They were forgeries; she had never seen them. He leaned back in his chair, looking from one warder to the other, and shook his head in resignation.

Once he was amused; it was when she admitted that she had left a public-house "slightly inebriated". He repeated the words to a warder. Somebody near heard him say "A lady!"

Throughout the trial he was reasonable. Smothered comments on witnesses, a reference to one as a villain... It was over at last – speech for the prosecution, speech for defence. He ceased to be the practical man of affairs. Everything right and proper – inevitable. Part of the speech for the defence pleased him very much. He said "Hear, hear!" very loudly, and was surprised that the applause was not more general.

The charge to the jury. The inevitable and invariable appeal to men who were steeped in every detail of the case to forget that they had ever heard anything about it; to be impartial, which is the eminent quality of Englishmen. Peace listened blankly to the charge, seemingly unmoved.

The jury were out twelve minutes, and they were agreed upon their verdict. The prisoner at the bar was guilty of murder.

Peace stood up, blinking round the court. He was overcome by the grandeur of the moment, and when the Clerk of Arraigns asked him what he would say why the court should not pass sentence according to law, he replied: "It's no use saying anything."

Which was one of the most intelligent things said in the court that day.

That was all. The black cap on the judge's wig. Where had he seen that before? At the Harbrons' trial, of course. It looked different when you were looking at it from the public gallery. A little point falls over the front of the wig. The clerk hadn't put it on straight; it had a rakish angle to it. The judge in his scarlet robes said what it was proper to say. He had had a patient trial; every argument that could be used in his favour had been used by counsel, to whose superlative genius he paid tribute.

This was the way he, Charles Peace, must go. He was to be taken hence to the place whence he came; thence he would be taken to the place of execution, and there he would be hanged by the neck until he was dead, and his body would afterwards be buried in the precincts of the gaol wherein he was last confined.

The judge expressed the hope that the Lord would have mercy upon his soul. Somebody said "Amen!"

Peace stood irresolutely, fumbling at his cap. The warder touched him on the arm. They always did that at every trial. They turned to go to the place whence they came, and thence to a place of execution.

Peace said nothing. What was the use of saying anything? There was no despair in that remark, just cold intelligence. It meant ever so much more than his supplication before Hawkins, Justice.

A great crowd gathered outside to see his removal to the place whence he came, but they were disappointed. A few people hooted, which seemed a little superfluous. They were hooting Peace because he had been a wicked man and had shot a man who was not so wicked. One man had been shot, the other man was going to be hanged, just to level things up. And Mrs Dyson would go across the Atlantic to proper oblivion.

Charles Peace was to die, the judge was to die, the two counsel for the prosecution and the two counsel for the defence, two of them painfully, were all to die, and the only one of them to be remembered was this ugly little blackguard, foul of mind and speech and thought, yet hiding in his toad head a jewel that none could appraise.

On the way to Armley he asked if he could read what the papers said about him on the following morning.

"I don't think you'd better see that," said the warder.

"Why not?" demanded Peace. "They're not going to leave me out altogether, are they?"

You never quite knew where you were with him. Sometimes the soiled rag of his mind lifted like a curtain and gave you a flashing vision of the radiance behind. Then the nasty, soiled thing fell down again, and you saw him materially as he was – a nasty little man.

Quite a number of newspapers glorified the law on the following morning and spoke learnedly of Nemesis and justice. They forgot to mention the fact that he played the fiddle… Nobody seemed to think that was a point in his favour.

So went Charles Peace on the first stage of his last lap, to the place whence he came, and all England was satisfied, and said: "Hanging's too good for him."

As if hanging was too good for anybody.

40

In the dark of the morning, a policeman patrolling the vicinity of Armley Gaol saw a man slouching slowly along. He passed the policeman, and a quarter of an hour later the officer observed him coming back again and challenged him.

He was a wild-looking man, unshaven, white-faced, sack-eyed. He wore a rough pea jacket, the collar turned up to his ears, and a pot hat. Most remarkable feature of his attire was a pair of kid gloves.

"I've got a friend inside" – he shivered in the cold wind which swept round the corner of the prison – "going to be hung... Charles Peace."

The policeman eyed him with an interest.

"Charles Peace, a friend of yours, eh? Well, what are you doing around here?"

The man shook his head helplessly.

"I can't keep away – that's the trouble," he said. "Went off to London and had to come back. Couldn't sleep...thinking of him in the condemned cell... My God, it was awful!"

The policeman thought the matter over, and found an explanation.

"So you thought you'd like to be near him, did you?"

The man nodded quickly.

And then the man behind the constable asserted itself. He had a wife who nagged him all the time for news of Peace. If a policeman did not know, and a policeman, moreover, who had the gaol on his beat, who would?

"Have you been in to see him?" he asked.

The man shook his head.

"No, I haven't been in to see him, and I'm not going. I don't want to see him…awful, ain't it – him living there, and he'll be dead in a week!"

"Three clear Sundays," murmured the policeman.

"Awful, awful!" quavered the walker of the night. "I've been here since three. I walk round and round, or as near round as I can get – until I'm ready to drop. He'll be sleeping – yes, he will; you don't know Charles. I see him sleeping the day he was pinched at Blackheath. With my own eyes."

"What's your name?" asked the policeman suspiciously.

"Carton – that's my name. I've got a good job in London, and a young lady, and a business of my own…master man. The landlord's done up the shop free of charge. The counter was there. Fried fish…and stewed eels. There's a lot of profit in it."

He glanced fearfully up at the walls of the gaol.

"Where's the condemned cell, sir?" he asked. "It'll be in one of the main wards, I suppose? A feller told me the execution place was just about there." He pointed. "I hear a young builder has got the job of putting up the scaffold."

"Don't you worry your head too much about hanging, my boy," said the policeman paternally. "We've all got to come to it sooner or later – I don't mean hanging, I mean passing away. You'll go mad if you think about things like this, it's worse than penny dreadfuls."

The next night he saw the same man and spoke to him. In the meantime he had reported the matter to his superior and had received certain instructions. Carton was told just where he could walk and where his perambulations were forbidden.

"You wasn't at the trial?" said the policeman.

Carton hesitated.

"No," he said; "my body wasn't there, but I was there! My body ain't inside that prison, but I'm there!"

He was looking even more unkempt than he had been when the policeman had seen him before.

257

"He wouldn't be here at all but for me – it's awful! It can't be worse to have murder on your hands…to wake up every morning from your sleep and say: 'There's a man in that condemned cell, waiting to be hung, and I put him there. He's having his breakfast with two warders looking on; and going to bed every night and saying: 'Well, in three or four nights' time I shan't be going to bed at all'; and waking up every morning and seeing the light come in, and saying 'I'll only see this about three more times.' – And I did it! That's what you can't understand and nobody else can understand. I didn't like him, and never shall like him, and he didn't like me. But that's nothing – there he is."

He pointed his gloved finger towards the gaol.

"I'll bet he's sleeping. I'll bet he's giving more trouble than any man inside! I'll bet he don't care a half, or a hundredth part, of what I care, or feel anything like I feel!"

The policeman thought over this matter, and reached the conclusion that we all had our troubles to bear. Carton apparently had other troubles, and he mentioned them casually. He had detected his young lady surreptitiously walking out with another man, a young clerk from Penn's Ironworks. And after he'd taken the shop and had it painted blue, and purchased the apparatus for fish-frying! A nice thing!

The story of this wanderer of the night came by obvious channels of transmission to the prison officials, and in some mysterious fashion, remembering that all news of the outside world was shut from him, to Peace himself. He derived considerable satisfaction from the knowledge.

"And so he ought to be," he said, referring to the man's misery. "After what I done for him! Took him in when he hadn't got a friend in the world, and looked after him – and what did he do to me? He put the police up to me – got 'em to swear my life away. He's more of a murderer than I am, because I didn't intend killing anybody and he did intend doing me in!"

He had grown a little gloomy, but was not more tractable than he had been. To the warders who watched him day and night he was a source of constant anxiety. They suspected his ingenuity, which might at any time put into his hand a weapon which would enable him to cheat the hangman.

One cause of his depression he revealed to the visiting clergyman.

"People have forgot all about Charles Peace now," he said.

He was conservative, something of a ritualist, and demanded, sometimes with acerbity, all the material and spiritual etceteras to which his position entitled him. The chaplain's visits were part of his rights. He went farther afield and sought the spiritual counsel of a Sheffield pastor to whom he was known. Because he was at heart an actor, and the circus blood in him still tingled, he must have the lines and properties which his setting demanded.

He was not a hypocrite, not even an opportunist. He was, in his crude way, an artist.

One morning he swung his legs out of bed, a light in his dog's eyes, a bright idea working confusedly in his mind.

"You'd better go back to bed," said one of the watchers. "It's only four o'clock."

"I'm going to write," said Peace, and dressed himself.

Write he did with a vengeance; for in the night there had come to him the spectacle of Harbron, working in a convict prison, under a life sentence for a murder he did not commit. Only Peace could know his own mind, but to those who have studied him it was not penitence, not a belated sense of justice, nothing, indeed, but a passion for the grand gesture and the knowledge that his act would set tongues wagging all over the world, which produced his confession.

For confess he did. To the minister who called that day; to the Home Secretary in more elaborate manner, illustrated by sketches of his own design, he told the story of Cock and the shooting.

All the penitent things he should have said he did say, but crowded them into the smallest possible space. His chief interest was to recall details exactly, and here in some respects he failed.

He would have let William Harbron die without compunction. The sufferings of this innocent man never disturbed his mind for a second. The grand gesture produced all he anticipated. The loss to him was that he could not read the newspapers and revel in the new-found sensation.

One sensation remained for him. Three days before the end, an application was made for permission to visit him. He was consulted, and, on seeing the name of his visitor, grew pleasantly excited.

"It's the woman I was talking to you about," he said exultantly. "All the way from abroad she's come – what did I tell you? They never forget old Charlie Peace."

The interview took place in the room proper for the purpose. Madame Stahm, in her stiff silk, sat at one end of the table, the bearded little convict at the other. She was very bright, beautifully human.

"I have come all the way from Switzerland to see you, my little friend. I heard you were in trouble, and from the newspapers I have seen that you have very few friends."

"After all I've done for people!" said Peace. "It's worse than Judas Iscariot, my lady!"

"I also am going to die," she said with a smile. "The doctor has given me six months – three months perhaps, if I was so silly as to take this journey. But three months or six months, what does it matter?"

Peace was interested.

"I shouldn't believe no doctors if I was you, my lady," he said. "A couple of bottles of medicine'll put you right. I used to take sarsaparilla."

She laughed softly.

"One doctor, two doctors, six doctors – they all tell the same lie!"

She did not speak English as fluently as she had done, had found some difficulty in finding the right word.

"Well, I have come, I have seen you, and I say 'au revoir.' Somebody in Switzerland will think of you whilst she thinks at all! My love to you, little man!"

She kissed her finger-tips daintily, this gaunt woman, and rose. Peace went back to his cell, cursing monotonously.

"If I'd only remembered it, and she'd stopped jawing about herself, I could have got hundreds of pounds out of her. As a matter of fact, I'm here because of her. Die? She won't die."

Somebody else did. They found him stiff and cold, propped against the wall of the prison, his head hanging drunkenly. It was on the morning, just before the big crowd began to assemble on the snow powdered road. The policeman who had met him before had missed him for a day or two, but recognised the pilot jacket and the gloved hands folded helplessly in his lap.

"His name's Carton," he said to the doctor who was called. "Is it suicide?"

The doctor shook his head.

"No, not so far as I can tell at the moment. It seems to me to be a case of exhaustion, possibly alcoholism."

The policeman had never heard the word and sought a translation.

"Booze," said the doctor coarsely.

The policeman had a romantic mind.

"Might it be broken heart?" he suggested.

"Don't be ridiculous," said the doctor.

Peace took his time over his toilet that morning. One of the warders, his nerves on edge, asked fretfully how long he was going to be. Those deep eyes of Peace transfixed him; the restive jaw moved from side to side.

"What's the hurry?" he asked. "Are you being hung or me?"

He was all for his rights. He was entitled to his leisure, to his smoke, to the best breakfast he could procure, to a glass of brandy if he wanted it. He was the most important person in Leeds. No king, no eastern potentate, could command such ceremonial. Politeness from governors, reverence from chaplains, attention from all the world. All England was standing still, its face turned towards the grim gaol at Leeds.

Reporters were flocking from the four corners of the kingdom; newspaper presses were waiting, the centre of small armies of distributors. At tens of thousands of breakfast tables people would be saying: "That rascal was hanged this morning."

Peace was conscious of this fact; he had already composed the speech which he would make to the reporters, and which would be printed all over the world. A speech necessarily charged with piety, because the situation demanded an acknowledgment of his penitence. It was the convention of executions that the condemned man should also offer advice to those whose feet were straying towards evil, and that he should cite himself, with a melancholy pride, as an awful example of the place to which wrongdoing brings a man. He would maintain all the best traditions.

So he thanked the governor and the warders, remarked on the coldness of the morning and the dullness of it, and hoped all his enemies would be forgiven, and mentioned a few he hadn't forgiven himself.

A man came into the cell, a man with a beard; stocky, not too well dressed, but obviously The Man. In one hand he carried a body strap; the other hand, rather podgy, was extended.

"I'm very sorry that I've got to do this, but it's my duty," he said.

Peace nodded approvingly, and Marwood, the hangman, waited; but the inevitable query did not come. Peace did not ask if it would hurt. He had always strongly disapproved of that question, and was true to his principles.

"I have to do this, and I hope there's no ill-feeling," said Marwood, busy with the body strap about the little man's waist.

"That's all right," said Peace...

The speech to the reporters was over. He mounted the scaffold with a firm step, because that was also part of the convention.

And here he was at the end of the path, upon a trap that slightly sagged beneath him, with a cloth upon his face and a rope round his neck. He had been taken hence from the place whence he came, and he was now at the place of execution. Everything according to plan and in order. He was hanged by the neck until he was dead.

On the afternoon of that day a prosperous hop merchant in Blackheath, rummaging through his desk, found a small bottle of crystals, frowned at them, rattled them, took out the cork and smelt them.

"I don't know where these came from," he said to his wife… "No, my dear, don't throw them on the fire: they may explode. Give them to the maid and tell her to pour them down the kitchen sink."

EDGAR WALLACE

BIG FOOT

Footprints and a dead woman bring together Superintendent Minton and the amateur sleuth Mr Cardew. Who is the man in the shrubbery? Who is the singer of the haunting Moorish tune? Why is Hannah Shaw so determined to go to Pawsy, 'a dog lonely place' she had previously detested? Death lurks in the dark and someone must solve the mystery before BIG FOOT strikes again, in a yet more fiendish manner.

BONES IN LONDON

The new Managing Director of Schemes Ltd has an elegant London office and a theatrically dressed assistant – however Bones, as he is better known, is bored. Luckily there is a slump in the shipping market and it is not long before Joe and Fred Pole pay Bones a visit. They are totally unprepared for Bones' unnerving style of doing business, unprepared for his unique style of innocent and endearing mischief.

Edgar Wallace

Bones of the River

'Taking the little paper from the pigeon's leg, Hamilton saw it was from Sanders and marked URGENT. *Send Bones instantly to Lujamalababa... Arrest and bring to head-quarters the witch doctor.*'

It is a time when the world's most powerful nations are vying for colonial honour, a time of trading steamers and tribal chiefs. In the mysterious African territories administered by Commissioner Sanders, Bones persistently manages to create his own unique style of innocent and endearing mischief.

The Daffodil Mystery

When Mr Thomas Lyne, poet, poseur and owner of Lyne's Emporium insults a cashier, Odette Rider, she resigns. Having summoned detective Jack Tarling to investigate another employee, Mr Milburgh, Lyne now changes his plans. Tarling and his Chinese companion refuse to become involved. They pay a visit to Odette's flat. In the hall Tarling meets Sam, convicted felon and protégé of Lyne. Next morning Tarling discovers a body. The hands are crossed on the breast, adorned with a handful of daffodils.

EDGAR WALLACE

THE JOKER

While the millionaire Stratford Harlow is in Princetown, not only does he meet with his lawyer Mr Ellenbury but he gets his first glimpse of the beautiful Aileen Rivers, niece of the actor and convicted felon Arthur Ingle. When Aileen is involved in a car accident on the Thames Embankment, the driver is James Carlton of Scotland Yard. Later that evening Carlton gets a call. It is Aileen. She needs help.

THE SQUARE EMERALD

'Suicide on the left,' says Chief Inspector Coldwell pleasantly, as he and Leslie Maughan stride along the Thames Embankment during a brutally cold night. A gaunt figure is sprawled across the parapet. But Coldwell soon discovers that Peter Dawlish, fresh out of prison for forgery, is not considering suicide but murder. Coldwell suspects Druze as the intended victim. Maughan disagrees. If Druze dies, she says, 'It will be because he does not love children!'

OTHER TITLES BY EDGAR WALLACE AVAILABLE DIRECT
FROM HOUSE OF STRATUS

Quantity		£	$(US)	$(CAN)	€
	THE ADMIRABLE CARFEW	6.99	11.50	15.99	11.50
	THE ANGEL OF TERROR	6.99	11.50	15.99	11.50
	THE AVENGER	6.99	11.50	15.99	11.50
	BARBARA ON HER OWN	6.99	11.50	15.99	11.50
	BIG FOOT	6.99	11.50	15.99	11.50
	THE BLACK ABBOT	6.99	11.50	15.99	11.50
	BONES	6.99	11.50	15.99	11.50
	BONES IN LONDON	6.99	11.50	15.99	11.50
	BONES OF THE RIVER	6.99	11.50	15.99	11.50
	THE CLUE OF THE NEW PIN	6.99	11.50	15.99	11.50
	THE CLUE OF THE SILVER KEY	6.99	11.50	15.99	11.50
	THE CLUE OF THE TWISTED CANDLE	6.99	11.50	15.99	11.50
	THE COAT OF ARMS	6.99	11.50	15.99	11.50
	THE COUNCIL OF JUSTICE	6.99	11.50	15.99	11.50
	THE CRIMSON CIRCLE	6.99	11.50	15.99	11.50
	THE DAFFODIL MYSTERY	6.99	11.50	15.99	11.50
	THE DARK EYES OF LONDON	6.99	11.50	15.99	11.50
	THE DAUGHTERS OF THE NIGHT	6.99	11.50	15.99	11.50
	A DEBT DISCHARGED	6.99	11.50	15.99	11.50
	THE DOOR WITH SEVEN LOCKS	6.99	11.50	15.99	11.50
	THE DUKE IN THE SUBURBS	6.99	11.50	15.99	11.50
	THE FACE IN THE NIGHT	6.99	11.50	15.99	11.50
	THE FEATHERED SERPENT	6.99	11.50	15.99	11.50
	THE FLYING SQUAD	6.99	11.50	15.99	11.50
	THE FORGER	6.99	11.50	15.99	11.50
	THE FOUR JUST MEN	6.99	11.50	15.99	11.50
	FOUR SQUARE JANE	6.99	11.50	15.99	11.50
	THE FOURTH PLAGUE	6.99	11.50	15.99	11.50

ALL HOUSE OF STRATUS BOOKS ARE AVAILABLE FROM GOOD BOOKSHOPS
OR DIRECT FROM THE PUBLISHER:

Internet: **www.houseofstratus.com** including author interviews, reviews, features.

Email: **sales@houseofstratus.com** please quote author, title and credit card details.

OTHER TITLES BY EDGAR WALLACE AVAILABLE DIRECT
FROM HOUSE OF STRATUS

Quantity		£	$(US)	$(CAN)	€
	THE FRIGHTENED LADY	6.99	11.50	15.99	11.50
	GOOD EVANS	6.99	11.50	15.99	11.50
	THE HAND OF POWER	6.99	11.50	15.99	11.50
	THE IRON GRIP	6.99	11.50	15.99	11.50
	THE JOKER	6.99	11.50	15.99	11.50
	THE JUST MEN OF CORDOVA	6.99	11.50	15.99	11.50
	THE KEEPERS OF THE KING'S PEACE	6.99	11.50	15.99	11.50
	THE LAW OF THE FOUR JUST MEN	6.99	11.50	15.99	11.50
	THE LONE HOUSE MYSTERY	6.99	11.50	15.99	11.50
	THE MAN WHO BOUGHT LONDON	6.99	11.50	15.99	11.50
	THE MAN WHO KNEW	6.99	11.50	15.99	11.50
	THE MAN WHO WAS NOBODY	6.99	11.50	15.99	11.50
	THE MIND OF MR J G REEDER	6.99	11.50	15.99	11.50
	MORE EDUCATED EVANS	6.99	11.50	15.99	11.50
	MR J G REEDER RETURNS	6.99	11.50	15.99	11.50
	MR JUSTICE MAXWELL	6.99	11.50	15.99	11.50
	RED ACES	6.99	11.50	15.99	11.50
	ROOM 13	6.99	11.50	15.99	11.50
	SANDERS	6.99	11.50	15.99	11.50
	SANDERS OF THE RIVER	6.99	11.50	15.99	11.50
	THE SINISTER MAN	6.99	11.50	15.99	11.50
	THE SQUARE EMERALD	6.99	11.50	15.99	11.50
	THE THREE JUST MEN	6.99	11.50	15.99	11.50
	THE THREE OAK MYSTERY	6.99	11.50	15.99	11.50
	THE TRAITOR'S GATE	6.99	11.50	15.99	11.50
	WHEN THE GANGS CAME TO LONDON	6.99	11.50	15.99	11.50
	WHEN THE WORLD STOPPED	6.99	11.50	15.99	11.50

Hotline: UK ONLY: 0800 169 1780, please quote author, title and credit card details.
INTERNATIONAL: +44 (0) 20 7494 6400, please quote author, title and
credit card details.

Send to: House of Stratus Sales Department
24c Old Burlington Street
London
W1X 1RL
UK

Please allow for postage costs charged per order plus an amount per book as set out in the tables below:

	£(Sterling)	$(US)	$(CAN)	€(Euros)
Cost per order				
UK	2.00	3.00	4.50	3.30
Europe	3.00	4.50	6.75	5.00
North America	3.00	4.50	6.75	5.00
Rest of World	3.00	4.50	6.75	5.00
Additional cost per book				
UK	0.50	0.75	1.15	0.85
Europe	1.00	1.50	2.30	1.70
North America	2.00	3.00	4.60	3.40
Rest of World	2.50	3.75	5.75	4.25

PLEASE SEND CHEQUE, POSTAL ORDER (STERLING ONLY), EUROCHEQUE, OR INTERNATIONAL MONEY
ORDER (PLEASE CIRCLE METHOD OF PAYMENT YOU WISH TO USE)
MAKE PAYABLE TO: STRATUS HOLDINGS plc

Cost of book(s): _____ Example: 3 x books at £6.99 each: £20.97

Cost of order: _____ Example: £2.00 (Delivery to UK address)

Additional cost per book: _____ Example: 3 x £0.50: £1.50

Order total including postage: _____ Example: £24.47

Please tick currency you wish to use and add total amount of order:

☐ £ (Sterling)   ☐ $ (US)   ☐ $ (CAN)   ☐ € (EUROS)

VISA, MASTERCARD, SWITCH, AMEX, SOLO, JCB:

☐☐☐☐☐☐☐☐☐☐☐☐☐☐☐☐☐☐☐☐

Issue number (Switch only):

☐☐☐

Start Date: **Expiry Date:**

☐☐ / ☐☐   ☐☐ / ☐☐

Signature: _____

NAME: _____

ADDRESS: _____

_____

POSTCODE: _____

Please allow 28 days for delivery.

Prices subject to change without notice.
Please tick box if you do not wish to receive any additional information. ☐

House of Stratus publishes many other titles in this genre; please check our
website (**www.houseofstratus.com**) for more details.